BEHIND THE PLAID

Book One – Highland Bound Trilogy

BY
ELIZA KNIGHT

Behind the Plaid

Eliza Knight

He dominated her mind. She possessed his soul.

Emma Gordon escapes from a troubling marriage in which she's completely lost sight of who she is. Desperate for independence, she leaves her husband while on a trip in the Scottish Highlands. Only thing is, she ends up hurled back in time to the 16th Century Castle Gealach and headlong into the arms of the handsome, intimidating Laird Logan Grant. Thrust into a world filled with treachery, danger and intensity she must summon the courage to find her way.

Logan is tormented by a dark past and harbors a secret that could tear his country apart. He's consumed with the need for control which wars with his longing for harmony. Unable to resist Emma's beauty and spirit and the calm that she invokes, Logan confesses he desires her—but only on his terms. He promises erotic encounters that will change them both forever, and quench their overwhelming desire.

Despite her own reservations, Emma longs to get close to the mysterious laird, even while she is desperate to return to her own era. She agrees to Logan's proposal to satisfy her curiosity, but in the end embarks on a daring, passionate affair that rocks her to the very core. Secrets are uncovered, souls bared, spirits transformed. Neither of them can hide behind the plaid.

Behind the Plaid

Eliza Knight

****
FIRST EDITION
March 2013

Copyright 2013 © Eliza Knight

BEHIND THE PLAID © 2013 Eliza Knight. ALL RIGHTS RESERVED. No part or the whole of this book may be reproduced, distributed, transmitted or utilized (other than for reading by the intended reader) in ANY form (now known or hereafter invented) without prior written permission by the author. The unauthorized reproduction or distribution of this copyrighted work is illegal, and punishable by law. The characters and events portrayed in this book are fictional and or are used fictitiously and solely the product of the author's imagination. Any similarity to real persons, living or dead, places, businesses, events or locales is purely coincidental.

Cover Design by Kimberly Killion @ Hot Damn Designs

ISBN-13: 978-1482531923
ISBN-10: 1482531925

****

Behind the Plaid

Also Available by Eliza Knight

The Highlander's Reward – Book One, The Stolen Bride Series
The Highlander's Conquest – Book Two, The Stolen Bride Series
The Highlander's Lady – Book Three, The Stolen Bride Series
The Highlander's Warrior Bride – Book Four, The Stolen Bride Series
A Lady's Charade (Book 1: The Rules of Chivalry)
A Knight's Victory (Book 2: The Rules of Chivalry)
A Gentleman's Kiss
<u>Men of the Sea Series:</u> *Her Captain Returns, Her Captain Surrenders, Her Captain Dares All*
<u>The Highland Jewel Series:</u> *Warrior in a Box, Lady in a Box, Love in a Box*
Lady Seductress's Ball
Take it Off, Warrior
Highland Steam
A Pirate's Bounty
Highland Tryst (Something Wicked This Way Comes Volume 1)
Highlander Brawn (Sequel to *Highland Steam*)

Coming soon...

Bared to the Highlander (Book 2: Highland Bound)
The Dark Side of the Laird (Book 3: Highland Bound)
The Highlander's Triumph (Book 5: The Stolen Bride Series)

Writing under the name E. Knight

Coming soon...

My Lady Viper – Tales From the Tudor Court
Prisoner of the Queen – Tales From the Tudor Court

Writing under the name Annabelle Weston

Wicked Woman (Desert Heat)
Scandalous Woman (Desert Heat)
Notorious Woman (Desert Heat)

Behind the Plaid

Mr. Temptation
Hunting Tucker

****
Visit Eliza Knight at www.elizaknight.com or www.historyundressed.com

Eliza Knight

Dedication

To my own Highlander, my soul mate—
living proof that real men wear kilts.
Love you!

Acknowledgements

Many thanks to Christi, Tara and Jenn for all of your amazing support!

Behind the Plaid

Eliza Knight

CHAPTER ONE

Emma

Inverness, Scottish Highlands
Present Day

The sunset was like a bruise. I stared at the evening sky as it changed from yellowish pink to black and blue. Not unlike my soul. Bruised. Battered. Hopeless.

If I'd known that I'd be sitting on a Victorian settee, complete with a beautiful cushion embroidered with thistles, at a bed and breakfast in the beautiful Scottish Highlands, gazing through a lace-covered window as I listened to Steven berate me when any other guest could witness it, I'd have never come.

Not that I had much of a choice. My choices were limited since we'd gotten married eight years ago—me just barely out of high school.

Behind the Plaid

From the corner of my eye, I spied, his mother Beverly whispering behind her hand to Steven who eyed me with contempt. She didn't like me. Never had. Not since I became Steven's charity case at age eighteen. Steven liked a good project. Trouble was, I wasn't a good one.

"Emma, are you even listening to me?"

I nodded but continued to gaze at the horizon. If I told Steven the truth, that I tried not to listen when he flew into a tirade, tried to float off into oblivion, that would only add fuel to his fire. At that moment, he was blazing. Whisky was partially to blame—the fact that he'd had several cups of it—and his mother just had to bring up the fact that we had no children.

A major issue within our marriage.

A promise I'd broken. To have his children, so he could pass down his fortune to his heirs. Steven was the last of his family. If he died, his money died with him. And there would be no one for him to leave the Scottish manor home he planned to buy, a tribute to his ancestry.

"You're a fucking failure, Emma." Steven's voice had risen. He'd grab me by the arm soon…drag me upstairs. "A dammed charity case that I should have left to drown in your disaster of a life years ago."

It was always the same. Belittling me. Lamenting of my uselessness as a human being. I hoped he would quit his preaching soon so I could drown myself in a glass or three of Chardonnay. White wine, because red stains my lips and teeth and only makes Steven angrier.

"Well, what do you have to say for yourself?" He stopped in front of me, hands on his hips, eyes bloodshot, sandy blond hair flying this way and that from having run his fingers through it so many times. Steven had never hit me, but that didn't mean he wouldn't. He'd threatened beatings often enough, and hurt me in other ways. But mostly his method was worse than physical brutality. Steven's method was deprivation. A lack of food, no friends, no job, no money. Forbidden to go anywhere unless he approved it, and most times, he didn't. I'd been a virtual prisoner for eight years and no one knew it. As time went on, his anger grew and his temper tantrums increased.

We lived in a nice little house on a cul-de-sac with a neatly trimmed postage stamp of a yard. Steven drank beers with the neighborhood men as they mowed their lawns on Saturdays. Sometimes a few wives came out to chat, bringing iced tea or lemonade. The one time I'd tried it, the glare I'd received from Steven had been murderous.

"Well? Are you too stupid to answer the fucking question?" His voice was loud, reverberating off the walls, and I feared the other guests would hear my humiliation.

My mind drew a blank. What could I say or do to make his pain and anger at our childless marriage better? Nothing. And if I admitted the truth as to why we had no children, that might just push him over the edge.

I tempered the urge to shrug and roll my eyes. Despite his attempts to squash my spirit, it still lingered in there somewhere. "I'm sorry, Steven."

He blew out a breath of disgust, whisky, fried cod and garlicky potatoes coming with it. I swallowed a gag and instead feigned an itch on my nose to keep my reaction from being visible.

"I'm sorry? Is that all you can say? I'm sorry?" Steven laughed bitterly. "Eight years and nothing to show for it. You've been a waste of my time."

Beverly nodded her agreement. If only they were aware… Steven would have probably killed me. After the abuse started, I knew I couldn't bring children into the world. Not with Steven. I was so miserable, I couldn't bear the thought of subjecting an innocent child to it. I visited the women's clinic on campus.

Behind the Plaid

They gave out birth control like it was candy, no questions asked. I'd had a steady supply ever since, my one saving grace.

"Get out of my sight!" Steven roared.

Head down, I wasted no time scurrying from the chair, and out of the sitting room. Our hostess stood in the hallway wringing her hands. When I rushed out, Mrs. Lamb opened her mouth to say something, but I shook my head. There was no need for her comfort or offer. I was embarrassed enough as it was. With silent but hurried steps in my practical ballet flats, I ran upstairs to the bedroom I shared with my husband and clicked on the dim light, waiting for my eyes to adjust to its flickering.

I gazed into the aged bureau mirror. A stranger stared back at me. She wore her long, wavy red hair hidden well in a tight bun at the nape of her neck. Wide, frightened blue eyes. Pale skin. Cheek bones jutting from thin flesh. A long, slender neck. Collarbones that could cut someone. When had I become so fragile?

Why did I look so ghostly?

This wasn't me. Couldn't be me. And yet it was. A stranger.

I'd been so full of life at eighteen. Until the day I lost everything—and thought I'd gained a loving husband.

A plane crash. Both parents and younger brother gone in an instant. I had no grandparents. My father was an only child and my mother's sister was always in and out of rehab for one drug related abuse or another. That left me. Alone.

Now I was dressed in clothes suited for someone well beyond my twenty-six years. A frilly-collared maroon blouse, buttoned at the wrists, and an ankle-length beige pencil skirt. I looked like my grandmother—what I could remember of her. Beneath the prim clothes was an even primmer pair of white underwear and a white no-nonsense bra. Nothing sexy. I wasn't allowed to look sexy on the outside. Wasn't allowed to think of myself as anything other than Steven's wife. Steven's maid. Steven's cook. Steven's punching bag.

I longed for something different. Dreamed of a life unlike this one. One with love, friendship, respect. One where I could feel beautiful, be free to be me.

I turned away from the mirror and let my gaze drift over the room. It was small. Wood paneled walls, a cream ceiling with a few water stains. A tiny, shuttered window, sheer ivory curtains with embroidered roses waving softly in the air from the ceiling fan.

The bed was small—a full, I think—and dipped in the middle from years of use. Steven made me sleep pinned against the wall as his larger frame settled into the middle of the bed. I didn't want to touch him as I slept, for fear of angering him. The quilt was hand woven by Mrs. Lamb, she'd told us when she escorted us to the room. Made with love and tears, she'd said. Hoped it would bring us love, but no tears.

I marched over to the bed and sat heavily. I felt hopeless. Out of control. There was nothing for me left in this world and yet I knew there had to be. At one time, I'd thought there was.

Now there was only this continued battle with my husband's bruised ego and battering words. It wasn't how I wanted to live my life.

A swish of sound came from the door and for a moment my heart stopped. Swift nausea came over me at the thought of Steven returning. He always wanted *it* after he was done raging at me. *It* being my body. A horrendous affair that, if I could, I'd never do again.

He brought me only pain.

But it wasn't Steven. Instead, a little white card skidded over the worn wooden floor, flipping once before landing with a corner stuck beneath the threadbare rug. Curious, I shoved off the bed to retrieve it.

MacBurns Cab Service. 01455 521216

Behind the Plaid

The old brass doorknob was frigid against my palm as I quickly opened the door, but there was no one in the hallway. Could it have been Mrs. Lamb? Steven's mother wouldn't help me. Maybe it was one of the other guests who'd heard Steven berate me over the past week. Or worse, heard my struggles and muffled, pain-filled cries as he exerted his husbandly duties.

The voices of Steven and his family floated up from the sitting room, loud, agitated. He would be up soon.

Shutting the door silently, I picked up the old rotary dial phone that sat on a scratched wooden desk. My fingers trembled and I misdialed at least three times before getting it right.

"MacBurns Cab Service," came a man's voice, heavy with brogue.

I slammed down the phone. I couldn't leave. I had nowhere to go. No money. No friends. No family.

My heart thudded loudly, blood rushing to my ears. I dialed again.

"MacBurns Cab Service."

"Hi, yes, I need a cab please." My voice shook and my teeth started to chatter. I clamped them tightly.

"When and where?"

"Immediately." I started to give him the address to Mrs. Lamb's B&B but instead changed it to the cross street. Somehow I'd have to sneak out and make it down the road without Steven seeing me. That only made my nausea return, churning the few bits of fish I'd nibbled.

"We'll get ye in a jiff."

The line went dead. Either a cab would be waiting for me and I'd climb into it, or the cab would wait and then drive away as I stared out the window.

I shook my head. "No. No. No." I had to leave. This was my chance. Perhaps Mrs. Lamb would distract Steven and his family long enough for me to escape. Once I was in the cab, I could figure out where to go.

I grabbed my carryon from beneath the bed and stuffed my meager belongings into it. Clutching my purse, I headed for the door, stopping in my tracks. Steven tucked cashier's checks and cash in the top drawer of his bureau, buried beneath his white underwear and black socks. Did I dare take some? All? If he found me... There would be no end to my chastisement.

There would be no end to it anyway. I was leaving him, and that was not a humiliation he would tolerate lightly or moderately. His only reaction would be volcanic.

I ripped open the drawer, yanked out a wad of cash and stuffed the bills into my purse with my passport. Slipped off my wedding ring and placed it where the cash had been.

My throat closed, terror so profound coming over me that my feet froze in place. Someone tapped at my door and I whimpered in fear.

"Mrs. Gordon?"

Acute relief washed over me, and my limbs felt weightless. My legs shook and nearly had me buckling to the floor.

"Mrs. Gordon... I believe there is someone waiting for ye across the way."

So soon? Had my host been keeping an eye out?

Swallowing back the bile forcing its way up my throat, I willed my legs to work, to walk towards the door and turn the ancient handle. Mrs. Lamb stood in the hallway, her gaze anxious.

"Come now, lass, your ride is awaiting."

I nodded. Mrs. Lamb led me along the dimly lit, narrow hallway toward the back of the house, and down a steep and tiny iron circular staircase. The steps seemed made for a child, no more three or four inches deep and only a foot wide. We ended up in her kitchen and she ushered me toward the back door, where her yard was pitch black.

Behind the Plaid

"Go with God, lass. Ye're doing the right thing." The woman nearly pushed me out the door.

As soon as my feet hit the dewy grass, I felt it.

Freedom. An insurmountable weight lifted from my chest. I was free.

Almost.

I took off at a jog down the street, tripping over my own feet as I looked behind me to make sure Steven didn't follow. Adrenaline pumped through my veins. Elation filled me, like I was floating. Ahead at the crossroads a nondescript silver cab waited, lights shining in the evening mist.

A burly Scot climbed from the car. He tipped his cap, showing his silver hair and held open the door for me.

"Can I take your bag, miss?"

"No, thank you."

"What about that one?" He pointed to the carryon I was going to toss into the back seat.

Not wanting to stall any longer, I thrust it toward him. "Just this one." Clutching my purse to my chest, I scooted all the way to the other side of the cab, slinking low in the seat. Just in case Steven did happen to race down the street, I didn't want him to see me.

The cab driver stowed my bag, slower than my nerves could handle. I tapped my feet, my fingers. Finally he slid into his seat, shut the door and faced me. "Where to?"

I froze. I didn't know. I could stay here in Scotland for a time. But eventually, I'd have to go back to the U.S. Just not back home to Washington, DC. I didn't want to risk staying here in Drumnadrochit, though. If Steven found me, or I got cold feet and returned to my old life... My toes tingled. Was I getting cold feet now?

"The airport. In Inverness," I proclaimed.

"Where ye headed?"

"Home." Or at least the country of my old home.

"U.S.? I can take ye to the regional airport in Inverness, and then ye can catch a flight to Edinburgh. There are no flights to the U.S. from Inverness."

I nodded, even though his answer made me panicky. That would be the first place Steven would look for me.

"Are there any trains to Edinburgh?"

"Aye, we've a national rail."

"Do you think they have a train tonight?"

"In a hurry, lass?"

I nodded and frantically looked out the window. The cab driver caught my nervous glances and turned onto the road, slowly driving away.

"I'm sure they've a train tonight. Usually one around eight." He tapped the dashboard clock. "Ye should make it."

I nodded, my breath catching. I was really doing this. "How much do you think the train fare is?" I didn't know how much I'd grabbed from the drawer, but guessed it was at least two or three hundred.

"Probably about fifty or sixty quid, lass." He glanced back, his eyes sympathetic. "Mrs. Lamb's taken care of your taxi fare, so ye've no need to worry on that account."

The woman had truly wanted to help me leave. Amazing.

The cab driver grew silent and I watched the darkened scenery with new awakened eyes. A drizzle started, rain drops splashing on my window, obscuring and blurring the view. Steadily, the drops fell harder, as if the clouds themselves wanted to cover my tracks. Deep thunder rolled, so colossal my insides vibrated with it. Lightning flashed, illuminating the sky and an imposing medieval castle alongside the road. The ride was bumpy, windy, and I clutched at the seat to remain in place.

My eyes were drawn to the soaring stone towers, crenelated tops. Rock crumbled in spots, revealing more stone and mortar beneath. The grounds were vast. A thick wall surrounded the

Behind the Plaid

castle. When lightning flashed again, I could see the raging loch beyond the castle. Loch Ness.

I'd not seen a monster there when we'd taken a tour two days ago, but I'd been so absorbed in the water itself, as if waiting for something to emerge from its depths. I'd even stepped in an inch along the edge, wetting my shoes and the hem of my skirt. Steven had been furious. I'd not known what compelled me.

I was drawn to it even now. My eyes were riveted by the stone towers and the main building itself—a keep, the tour guide had called it. Seemed fitting as it would keep people in or out.

"What is the name of this castle?" I asked the cab driver, unable to recall it myself. When we'd visited a couple days prior, I'd been too occupied with Steven's cross temperament.

He slowed the car, heedless of the honking drivers behind us. The cabbie rolled down his window and waved them around us, before pulling over to the side.

"That's Gealach Castle, lass."

"Gealach," I repeated, imitating his brogue.

"Aye."

"Will you wait here for me?" I asked, a powerful urge to walk along the ruin taking hold. It was stupid, given that Steven may be following me at that moment. But I didn't care. I *had* to do this.

"'Tis raining lass. Ye'll not want to go out there now."

"I'll just be a few minutes." I didn't wait for him to respond. But instead yanked on the handle and pushed the door open, holding my purse over my head as I ran up the embankment. The castle was closed, a metal gate blocking the path, but luck was on my side—someone had forgotten to lock it. I yanked it open and ran through. My flats sank into the grass, slipping on the wet earth.

My blouse and skirt were quickly drenched, gluing themselves uncomfortably to my skin. Still I ran toward Gealach. I don't know what drew me, but it was strong. Like someone literally moved my limbs for me. Thunder rolled, shaking the earth and making my legs tremble. Lightning lit up the night sky.

"Miss!" I heard the cab driver call behind me.

I waved my hand in the air, dismissing him, as I kept moving forward. Chills swept over me. A swift wind blew the cold rain. Yet, I did not stop until I reached the gate. Lightning struck somewhere close by. I hesitated. What was I doing? This was insane. Was my newfound freedom making me crazy?

No. I had to go inside. I just had to.

Thunder reverberated across the stones, making it sound even louder, and sharp pelts of rain hit my face. I crossed over the sturdy bridge with iron rails across what was once a moat toward the castle gate. One more step forward and I was beneath what was left of the stone gate, just as lightning struck. Sparks shot into the air from the iron spires on either side of me.

Stunned, I fell to the cobblestone and the storm ceased.

CHAPTER TWO

Logan

Scottish Highlands
Mid-summer, 1542

The bedchamber was rife with the scent of rutting. Lots of rutting. The sun had barely risen and the golden light of morning streamed into the room, pulling back the cloak of darkness from numerous legs, sprawled and entwined. The fire was banked and the candles had long since burned through their wicks, wax dripping over the holders to lay in hardened lumps.

"A lovely gift," I chuckled, staring with renewed interest at three of the maids draped around me on the bed.

Being a Highland laird and chief was no easy position, but somebody had to do it. All the better that it was me—born and raised to be formidable, powerful, dominant. With a wide grin, I noted how very true those words were.

One of the lasses stirred and murmured her appreciation. But 'twas I who was truly appreciative. I'd needed a good night of sport and wickedness away from the strife of running the clan. Away from the bleakness that was my past — thoughts that always blackened my mood like a rotted carcass.

King James V of Scotland was a good man. And I knew his gift — these wenches — was a bribe. No one's sovereign sent them a wagon full of ripe and willing females if they didna want something.

But I would gladly serve my king, and last night I think I served him rather well. I chuckled again at the thought, my cock growing hard as memories of plunging deep inside one and then another of the lassies came to mind.

I cupped a handful of plush breast in one hand and an arse in the other. "Mmm... Any one of ye wenches awake?"

Several lasses tittered, claiming they were ready for another go at the Laird of Gealach. Those who'd slept on the floor rose to join us on the bed.

A wide, lascivious grin creased my lips. I commanded, "Come and let me grant ye your every desire."

Within moments, my full cock was wet and hot within the slick heat of a blonde's tight sheath. Another pressed her mouth to mine, while two others stroked and licked over my body. Opening an eye, I caught sight of the brown-haired lass trying to gather her clothing on tip-toes, intent most likely on sneaking out. Pausing mid-kiss, I called out, "No need to rush off, lass, there's plenty of room for ye!"

Her face flamed, but she dropped her garments and scurried back to the bed. I reached out for her to kiss me. She'd been more on the timid side, most likely new to the harem King James kept.

Behind the Plaid

Ah, what a life. One I intended to keep. If any knew the truth of my past, they'd know I wasna truly meant for it. Despite all outward appearances. Despite the man I called Da, the previous Laird of Gealach. I fought to the death anyone who threatened my domain. And it happened more often than not. Luckily, Death's grip had been for my opponents rather than for me thus far. Was that skill, or was that Fate? I'm confident in myself, my sword, and my strength, even I wouldna turn my back on Fate.

The king advised me to keep Gealach and her secrets safe. To make sure no one passed into the kingdom without my approval first. Thus far, I'd made good on my word. Any bastard that got in my way would burn for it.

The clan knew what was at stake and followed me without question. But even so… There were many willing to take on the infamous Laird of Gealach. Many willing to risk their lives for a cause they deemed worthy. But I have always been and would always be, stronger. Swimming, a daily caber toss, weapons training, and hand to hand combat keep my body conditioned. My men were the best of the best. Elite. Many an allied laird sent his warriors to me for training. A hefty price in coin they paid for it, too. Didna hurt to have as many allies on the field as possible. Especially with the ever present threat of England drumming on our backs.

But those enemy clansmen, mostly the Lairds of the Isles who wished to challenge King James' rule, or those who wished to take my place, were too absorbed in their greed to realize I was unbeatable.

Fools. All of them. If even one realized who I truly was, the power I wielded, they'd nay set foot on Gealach lands. They'd abandon their weapons and their foolish notions and run for the hills. Gealach would be a peaceful place. But no one was likely to tell my enemies the truth. Three had died with the secret. The one other living soul who knew the truth would nay speak it, as it would bring about his own ruin. If he were to perish, my secret would be forever buried. My secret was protected. And so was my right to rule this place.

But peace wasna the way of it. Instead, Gealach was often plagued. A tireless life I led. And so, aye, when a wagon full of lovelies was spilled at my feet, I eagerly grappled up the warm flesh and tantalized them all with my prowess until each of us was sated and without breath.

The blonde switched places with the timid one who rode me like a tigress, rubbing her mons against cock like a wench on a mission. The others continued to tease me, and I touched and kissed where I could, not wanting anyone to feel left out. There was enough of me to go around. But when one of the lasses put her mouth to my sac...that saw the end of it. My ballocks clenched tight and I roared with release.

Moments later, a light tapping sounded at the door. The morning's revelry would have to come to an end despite that I could go another round or two. We'd yet begun to work on the rather naughty activities I dreamed up overnight. "Up with ye, lassies. I must be about my day."

I opened the door a crack to see my second in command in the corridor, armed and ready. Ewan was as tall as I and boasted the same breadth of strength in his muscles. A must for the man who had my back. But there, the likeness waned. He was light where I was dark—blond hair glowing like the gold in my treasure box, whereas mine was as black as the iron lock keeping the treasure secure. Eyes light, icy blue, in steep contrast to mine which matched the darkness of my hair. "Ye said to wake ye at dawn, my laird."

"Aye."

Ewan wiggled his brows as a few of the lassies giggled and moaned. I just grinned. "I suppose they'd like some privacy." Grabbing my plaid I opened the door a bit wider to give Ewan a peek at the erotic spectacle, then stepped into the hallway, arms crossed over my chest.

Ewan shook his head. "My laird, a lovely gift the king has sent ye."

"They may entertain ye if ye like."

Ewan shook his head vigorously. "Nay, I couldna, as much as I wish it. Scouts are back and requesting your audience."

Damn. I hoped they wouldna be back so soon. The fact they wanted an audience didna sit well. "Och. Take them to my library. Tell them I'll be down in a moment. I need to get my boots on at least."

Ewan chuckled. "Be sure not to get too distracted on your way out of the chamber."

As much as I wanted to bury my face in the brunette's ample bosom while the raven haired one rubbed hers on my back, duty called. I stepped back inside, groaned aloud when they beckoned me, and groaned louder when I declined. "'Haps next time lassies." I slapped each of them playfully on their arses, sucked greedily at a few turgid nipples, finished getting dressed and left the chamber, my plaid fully tented in the front.

Despite the early hour, the castle was already coming to life. I could hear the maids opening chambers and singing as they dusted and straightened bedding. Even though most of the chambers were empty, I required they be kept in order in case any guests arrived. We were known to have unexpected visitors on occasion and with Gealach being a major political appointment, I wasna about to turn anyone away.

The echo of my boots sounded off the stone walls as I descended the wheel stair. Gealach had been built for defense, from its thick, impenetrable walls to the design on its staircase. The counter-clockwise direction of the stairs was so those who attacked had to fight with their left hands and those who descended must fight with their right. We'd never been breached except in one case where I'd encountered a left-handed maggot—a traitor within our midst. Good thing I could fight just as well with both arms.

Mayhap I'm a glutton for punishment, but I enjoy fighting my battles uphill. The harder I have to work to win, the more grueling the fight, the more satisfied I am with victory. I chuckled, likening it to making love. The harder I worked, the more effort put into it, the better it was for us both in the end.

I paused on the second floor to glance out the slitted window at the glow of the morning sun and how it lit everything in its path. Our lands were mostly covered in grey. A sunny day was rare and to be treasured. Dreamlike moments like these, when the land's beauty was shown in such an austere way made me supremely grateful to be alive. I took a moment to breathe it all in. A side I never let anyone see.

And a side I tried not to indulge too often. Death was always in the forefront. A warrior's life was never guaranteed to be long.

Turning toward the closed oak door that led to my library, I opened it, pleased to see that someone had lit the torches. This corridor was always dark, housing not only my library, but a larger meeting room for private sessions with various leaders, my treasury and my own personal armory. I nodded to the guards who waited beyond the door—best to surprise anyone who thought to venture past the forbidden entrance.

The men greeted me with grins that practically shouted questions regarding the guests in my chamber. If they were nay on duty, I'd offer them a chance to sample the wares. But alas, I needed them to guard this sacred corridor.

Ewan stepped from my library. "My laird, Tavish and Collum await ye."

I nodded, entering the library to find two of our most prized scouts on the edge of their seats. Both of them sat rigid, weariness written into the creases of their furrowed brows.

"My laird," Tavish said, jumping up and then bowing. Collum followed suit.

"Sit, lads. Tell me what news."

They nodded, unruly brown locks whipping in and out of their faces. The lads' skin was darkened, attesting to the time they spent roaming the Gealach holdings. Wiry but strong, the scouts were hard runners and even harder riders, able to shoot an arrow from a swiftly weaving horse and always hit their marks. Regaining their seats, Collum's and Tavish's feet began to tap with anxiousness.

"Ships, my laird," Collum burst out, licking his cracked lips and swiping at his freckled nose.

"Galleons?"

"Aye, my laird. Half a dozen, I counted."

"And I counted eight." Tavish added, swiping at his nose. An odd habit they both tended to do when on edge.

"Well, which is it? Six or eight?" I tried not to be irritated with the men.

Collum held up his hands and shook his head. "Eight, my laird. Tavish here could hardly count he was too busy—"

"I am never too busy to complete my duty! If ye hadn't been—"

I rolled my eyes. Collum and Tavish were not only my best scouts, they also happened to be twins. And they fought like wildcats for place as leader over one another. I walked behind the two and slapped a hand on each of their shoulders which gained their attention, letting them know who was in fact the dominant one in the room.

"Enough. Whether it was six or eight, we'll know soon enough. Where did ye see them?"

"In the River Oich just to the north of Loch Ness, my laird."

Their answer disturbed me. The enemy was close. They'd had to pass a few other strongholds. Had they bothered to stop and fight? Was it possible some of their number were actually allies to Gealach—intent on working with myself and my men to take down the enemy ships they trailed?

Damn the Lairds of the Isles. They certainly did complicate matters.

"Flags?"

They both shook their heads. At least they could agree on something. Too bad it wasna the answer I desired.

"Anything distinguishing?"

They shook their heads in unison. "Regular gun boats, my laird," Collum answered.

"Aye. Nothing so fine as the *Salamander*. But I did see the guns through my looking glass, about seven on one side and three on another."

The damn galleons better not be as fine as the *Salamander*, King James' own vessel, which had brought his bride, Mary of Guise from France a few years ago. Still, ten guns total was a sizeable vessel.

"Were ye well hidden?" 'Twas best to defeat an enemy if they didna think ye expected them. They'd be cockier that way. Cocky men always made mistakes.

"Aye, my laird," Tavish answered. "In our usual spot. As we rode over the Great Glen, we caught sight of vast slashes of white in the sky. Ship sails. We left our horses to graze and crawled atop a ridge to peek over the side toward the north of the loch, and there they were. Six ships."

"Eight," Collum corrected.

Ignoring their renewed argument, I walked to the window on the opposite wall, my battered and aged oak desk between me and the scouts. I stared out at the loch below. She churned, the frothy white tips of her waves growing wider as she swirled and bashed herself against the cliffs. From my vantage point I could just make out a half dozen black dots on the horizon. Six. "This means they came from the North Sea. Passed through Loch Lochy and Dunrobin Castle. Laird Sutherland is an ally.

Behind the Plaid

We willna let them pass by Gealach." It was hard to know if the enemy galleons were after what was buried within Gealach's walls or if they were intent on invading Scotland as a whole.

Part of me wanted to let them pass. To run back up the stairs and bury myself inside one of those wenches. To forget the powerful weight of my duty to the crown. The responsibility that had been heaped on my shoulders at birth. A pact forged in blood.

I turned around and glanced at Ewan by the closed door. "Alert the men." Glanced back out the window, watching as the trees swayed with the wind. The sky had turned from orange to grey. "Looks like a storm is brewing. All are to be prepared. Our guests could arrive in the next few hours."

Given the storm, the strong winds would push their sails, making the galleons arrival sooner than expected. Littering our sandy beaches with the filth and stench of their betrayal. Who the hell was it now? Who would dare?

Unfortunately, the answer to that question was too many…

No matter. I was prepared to keep Gealach, and to safeguard its secrets from all who wished to plunder her.

CHAPTER THREE

Emma

I blinked open my eyes, staring down at my hands laced in the green grass. Splatters of mud caked and dried between the folds of my knuckles and in-between my fingers. The rain had ceased and the ground itself was dry. A cold fall wind swept through my unpinned hair and down the neck of my blouse to chill my spine. Daylight had come.

How long had I been passed out? Didn't feel like long. Seconds maybe. Why hadn't my driver ever come to fetch me?

Pushing up onto my knees, I glanced over my shoulder at what had been a rather modern bridge, to find the iron handrails replaced with wood. The once empty moat was now filled with water. The hill leading down to where the road had once been, and the city... It was gone. Only medieval-looking cottages and fields covered the small Scottish town. No taxi. No driver. Not even my suitcase. The only thing I had was myself and my purse.

I'd curse the driver for leaving me, but judging from my surroundings, he didn't exist. Or he'd somehow disappeared — along with the asphalt road.

I stared, unthinking, numb. Slowly turning back around, I gazed up at Gealach Castle, my eyes widening. The castle looked different. Stones that had been crumbling were magically back in place. Birds could no longer swoop into the openness of the decaying keep as a thick wooden shingled roof kept them out.

Gealach was no longer in ruin. How could that be? I'd visited just a couple days ago and stood in the great hall looking up at the sky covered with greying clouds, marveling at how the structure had remained and weather was free to enter as it pleased.

An eerie silence hushed over the deserted grounds. As if time stood still.

I must have hit my head on something as I fell. I desperately looked down for a rock or log. That was the only explanation. I was either hallucinating or in a dream. Except…my explanation nagged at me. The heat of the sun warmed my skin. The dirt on my hands that I flaked off with my nails felt real. There was nothing but soft grass below me. Nothing to knock me out.

Perhaps I'd been struck by lightning?

My head ached. I must have injured myself somehow. But there was no particular spot of pain—it hurt all over like a migraine. I sat dejectedly, legs tucked and rummaged through my purse for a small bottle of ibuprofen. Popping them into my mouth, I swallowed them dry. The pills lodged in my throat and I coughed, trying hard with whatever saliva was left in my mouth to swallow the damn things. I just wanted to cease the pounding in my head. The bitter taste of the pills' coating rose up my throat and I shivered.

What the hell was going on?

Well, I couldn't just sit here. I couldn't wrap my head around any of what was happening. Couldn't fathom the conclusions I'd started to come too. There had to be another, more believable, explanation. Perhaps in the dark and rain I'd mistaken this place for Gealach. My driver had gotten irritated and left. I'd just have to walk down into the village at the bottom of the hill, find out where I was and call another taxi. I'd have to hurry, too.

No doubt Steven and his family had begun a search and had hours of lead time. A sudden fear snaked around my spine, gripping it, nearly making me fall over as though it'd snapped.

What if he was in the village already? Waiting for me?

I shook my head. I couldn't go to the village. Turning around, I did the next logical thing. I would find the visitor's desk inside the castle and use their phone to call a cab. I felt inside my pocket, McBurns' card was still there. I could hide out inside until the driver arrived and then make my escape.

As I turned to head toward the castle, a cacophony of noise trumpeted in my ears—but only for a split second. The air around me shifted, visibly, making me dizzy. It appeared to warp, swirl. Then there was nothing. No sounds, no wavering air. I put my hands out in front of me, completely unsteady.

I was beginning to worry. What was happening to me? Was I having a complete mental breakdown? I just needed to get a cab. Be on my way to the train station. Taking a few more hurried steps, I made it to the center of the courtyard when the racket sounded again, catching me completely off guard. It was loud—hammering, shouting, clanging. Then gone.

I closed my eyes as the air once more shifted in and out, like a strange warping, a black hole.

Behind the Plaid

"Inside. Inside. Inside," I chanted, forcing my feet to move quickly. The sounds and shifts of space came quicker and quicker. A buzzing, then silence, again and again. I crawled up the stone steps, unable to stay upright, my eyes feeling as though they'd pop from head, so much pressure built up behind them.

On my knees I reached up, hands shaking, fingers unable to connect with the large rings of the front door. They kept missing, scratching down what should have been ancient oak, but instead was strong and newly polished. Finally catching hold, the cold metal bit into my fingers as though covered in ice, and I flinched, yanking. Nothing happened. Tears of frustration stung my eyes.

I tried again. Hit at the door with my fists—creating a dull thud. The wood was so thick. Perhaps if I stood, I could put my weight behind it as I yanked. The doors were at least twelve feet high. Somehow, I managed to pull myself up, grasping the metal rings and preparing to yank as hard as I could.

Just as swiftly, the door flung open and I was knocked backward. Unable to catch my balance, I fell down the wide stone steps. My hip hit particularly hard. Landing flat on my back, my eyes glazed with pain and shock, I stared up into the black eyes of a giant.

Tall, wide with muscle, the man wore a green and red kilt, pleated and wrapped about his hips. A linen shirt covered his thick, muscled arms and the end of his plaid was tossed and pinned to one of his broad shoulders. His dark hair was pulled back, tied at the nape of his neck by a bit of leather. Chiseled, hard features, thick square jaw, and a mouth that made me blush.

A raw sensuality emanated from his gaze, sparking something dangerous, carnal and forbidden within me. The feelings were overwhelming, urgent and unknown.

Steven had never made me feel that way. And never from something so normal as a pair of eyes connecting. But there was nothing normal about this man. He was intense, compelling... I felt myself being drawn inside.

He said something in a bizarre language I didn't understand. Gaelic maybe? I shook my head, swallowing hard and trying to break my stare. But there was no use, I couldn't stop looking. He walked down the stairs toward me. On closer inspection I could see his eyes weren't black but an intense, dark blue.

"What are ye doing here?" he asked, his Scottish burr strong.

He spoke English too? Thank goodness... I opened my mouth but no words came out.

He held out his hand, his lips thinned into a grimace as our flesh touched. My small palm fit inside his larger one, sending a fresh batch of shivers up my arm. He was warm, in great contrast to my frigid digits. With no effort at all, he pulled me upright, and I noted how the top of my head barely reached the middle of his chest. The man had to be at least six and a half feet tall.

"I... I need to make a phone call," I finally stammered.

"Phone call?" he asked, slashed brows narrowing in suspicion and question.

But before I could respond, his men shouted all around us, overwhelming my senses once more. The pounding in my head had dissipated some when I concentrated on the giant who'd knocked me down the stairs, but with fresh shouts and clangs of metal the pounding returned tenfold.

"Lower the portcullis! Shut the gates!" the giant ordered.

Men ran here and there, obeying his orders. Flashes of plaid and weaponry.

"Ye, get inside," he ordered, his eyes on me. "Stay hidden."

Behind the Plaid

On timid feet I rushed up the stairs, ignoring the bruised and tender aches on my hips, legs, back and arms. I didn't know what was happening, but the demand in his voice, the rush of danger, all had me running. Could be a terrorist attack, or a bear or some such. I didn't know, and I wasn't willing to find out.

The inside of the castle was dark, dank. A draft blew around my ankles as the heavy door closed with a quiet hush, finishing with an echoing bang that reverberated off the stones and rafters. I waited a few moments until my eyes adjusted, then headed straight across the foyer down a few stairs into the great hall. The place greatly resembled Gealach, even though I knew it couldn't be. There must be plenty of Scottish castles that looked alike.

My ballet flats made no sound as I walked deeper into the empty great hall. The walls were covered in tapestries of battles past and massive displays of weaponry, stuffed wildcats, bears and various other animals.

The hall smelled… odd. Old. Like peat, stale beer and an underlying earthiness. Hands on my hips I turned in a circle, not seeing a phone or a reception desk, nor anyone to ask. Seemed everyone had run out when the handsome and commanding man had knocked me down. Just thinking about his strong hand as he lifted me sent fresh, enticing chills to cover my flesh. Both exhilarating and frightening, waking some dormant side of myself that had lain silent since marrying Steven.

As much as I sensed I could sit and muse on the darkness of his eyes, or the raw power that came off of him in waves, or the fact that it made me feel wholly unlike myself, I couldn't think about the man now. I needed to find a phone.

I walked back toward the main door, a particularly bruised spot on my hip aching with each step. I grimaced up the three foyer stairs and stopped dead in my tracks.

Through the doors I could hear shouts of pain, screams, horrid noises that had me covering my ears and ducking. Something was horribly wrong. The castle was under attack. But by whom? What would anyone gain from attacking an old tourist trap?

Not knowing where else to go, refusing to accept what appeared to be the truth—that somehow I'd traveled through time—I turned to the right and ran up the circular stone stairs, feeling as though I was climbing high in the sky. The metal handrail was gone from here, too. Round and round I went, tripping over my feet and slipping on the smooth stone. I went down hard on one knee, wincing, crying out. My hand caught against the damp stone wall, rock slicing into my fingertips. Light shone through an arrow slit, and I pulled up on the ledge to look outside. The ledge was about a foot and a half wide, a few feet tall and four feet deep. Big enough for me to climb inside to peek out the long gap in the stone.

I hoisted myself into the alcove, the sounds of whatever horrid fight waged outside, echoing off the stones. What I saw shocked me.

A full battle. It looked so real, sounded even worse. Swords, axes, bows, maces, daggers, shields. The men flung their weapons with ease and skill. Clangs and clashes vibrated the very air. A shock of terror passed through me, my palms sweated and my heart skipped a beat. There was blood. Lots of it. Staining white linen shirts, staining flesh, staining the ground.

The shouts of pain, streams of blood, were all too real. There was no denying any longer what had happened. I was no longer in my own era... I watched with dawning horror as the battle raged on.

Then I spotted him. The giant. He swung his sword around his head, the length of which I didn't think I'd be able to lift, let alone wield as he did. His dark hair had come loose from its tie,

Behind the Plaid

waving wildly around his face and shoulders. Even from this distance I could see the muscles of his body working in a way that was sensual and dangerous at the same time.

With frightening clarity, I imagined this battle gone, and me touching him. Stroking my hands over the dips and ridges of his body, luxuriating in the smoothness, the taut sinew. My cheeks heated to burning. Desire. That was what ran rampant through my mind. I'd not known desire in years. Not been interested in sensuality, sex. For me it had been an unpleasant duty, never something to be enjoyed. How was it possible?

This man, this stranger... He'd awakened something inside me. As he swung his sword, taking out one man and then another, shouted commands to his men, my sense of terror dulled and was replaced by a calmness, a need. A hunger.

That alarmed me even more. I didn't know where I was. What was happening. What my future held. And yet I was calm. I tore my gaze from the fray and stared at the mortar between the stones. Had the absurd thought that I should look for a phone. Look through the various chambers. Anything except stare out the window. As if I could will the obvious away.

Part of me knew it was no use. This place didn't have electricity. I'd noted that by the flaming torches bolted into the stones. No electric light. All natural. No light switches, no plugs hidden behind pieces of furniture. No vents. No exit signs.

Even historic villages in modern times made some provisions for safety. But I saw none of that here. I swallowed, smoothing the hem of my mud-splattered skirt and noting that the whole of my skirt was caked with flecks of dirt. My bare ankles, too.

I had nothing to do but wait. Deep in my soul, I knew I had to speak to this man again. That he could help me. That he'd know what to do. I didn't like putting my life in his hands, but this was different than when Steven had offered to help me eight years ago. I sensed now that Steven's assistance and subsequent offer of marriage had been sinister. He'd seen a vulnerable, malleable girl. A person in need, and someone he could trap, use. He needed someone that made him feel better about himself. Steven needed someone to do everything for him, and yet he offered nothing in return.

Flicking my gaze outside once more, I could see that the battle had subsided. The large man still issued commands, but what was left of their enemy took off running through the gate, over the bridge, across the moors and into the woods beyond. Grey clouds in the sky moved swiftly, clashing together, churning. They were so low, an eerie fog filled the courtyards.

No one followed the men who ran. No one returned to offer congratulations on a well done show. Those who lay still and bloodied upon the ground did not rise. In fact, the leader pointed and warriors lifted men by their arms and dragged them into a pile.

One body on top of the other. A mass grave.

I shuddered. This man was ruthless, and yet when he'd offered me his hand, he'd been gentle. His voice, while dominant and commanding, had undertones of interest, sensuality. His eyes were intense, inviting. I wasn't scared.

And I probably should have been.

In all actuality, I should get my rear off this ledge and find an exit and run away. Toward the village. Find help.

But I didn't move. I stared, mesmerized outside of the arrow slit window. Watching, becoming familiar with his movements, his voice.

I gasped as he turned up to glance at the castle, as if he sensed my eyes upon him. Heat suffused my cheeks. I didn't turn away. I couldn't. I doubted he could see me, perched as I was two to three floors off the ground. But I could see him, and there was something on his face that made me feel like he sensed me.

Behind the Plaid

He walked toward the castle stairs leading up to the big oak doors. My heart sped up. My mind raced. My breath caught. I knew he was coming for me.

CHAPTER FOUR

Emma

For the span of several heartbeats I sat unmoving, unable to catch my breath.

He was coming. I felt it in my bones. I scrambled from the window ledge, my feet landing on the stone stairs with surprising agility, as if my limbs wanted me to move. To escape.

But it wasn't from fear, that I was compelled to escape. It was for the exact opposite reason, because somehow, the connection, the interest, the compelling force that almost made me turn and run down the stairs toward him, frightened me worse than even Steven's worst berating.

So, up I ran. Round and round, grappling with an arched, metal studded door that led down a dark, cold passageway. Only the light from an arrow slit every few yards to my left

Behind the Plaid

guided me. Each torch sat starkly naked and dead of flames in their iron casts. There were doors on the right, all closed and seemingly forbidden.

From behind, I heard the door open and then the sound of boots walking steadily on the stones behind me. He was here. I battled with running, trying to open a door, and with simply stopping. I opted for the latter. I would have to confront my fate instead of running from it.

I'd never confronted my fate in my life before. Never stood up for myself. Perhaps this was a new beginning. A chance to test myself. To be me.

I ceased running, standing in a dusty shaft of light, hands clenched at my sides, my breathing erratic. Feet rooted in place, I couldn't force myself to turn around. Couldn't face him. Had to work up the courage to do so. The booted steps clunked, and I could hear the scrape of metal from his weapons as they swung. Gooseflesh rose along my limbs, and scandalously, my nipples tightened. I bit my lip, pleading with my body to calm.

"Lass," he said directly behind me. His voice was deep, gravelly. The sound stroked with roughness over my flesh. I resisted that urge to rub away the prickles on my skin.

I nodded, unable to speak. But that wouldn't do. I had to speak. Had to find that semblance of freedom I'd once lived by. Easier said than done.

"Why do ye run?" He stood so close, his breath shifted my loose hair at my neck, sending shivers to rush along my spine.

"I...I don't know."

"Are ye afraid?"

I rubbed my arms in an effort to quell the chills. "No." I wasn't afraid of him...I was afraid of myself.

"What are ye doing here?"

That was the same question I wanted answered. "Where is here?"

"Ye answer a question with a question?"

I nodded, not budging.

He chuckled softly, and warm fingers swiped the hair away from my neck, leaving that tender flesh exposed. My breath caught, intensely curious about what he would do and at the same time wanting to run away.

"Gealach Castle."

My stomach plummeted to my ankles. The truth revealed at last, and not at all what I'd hoped for.

"Impossible," I whispered.

"'Nay, 'tis true."

What I'd been thinking all along—that somehow I'd been plummeted through time to this place came crashing into my consciousness with knife-like clarity. I was no longer in my own time. However impossible. I shook my head. It *was* impossible. Should be impossible. A dream. Had to be a dream. No, this wasn't a time-travel thing, this was me passed out in a ditch somewhere, suffering madly for it.

"Why do ye shake your head? Where are ye supposed to be, lass?" His fingers trailed lightly over my shoulders. "Ye're dressed as a peasant, yet your bearing, your hands"—his fingers slid down my arm to catch my hand into his, his thumb rubbing circles in my palm—"they are those of a well-bred lady."

"I'm not…supposed to be here." Or was I? Maybe somehow Fate had deigned to give me a second chance at life, knowing there was nothing left for me in my own time.

"Are ye sure?"

No, I wasn't. A huge part of me wanted to be here. To have his breath on my neck, his caress on my hand. I'd never felt so… I don't know. I couldn't describe it. He was intense, but gentle. He exuded power, yet I wasn't frightened. I liked his attention. Wanted more.

"What is your name, lass?"

Behind the Plaid

I swallowed around the lump in my throat to keep from croaking in answer. "Emma." Unexpectedly, my voice sounded not its own. Sensual. Raw.

I sensed him coming closer. "Emma," he whispered against the shell of my ear.

Shivers wracked me, even when I tried to still them. This wasn't right. I had to leave. What was I doing, letting a stranger, a blood-thirsty warrior whisper in my ear? But my feet remained rooted to the floor and if it could, I swore my flesh would leach out for more of his touch.

"Where are ye from, Emma?"

"Washington," I answered, even knowing he wouldn't know where that was.

"Washington? I've heard of no such place. Are ye lying?" His voice had taken on a sinister note.

"No, it's across the ocean."

"I see. Ye're way of speaking is...odd."

He couldn't place it, that was obvious. He'd probably never heard an American accent. Then it occurred to me—I didn't even know what year it was. America might not even exist. But that wasn't nearly as worrisome as the fingers that trailed up and down my arms sending my nerves into a frenzy of contradicting sensations. A battle of want and recoil.

"Will you help me?" I heard myself ask.

"Aye."

Relief sank deep, even though I had no idea how he'd help me, or how I could ask him to return me to my time. I'd come during a thunderstorm. Maybe the only way to return was through a thunderstorm.

"Will there be anyone looking for ye?"

I nodded, because there was, even if I never wanted to be found. Even if Steven never made it to this place. This time.

"Who?"

Dare I answer? No. I didn't want him to know I had a husband. Didn't want him to stop touching me because of it. Shocking thoughts... I'd surely suffer for having them. But wasn't it true that if I had traveled back in time, Steven didn't exist? He'd yet to become a thought, let alone a man. He couldn't torment me here. Make me cringe with self-loathing.

I shook my head. "No one."

The man didn't ask me to explain or remind me that I'd just told him someone was. He accepted it. Relief sagged over me, making me feel even more comfortable in his presence.

"Do ye know who I am?" he asked, his hands stopping on my shoulders to knead the tension gently away.

I had a hard time not moaning at the sensation. I hadn't realized how knotted my muscles had grown. How thick with tension. "No."

"I'm the Laird of Gealach."

I dragged in a slow breath. The laird. The man in control of this castle and the land all around. A powerful man.

"What am I to call you?"

"Call me, 'My Laird'."

"What is your given name?" I knew it wasn't customary for him to share it, and he might punish me for asking, but if I were to call him My Laird, at least I wanted to think of him by his given name.

He stiffened, and I heard his intake of breath. I waited for him to berate me, to punish me, but he didn't. Instead, he answered softly, "Logan."

I repeated the name in my mind, letting it roll around. The name matched him. Was as strong as he was. Sensual as he was.

"Thank you, my laird."

"Why do ye thank me?"

"For sharing it with me."

He grunted, still massaging my shoulders. I was slowly becoming delirious with the way he made my muscles melt and the heat of his body. Exhaustion slipped over me like a cozy, well-worn blanket, and I was ready to curl up in his arms and sleep.

"Come. Ye need to get cleaned up, fed and rest," he said, seeming to read my mind.

He gripped my elbow lightly and twirled me around to face him. My eyes came face to chest, and slowly I raised them to meet his. His dark eyes were so intense, addictive, I could have stared at them all day. His mouth was set firm, yet soft. I had the unreasonable urge to kiss him, and leaned a little closer. For a moment, I thought he might kiss me. His lips parted, his eyelids drooping slightly. But Logan seemed to have more sense than me. He turned, urging me to follow him, his hand at my elbow.

We walked back toward the staircase and when we reached it, he lifted me into his arms, my sore hip pressed to the hardness of his torso. The ache in my bones dissipated with the warmth of his body. He lifted me with little to no effort, healing me with his easy charm.

"You don't have to carry me, my laird."

"Ye were limping."

I'd hardly noticed. "Are you not sore from your…battle?"

He gave me a wicked grin and a wink. "Never."

Holy of holies… My heart skipped a beat. The man was simply breathtaking and wielded a magnetism I was having a hard time ducking from. I didn't believe in things like fate and love at first sight, but even in the cab I'd had the overwhelming need to come here. And now I wasn't compelled to leave. I didn't know why. I was only aware that I wanted to stay, that I wanted to get to know this man.

We went down one flight, passing the window well I'd sat in, and then through another heavy door leading down an equally dark corridor. Logan came to the end of the hall, the last door, and without jostling me, opened it. The man exuded strength and dexterity. We entered the large room with high ceilings, multiple windows, and an overwhelming hearth.

More overwhelming was the size of the bed he laid me upon. Four thick posts, carved with designs that told of a history. Warriors, animals, weapons, battles, feasts. I was overwhelmingly curious, but did not have time to ask him about the carvings.

"Stay here," he commanded.

I lay back without argument, glad for the softness of the plaid coverlet and plush pillows. My aching muscles welcomed the softness, too, and my eyelids drooped. Maybe, if I drifted off to sleep, I'd wake upon the rain-soaked earth, my cab waiting patiently for my return.

But it wasn't to be. Moments later a team of servants bustled into the room. No Logan.

I watched with half-open eyes as they filled a wooden tub with steamy water, set out a platter of succulent meat, cheese, steamy bread and a bowl of fruits. A single goblet was set beside a trencher and filled to the brim with plum-colored wine.

Single. This was for me and I was to eat alone.

A hearty, middle-aged woman advanced on me. "Lady Emma, I'm Agatha, sent to serve ye. Come now, to the bath. His lairdship has requested we attend ye."

Lady Emma? Attend me? Why was I receiving such special treatment? Logan had no idea who I was, and yet he'd have me treated like a queen. It was more respect than I'd ever received from a man in my life—save my father before his tragic death.

I nodded and climbed from the bed, walking toward the water. Another maid dripped scented oils and sprinkled herbs into the water. Rose. Jasmine. Verbena. A luscious bouquet that had my flesh tingling to get inside of it.

Agatha reached for the buttons on my blouse, but I batted her hands away. "I can do this myself," I said, not wishing her to undress me. "In private." There were half a dozen maids in attendance, all of them staring at me. Heat prickled my cheeks. I smiled wanly, trying to seem as though I weren't so paranoid about their task. I simply didn't feel comfortable undressing in front of a bunch of strangers.

Agatha just raised her eyebrow and looked at me as though I were a peevish child. "My lady, the laird has requested us to attend ye."

"What does that mean? I can attend myself," I said petulantly, already feeling like I was losing the battle.

Agatha shook her head, hands planted on thick hips. "Whatever Laird Gealach wants, we are to obey."

But I didn't have to obey. I wasn't even from here. I shook my head and crossed my arms over my chest, as if to protect myself, hoping they would all just vanish. Agatha put a wrinkled, gentle hand on my arm.

"My lady, please. We willna harm ye. We are to see ye have a nice bath, warm clothes and a hearty meal. 'Twill do ye good."

I stared at her. Wondered if I ran would the women dodge or lunge to catch me? As if on cue a shift in the wind blew through the open windows, sending the scents of the herbal bath to tease my nose. I longed for the bath. Longed to scrub the mud from my hands and legs. Giving in, I nodded.

Agatha proceeded to strip me, handing my garments to another maid, both of them not bothering to hide their curiosity at my undergarments. When I was fully nude, feeling completely exposed. I did my best to cover my breasts and crotch, however feeble my moves were. All the women murmured as they took in my trim figure. Agatha prodded my bruises and clucked her tongue. Pointed at the dark blue Celtic rune tattoo on my hip I'd gotten in a moment of teenage rebellion. She muttered something in Gaelic to which they all responded, their eyes eagerly devouring me. I flinched, trying to get away from her—from all their prying eyes—wondered why she thought it so normal to see me naked, standing here, then realized that in whatever time this was, such a thing *was* normal. The only one embarrassed was me.

She issued an order for another maid to fetch oils, then all but lifted me into the tub. I sank into the heated water, letting the scents and warmth sink into my bones. Mumbling my pleasure, I laid my head back against the rim.

If this was a dream, it was a glorious one I'd no wish to wake from. I sent my thanks to Fate for being so kind in sending me back here to this place, with these people.

I was thoroughly scrubbed from my toes to the top of my head, my skin, including my scalp tingling, refreshed. When I stood to be dried, several women rubbed linen towels over my flesh, then massaged oil into my skin, focusing especially on the bruises. The oil smelled of sweet herbs, and soothed my tender flesh.

"'Twill help with healing," Agatha said. "Your legs are so smooth."

"I shaved them," I answered absently.

Agatha pursed her lips. "I thought only men shaved—and their faces at that. Never heard of a woman doing such."

I shrugged. "Where I come from it's standard." And I did it each day, hoping my attention to hygiene would impress Steven, but he didn't care. There was always something wrong with me. Why had I tried so hard? But I knew the answer to that—I wanted him to accept me. To praise me. And part of me still did.

"And this, too?" Agatha asked, her eyes centered on the sparse auburn curls between my thighs, shaped into a racing strip.

My face flamed red. I'd not thought they'd look. I suppose I should have known they would. "Wax."

"Wax?" The maids all murmured their confusion at that.

I just nodded, not wanting to explain to them the intricacies of a bikini wax. Just when I thought they would stare at my

Behind the Plaid

pubic area all day, one of the maids pulled a nightgown over my head. The material was soft, thin against my freshly scrubbed skin, and I felt strangely beautiful, sensual in it. Another maid knelt before me and lifted each of my feet to place silken slippers on them. They were a little big, my toes wiggling freely.

Agatha held up a red and green tightly-woven, wool plaid robe. Black Celtic designs were embroidered on the plain green fabric of the collar, hem and sleeves. I slipped into its warmth, then she settled me before the gigantic hearth. A small blaze — almost humorous in its size against the cavern — lit the space.

"Why such a tiny fire?"

"'Tis too hot in the summer for a large one, my lady."

"Why bother?"

"'Tis too drafty without it, and with ye being in the bath, we didna want ye to catch your death."

Agatha ran a comb through my wet hair, snagging on a few knots and gently working through them. As she did so, another maid approached me with a glass of wine in hand.

"My lady," she offered.

I greedily took it, even though it had to be afternoon — and I'd never had wine before six o'clock. The wine was thick, not watered down, tasting tangy and yet smooth. A contradiction, like everything about Logan. It warmed my belly and soothed my soul. I took another healthy sip, very much enjoying it. "What kind of wine is this?"

"'Tis from France, my lady. Laird Gealach only drinks the best wines."

The wine didn't have the same vinegary taste most of the wines Steven bought had. It was smooth, refreshing, enchanting. The tannic aftertaste a welcome bite to the tongue.

"Where is Laird Gealach?" I mused as my hair was braided and piled on top of my head.

"Dealing with the attack no doubt, my lady," Agatha answered.

I imagined him, chest puffed, eyes narrowed as he let whoever dared go against him feel the weight of his wrath. "Who attacked the castle?"

"'Twas a raid by a bordering clan. Looked like MacDonalds."

"Why would they attack?" I was starting to feel particularly warm and fuzzy from the wine and my bath. I should probably eat some food soon.

"Gealach is a powerful castle—one of the largest strongholds in the kingdom. It has been situated here on the loch since the beginning of time. We're the guards of Scotland. Many would seek to take that power away. King James has entrusted our laird to keep things in order."

"Hmm…" I took another sip of wine, realizing the cup was empty and I felt a bit like I was floating. "Which King James?"

Agatha gave me a look like I'd lost my mind, and I waggled the cup of wine in hopes she'd chalk it up to that.

"King James V of Scotland."

I smiled and inclined my head in thanks. James V… If only I could remember when he was King of Scotland. Inside my skull buzzed from the wine. I tried to remember all I'd learned in our short vacation and in the books I'd read before we traveled. The king's name rang a bell, but all I could think of was that it must have been sometime during—

"Come and have a bite, my lady," Agatha encouraged. She led me to the table which had been set out with enough food to feed an entire family—of a dozen.

"Won't you join me?" I asked.

All six of them shook their heads no, but proceeded to watch as I tore a hunk of bread from a loaf and nibbled. It was different than any bread I'd tasted before. Fresh, thick, hearty, surprisingly still warm in the center.

Behind the Plaid

"Shall I serve ye?" Agatha asked.

I shook my head. The woman had served me enough already, I could get my own food. Using a three-pronged fork and knife I cut a piece of meat, speared it and placed it on the silver trencher. It was roasted, succulent, juices oozing from within and smelled of fresh herbs and garlic. My mouth watered and my tummy rumbled. I didn't realize how hungry I was until then. Unable to help myself, I stuffed a chunk of the venison in my mouth, not caring that some of the juice dribbled down my chin. Steven would have never stood for that.

But he wasn't here. And I was hungry.

I ate like a glutton, no doubt making the maids wonder at my manners. When I was finally full on delicious food and even more delicious wine, I leaned back in the chair and stared up at them. My eyes were growing heavy. It'd been night when I flashed back in time. Though it appeared to be late afternoon by now, I'd missed a full night's sleep. The combination of wine, emotional trauma and the unbelievable had sucked the energy from me. I was thoroughly exhausted.

"Please express my pleasure to the cook," I murmured.

They nodded, bowing their heads.

"To bed now, my lady. His lairdship will wish ye to attend him soon."

And that woke me right up.

CHAPTER FIVE

Logan

The loch was frigid and churned with such ferocity that it seemed as though she felt the underlying fury sluicing off my skin. An ire that was always present, keeping me balanced on the edge of a sword's blade. Blackness, save for the sliver of moon and a sprinkling of golden stars, encased the sky. Night swimming was routine for me. Nearly daily, even when snow fell upon my head and chunks of ice floated upon the top of the water. The cold focused me. Helped me to think, to work through whatever issue needed deciphering.

Right now that issue was a certain beautiful, red-haired, supple creature housed within my castle.

I dove deep, letting the cool temperatures of the water sink into my skin, down to my bones, washing the remnants of battle sweat, blood and muck away. Letting it quell the heat that raged in my veins from the aftermath of the attack and my encounter with Emma.

Emma.

Who was she? How had she ended up upon the stairs of Gealach Castle? Images of her tumbling backward, end over end, long, shapely legs exposed. Breasts stretched across the front of her blouse. Heaving breaths accentuating those breasts. Though she'd yanked her skirt down, I'd caught a glimpse of an arse built for gripping in the throes of passion. She'd looked up at me with her large, almond shaped blue eyes. Seductive eyes. Soulful eyes. I felt as though she saw right inside of me, to the very core of my darkest secrets. And yet she hadna run, she'd let me take her hand in mine. Even after the battle, when I'd found her running down the corridor of the castle, headed nowhere, she'd stopped. Waited. Let me touch her. Let me breathe in her sweet scent.

Ballocks, how I'd wanted to crush her to me. To kiss her. To claim her for my own.

There was something about her. Almost as if her soul reached out to mine. Like we were connected, but 'twas impossible. I'd never met the lass in my life. Pushing harder in the water, I touched the bottom before shooting back to the top, lungs burning for a breath of air. Finally, I burst upon the surface, taking that much needed breath, flicking wet hair from my face.

"Who are ye?" I asked, looking up at the castle toward the chamber she occupied—the one that connected through a secret staircase to my library and another secret panel to the chamber next door—mine. The room was meant for the Lady of Gealach. Why had I given it to her?

I convinced myself 'twas because I wanted to keep an eye on her, and what better way than having her connected to the two rooms I used most?

However, another part of me suggested a separate reason... I wanted her.

More than just a claiming, more than to touch her, stroke her. I wanted her for... My heart skipped a beat, pushing blood forcefully through my body and straight into my cock. Rigid, straining, nearly painfully so with the need to fill her. To teach her. To have her submit to me and set us both free.

I shook my head, water droplets flicking into my eyes. Thank ye Gods for the refreshing water of the loch. Exercise was the only way to cure the surge of heat in my veins. I pulled my arms through the water, rotating my shoulders, twisting from side to side, legs kicking powerfully. A mile down the loch and back.

The ships we'd commandeered loomed from the docks like monsters in the dark. They were silent. All who'd occupied the vessels either dead or in my dungeon. The battle had been quick and easy, especially since we were prepared. We watched patiently from the battlements as the forces laid anchor, climbed from their rope ladders into the row boats and came to shore. My men were eager, ready then to storm the beach, but I wasna. I wanted the bastards to think they had the upper hand. And my plan worked.

Not as many warriors disembarked as I'd thought. Perhaps the number of ships was meant to scare, or they thought they'd have quite a bit to load when they'd vanquished us. Perhaps taking our people back to the Isles as slaves. I had no idea, nor did I care at the moment. I was simply astounded to see that not as many had climbed into the row boats. Maybe a hundred at most.

And still while they climbed the cliffs, we dared nay move. As soon as the first man set foot on the dawn's dewy grass, I issued a silent order to descend into the bailey. The crofters and clan members had long since been told to hide, to make the castle appear as though it were uninhabited by anything save spirits. Had been eerie for certes, to see and hear nothing but the gentle breeze. Then a crash of thunder hurled from above, lightning whizzing down to spark at my boots. 'Twas the most violent storm I'd seen yet—without rain. I took it as a sign from God, we would prevail. He would strike those heathens down. My men agreed.

We left the castle, running into Emma along the way. Her presence still bothered me. I'd not seen her come over the Great Glen. For certain I would have. 'Twas as if one moment there was no one and the next... she appeared as though from the mist. Perhaps delivered from the sky herself to tantalize me. Sway me. Disturb me.

My eyes once more fell on the well-built war ships, almost ancient in appearance with their swooping Viking design and dragon bows. But the wood was new. Polished, cared for. The design was meant to entice fear. To bring out the memories of Vikings invading these lands. Ravishing the women, annihilating the men, enslaving the children.

A cruel master of these ships. Could only be one man. My greatest enemy, besides the truth—MacDonald.

Laird MacDonald had been after Gealach for years, his father before him warring with my own in a conflict centuries old. Even though the MacDonald had to come to Gealach by ship, that never stopped him. And there was more incentive now behind his recent attack.

More than merely a centuries old conflict, more than simply to take.

The king whispered to MacDonald of Gealach's secrets when well into his cups. I'd stumbled across them late one night at Stirling when the king called all his leaders for his annual assembly, where we all agreed in treatise not to war with one another and to remain loyal to our king. MacDonald sneered in my direction as he swore upon the heavens to uphold the king's decree.

He was a liar.

The bastard filled the king's cup as I heard them whispering before the hearth in the king's inner hall. Everyone else had long since been dismissed and gone off to drink, gamble, or spend the eve with a wench or three. I sat in a darkened alcove, had been there for a while—enjoying my latest gift from the king. James would have never let anyone else entertain a wench in his inner hall. When she was gone, I remained. And listened. MacDonald was completely sober, his cup bone dry as he pretended to sip. I knew this because he never refilled his own cup. As many sips as he'd taken, he could have drunk an entire cask of ale. I suspected MacDonald of inebriating the king before, and now, I saw for myself as he filled the king's cup with whisky splashed with a drop of ale to keep him talking. The bastard pried the king for information, speaking jovially, laughing, pretending to be sotted, but his eyes were bright, clear.

He asked the king about Gealach, wanting to know more about me. How to defeat me—though he didn't ask outright. He simply asked the importance of the place the king prized most. While the king had been foolish enough to divulge of our buried treasures, he'd at least had the wherewithal to keep the biggest of Gealach's secrets to himself. Else, I'd be dead already.

Floating in the water, I glanced down at my hands, at the thick gold ring on my right ring finger. Celtic knots surrounded a single large ruby. King James gave me the ring on my seventeenth birthday. When the young king slipped it on my finger, he gave with it the news that turned my life from one of proud, eager son, to one of terror and tragedy. I still recall the look on my mother's face when he'd graced our doorstep, presumably to offer his condolences to the late laird's family and to require the allegiance of the new laird—me. She'd looked panicked, petrified. Glancing from one of us to the other— already knowing what was to come, and yet perhaps having hoped it would never come to pass. Mother had then fainted straight away and never recovered. The physician said her heart simply stopped beating.

At that moment, I loved James and hated him at the same time. We shared a common bond, one I could not ignore. One forged in blood. One he'd learned after having escaped the clutches of his step-father's greed. He needed me. Needed an ally, a protector. I hated him for what he'd done to my mother.

The king had not stopped giving me gifts since. A guilty conscience, perhaps. Bribery to remain on his side when I might loathe him for being what he was to me—not just my king.

Anger sliced through me as I watched the ships gently sway in the moonlight. MacDonald had not come with his men. He'd not sent all of his men either. This couldna be the end of it. 'Twas only the beginning.

Trusting in MacDonald was apt to get any man killed. Not even my king—although I'll never admit such to anyone. I dare not think it too often to myself. A man was best to believe that all surrounding him were his enemies. The only person I trusted completely was Ewan—yet even he knew naught of my buried secret.

Walking up onto the beach, cold sand pushing between my naked toes, I grabbed for my plaid, pleating it around my hips and belting it in place. No easy feat as many had to lie upon the ground. I taught myself young to dress quick and on my feet. Difficult, but not impossible. I stood upon the beach taking in the sights and sounds. Relishing the freedom that came with my position as laird and yet, I was still bound. Tied. Not truly free.

Shadows from the sliver of moon, danced all around, making leaping black figures frolic upon the damp cliffs. The crashing of waves and soft trill of wind was a welcome song.

I glanced up at the castle. My eyes riveted on the darkened windows of Emma's chamber. Not even a flicker of candlelight. 'Twas after midnight. She'd be asleep, the maids having followed my orders to see her bathed, dressed, fed and tucked into bed. The woman had been exhausted, evidenced by the dark purple smudges between her eyes. 'Twas apparent even in the way she'd walked, swaying a little on her feet and a slight limp from having fallen. When I'd lifted her in my arms, she'd weighed no more than a feather and her form molded perfectly to mine.

Lush, warm, feminine curves. Her clothing odd, her accent disturbing. She'd said she was from Washington. A place across the sea. Was she from the New World? I'd heard rumors the Spanish were exploring vast new continents halfway to hell and back. Why was her accent disturbingly close to the Sassenachs?

Where she was from, that didna explain how she ended up on the stairs of Gealach Castle. There were only four reasons for someone to climb my stairs—by accident, sent by an ally, sent by an enemy, or to attack. I prayed it was the first reason that put her within my grasp. If she'd been sent by an ally she would have mentioned it. The latter two only made me want to batter the MacDonald men harder.

I dinna believe in coincidence.

"*Mo creach,*" I cursed to the sky. "Why do ye test me?"

Was it the heavy burden I'd been dealt? The truth of my birth that plagued me? My whole life seemed a test. A test of patience. Fortitude. Strength. Loyalty. Intelligence. Even Emma was a test to what I could stand. Beyond an affair, she couldn't be mine. King James would choose a wife for me. And I had my suspicions about why Emma had suddenly appeared. The disappointment of her not being meant for me hit deep. And unreasonably so, since I'd nay idea who in holy hell she was. Mayhap 'twas because I wanted her for myself. To have just one thing I could savor. Something to believe in that was innocent of guile, and wholly sensual. She'd responded to my touch instantly. Her skin pebbling beneath my breath, her body shivering. Nearly panting. Nipples budding.

Behind the Plaid

Merely thinking of her had my cock hardening, lengthening. Lord grant me patience. A few clouds wafted over, covering what little light the sliver of moon had illuminated. Before a storm broke, I headed for the hidden stair cut into the cliff that would take me to the top. Rounding a jumbled bit of tall rocks and slipping into the crevice that was wide enough for only a man, I climbed the always slippery steps, my bare toes feeling the familiar moss and algae that grew with abandon upon the stairs.

When I reached the top, the wind picked up, my plaid billowing out and then plastering to my thighs, a constant give and take with the erratic and fickle winds. A rather intense storm it would be judging from how swiftly the clouds came in.

I'd not sleep well this night. Every broken bone I ever had—and that would be many in my thirty years—ached on nights like this. The only thing that quenched it was whisky and women. I'd no interest in the first and hoped to rectify the latter with a visit to my comely guest.

Was she warm and soft, huddled deep within the blankets? Or did she sit in the dark, plotting her escape?

A sudden thought wrenched inside me. What if she was sent as a spy—and as I stood here upon the glen she rifled through my library? A spy would have thought to look for a secret staircase.

"Och, ballocks!" I raced toward the castle, proud to see the men upon the battlements and gatehouse stay their ground despite the impending storm.

Why had I not thought to leave a guard at her door, or even told one of the maids to keep guard inside? Hell, a guard *in* her chamber!

Her beauty was distracting. Her curves an enticement I'd not found the will to turn away from. Emma would make the perfect spy. She could slip inside my bed, tire me with erotic prowess and then search the castle unfettered to find whatever she'd been sent to retrieve.

I wouldna let that happen. Midnight or nay, I had to find out who she was and her purpose. Had to get the thought of her lush breasts from my mind. The thoughts of what treasure was hidden between her lithe thighs. Her wet, pulsing cunny clenching my cock. I groaned aloud as I slammed into the castle, taking the wheel stairs three at a time. This night I'd touch her, quench my thirst by partaking in the pleasures she had to offer.

Spy or nay, she was going to answer my questions and then warm my bed.

CHAPTER SIX

Emma

In the middle of the night I woke, prickles of fear skidding over my neck. I gasped, eyes wide, but could see nothing. I sat straight up, feeling blind, scared. It took several moments for my eyes to adjust to the darkened room. The fire that had been banked when I'd been put to bed was dead and there were no candles lit. The only light came from the windows, sending slashes of silver to cut across the floor and pieces of furniture. One particular shaft fell over the bed, slicing across my knees, and another by the door…

Illuminating a figure.

A rather large figure, but I could make out nothing other than size in the shadows.

"Who…Who's there?" I asked, trying and failing to keep the fear from my voice.

The figure took a few steps closer, arms crossed over his massive and imposing chest. Logan. I blinked rapidly, trying to wrap my head around him being in my bedroom.

"You scared me, my laird," I admitted.

He didn't speak. A rather imposing and sensual man looming in my doorway.

Shivers stole over me, taking my breath once more. I pulled the covers closer, seeking their warmth, for there was no protection in the fabric, nor in the humongous four-poster bed. What could he possibly want? Had he come for me to...attend him, as his maids had assured me he would? The thought was tantalizing, awoke some part of me that had lain dormant for years. But at the same time I was filled with terror. What if he found me lacking in beauty as Steven did? What if he thought my body too thin and boyish? The red curls between my thighs repulsive?

"I needed to speak with ye," he finally murmured.

"What time is it?" Not that it mattered, but I'd lost all sense of time and place.

"After midnight."

I nodded, trying to ignore the big question—what was so important that he chose to wake me in the middle of the night? Instead, I settled for trivial conversation. "Thanks for the delicious meal and the bath."

"I was glad to see to your pleasure."

A different type of shiver stole over me—electrifying. Why did his words have to sound so...wicked?

"This chamber is...nice." I didn't want to say huge, masculine, imposing. I felt stupid for saying anything at all, but the silence was killing me, and I tended to speak when nervous.

But in that instant I saw the flash of his white teeth in a sliver of light as he stepped forward. I was again reminded of what a handsome man he was. His chiseled features even more

Behind the Plaid

pronounced in the moonlight and with a dark shadow of stubble across his strong jaw.

"I'm glad ye approve. Apologies for waking ye." His voice was soft, sincere. "I had much to deal with after the attack and I'd not intended to find ye asleep—or to come so late."

"Do you often stay up past midnight?" I asked, curious about his habits.

He shrugged, the motion drawing my eyes to his muscular torso once more. "Only when I have a lot on my mind."

"Do you have a lot on your mind?" I had a particular feeling that whatever thoughts he had on his mind had to do with me—but not in a way that was cruel or resentful. Logan was nothing like Steven. The two differed in nearly every way.

"Aye. Ye in particular."

Logan uncrossed his arms and bent by the hearth, stoking the deadened embers and obviously taking note there was no life left in them. He added peat logs and lit them with a flint. Wafts of the earthy scented smoke reached me, having an almost drugging effect. The light of the fire gave the room a warm glow, and better outlined Logan. It looked like he'd had a bath—his hair was damp. He wore no linen shirt, only a plaid wrapped at his waist. A short sword was at his hip, but he appeared otherwise unarmed.

My gaze landed on his eyes, still shadowed with his back to the fire. I wished I could see them more clearly, to know what he was thinking. To prepare myself for whatever it was he would say. Instinctively I knew he wouldn't berate me as Steven did. But even still, despite not having known him long, I didn't want to disappoint him.

"What is it you…needed, my laird?"

He took in a short draw of breath at my question. Perhaps it would have been unnoticeable to anyone else, but my eyes were glued on him, my nerves tuned in to each of his movements, reactions.

"What is it ye're willing to give?"

What a question. To which I had no reply. "I'd not thought about it," I answered honestly with a frown.

He chuckled. "Shall I tell ye, then?"

I nodded, even though part of me dreaded what he might say.

"Ye are a stranger here. From a faraway place. The moment ye graced my door, enemies attacked. I want ye to give me the truth, Emma."

The way he said my name was a dark stroke over my insides. It wasn't threatening, even when it was demanding. I liked hearing him say it, the way his brogue caressed each letter.

"I can give you that." *Or a version of it.*

"Tell me then. Who are ye? Why did ye bring the enemy to my doorstep?" Logan came around from the foot of the bed to the side I sat on. Standing just a few feet in front of me, he leaned a hip on one of the thick posters, his muscular arms crossed over his chest. With his face now only half in shadow, the other half dancing orange from the flames in the hearth, I could better assess that he looked merely curious.

I shook my head, held my hands out in supplication. "I truly had no knowledge that men were coming to attack. I've no idea who your enemy is, or why they were here. I can promise that I didn't bring them, nor do I have anything to do with them."

He studied me, eyes roving over my face, my chest—my nipples wickedly growing taut as his gaze hesitated there. I bit my lip as tingles zinged from the two naughty peaks, pulling at some place deeper within.

"Why did ye come here, then?"

"I was…" I had to tell him something. A version of the truth. Sticking to what I knew would help me keep my story fresh in my own mind. I wasn't one for lying, and Steven always said that my lies were fully visible on my face. Like I was a book, anyone could read through me. "I was running away."

"Running away?"

I nodded. "Away from my…life."

"Ye were not happy?"

I shook my head. I wasn't. I was miserable. Tears prickled the backs of my eyes, my throat was tight and I forced my fingers to stop trembling by digging them deep into the blankets.

"Why?"

I couldn't answer. Didn't know this man, and certainly didn't want to share with him the embarrassment of a nearly a decade of being told I was worthless.

Seeing my hesitation, he continued, "What were ye hoping to gain here?"

"I—I don't know. I saw the gate, the walls, the keep. Remembered that it was Gealach and so I ran toward it."

He seized on my words, his own coming out clipped and suspicious. "How did ye remember it was Gealach?"

Honesty. "I was here…before."

His darkened gaze bore into mine as though he would see inside my soul. "When? I dinna recall seeing ye."

I shook my head, nerves whizzing around like crazy, feeling completely out of control. One misstep and he might throw me out into the wild, or worse, into his dungeon. I'd seen the dungeon of Gealach when visiting with Steven. Seen how dank and dark it was. A hole in the deepest bowels of the castle. No light entered there. No way to get in or out. I would simply be tossed with the rats, spiders and God knew what else.

I was making a muddle of it. But sticking to the truth was the easiest thing, and so far I hadn't lied at all. Willing myself to gain some calm, I spoke in a surprisingly clear voice, "Well—" I searched for something. "We didn't come through the gate."

"We?"

"M—" I was about to say, *my family*, but I didn't want him to ask me about them, to try and find them. He'd never have any luck. But if he knew of their existence he might try to locate them—however futile.

When I didn't speak again, he prompted, "Merchants?"

"Yes." An obvious lie, as my eyelids lowered and I tried to hide from it. Logan's gaze shifted a bit, seeming to let it slide, surprising me. "We weren't here long."

"Long enough to like what ye'd seen?"

"Long enough to know that you are a good laird and that your people respect you, care for you."

His chest puffed a little at my praise, but still he kept his gaze guarded. Logan was an intelligent, shrewd man—however suspicious. "Aye, they do." He shifted closer, his hip resting on the mattress.

My heartbeat skipped and my temperature went up a notch. But I didn't know if that was from his closeness or the growing warmth of the fire. He was so large, powerful, filling up my personal space and owning every breath.

He stared at me for several assessing moments. "Do ye want to stay then, Emma?"

I licked my dry lips. My throat swollen with a lump. "Yes." My voice came out a hoarse whisper.

He came a little closer, this thigh brushing against mine as he leaned against the bed. I had to tilt my head to look up at him. "I want ye to stay."

He did? My eyes widened. The words floated between us. His admission. My admission. It seemed we were both in deep, but *in what*, I didn't know. Couldn't fathom. Felt at a complete loss for what *this* was. All I knew were the blanket facts that anyone could guess. But then again, I had seen a part of Logan that made me trust him. A part that connected my soul to his. He was compassionate, intense, and though he knew nothing about me, was willing to allow me to stay and offer me his protection.

"I dinna want ye to be unhappy." His words, while simple, edged deep. Steven had never cared about my happiness. Even *I* had not cared so much about my happiness over the last eight years. Just that short phrase, that short desire to see me pleased had an incredible effect on me. One I was sure Logan wasn't even aware of.

"But what am I to do with ye?" he asked, his gaze once more traveling over me.

My toes curled, and I squeezed my thighs tightly together. I could tell what he wanted to do with me. I just wasn't sure I really wanted it. My body did. My mind was another story—one that was slowly opening up to the possibilities that Fate had given me. "I don't know." Honestly.

"I have an idea." His voice was a soft caress, enticing. "I'll keep ye for myself."

"For yourself?" I swallowed hard, past the lump lodged right in the middle of my neck.

"Aye." He sat beside me, his hip touching mine, heating me thoroughly. "I can see the pulse beat in your neck." Reaching out, he touched the exact spot. The calloused tip of his finger was warm and my heartbeat increased at his touch, as though the beat would leap out just for him. He leaned closer, his face an inch away. I inhaled his scent—clean, salty—and closed my eyes. His breath on my face, warm, smelled faintly of whisky and spice. His lips, firm yet lush, brushed over mine.

His kiss wasn't demanding or overpowering. It was light, sensual, seeking permission. His tongue teased in a touch and withdraw pattern against the corners of my mouth. Logan tasted, but didn't require entry. He was leaving it up to me how far he'd go. For now I was content to press my mouth to his and feel the soft flicks of his tongue on my lips. To take in his masculine scent, to be the one with the power to alter the kiss from sweet test to carnal exploration. He didn't touch me otherwise. His hands rested on the mattress beside both of my hips, the deep depression of his weight caused me to tighten my muscles to stay upright.

What surprised me the most was that I didn't pull away. My insides thrummed, my mind buzzed and I was thoroughly enticed to keep kissing Logan. I'd never wanted to kiss a man more.

After several moments of him nibbling at my lips, I parted them slightly on a sigh. Logan didn't immediately invade. He gently swiped his tongue inside, then out, teasing me to open further. I did, my tongue tentatively touching his. It was velvet soft and hot. Sensations, delicious and wicked whipped along my insides. I tilted my head slightly, deepening the kiss, suddenly wanting him to consume me.

As if sensing my urgency, he grasped me face in his hands, threading his fingers in my hair and quickly claimed my mouth in a kiss that was altogether intoxicating and mind-blowing. I soared, weightless, filled with prickling need. My nipples were hard as stones, my thighs clenched so tight they quivered. I was wet, filled with a craving that seemed so intense as to be like a drug, an addiction.

"Do ye want to be mine?" he said gruffly against my mouth.

"Yours?" I couldn't stop repeating him, my tongue flicking against his, my hands rubbing up over his muscled arms, taking in their strength, their sheer size and wanting to rub my naked flesh upon his. My mind simply couldn't wrap around what he was saying. But one stark fact blared insistently through my brain. I shook my head. "I...I don't want to be anyone's property."

Logan chuckled softly, deeply, running his fingers down my neck and over a breast, softly thumbing one of my nipples. I gasped with shock at the pleasure. How could my body respond to him like this? How could he... I expected him to yell

Behind the Plaid

at me for the answer I'd given. Call me ungrateful. Banish me from his castle. But even knowing all that, I felt lighter. Liberated somehow. I'd spoken my mind for the first time in years—even while under the spell of his touch. I didn't want to be his to walk all over.

"I'm not asking for ye to be my property, lass." He nuzzled my neck, sending goosebumps to rise along my arms and legs. I shivered, wanting to feel his hot tongue flick over my pulse beat. "I'm nay asking for ownership. I just want ye to belong to me and no other. For now." His tongue flicked out and I moaned softly.

But I couldn't speak, discern his thoughts or my own with him driving my body toward places it'd never been before. No matter how tempting and delicious. I gently pushed him away. And while I'd been bold with my kiss, I'd only just begun with my words. Instead of staring at my lap like usual, I raised my eyes to his, taking in their dark sensuality, feeling it warm my blood. How was it possible that staring into those eyes, his fingers stroking along the column of my neck, that I wanted to be his? Remaining bold—at least for me—I asked, "Isn't that the same thing?"

Logan shook his head, with gentle pressure on my shoulders he pushed me back on the bed. I didn't resist. I didn't want to. My curiosity soared, my breath hitched. Would he kiss me again? Touch my breasts? Touch my... I was so wet, burning with a need I'd only just begun to realize even existed. I wanted him to kiss me more. To caress me. But that was all. Wasn't it? I didn't want him to hurt me. When Steven made love to me, it always hurt. And he was the only man I'd ever been with.

I was quickly discerning that Logan was nothing like Steven. My response to Logan was different—hot, wicked desire. Perhaps it was only that I'd been asleep, and was overtired. I could make all the excuses I wanted. They weren't the truth. I could not lie to myself. Logan drew me in—from that moment in the cab when I'd seen Gealach looming up in the night sky and needed to run toward it. I didn't know how long I had here, in this time, at Gealach. Perhaps come morning I'd be lying once again in the dewy grass outside the present day crumbling castle. I didn't want to give up on what was plainly in front of me. A night of passion with a man who might teach me all there was to know about... About what? Certainly not love—but desire, tenderness and the power of control.

"Were ye married, lass?" His fingers trailing over my shoulders were as soft as his whisper. I wished my nightgown lay crumpled on the floor.

I nodded, unable to form words, for now he was stroking idly up and down my arms.

"Are ye still?"

Technically...no. Steven had yet to be born—and even in my own time I'd left him. I shook my head.

"Widowed?"

I paused a moment before nodding. I couldn't exactly say that my husband lived in another time. No doubt he was tearing Scotland apart looking for me. Or could I hope that he'd left well enough alone?

"When ye're married, ye're owned by your husband. And even your husband is owned by ye. Ye're bound forever, unto death do ye part. He can do as he pleases to ye, aye?"

I got the underlying impression that Logan feared a bond that couldn't be broken—the reason he stated he only wanted me *for now*. He didn't say it outright, and I could have been completely wrong, but there was something in the way he said it. That marriage represented something permanent he wasn't willing to enter into. We appeared to share the same feelings—I feared being bound to anyone permanently, and so did he. "It would appear that way, but it doesn't seem right."

Logan's lips twitched in a smile, and his fingers caressed slowly over my ribs. "I agree. But nevertheless, in the times we

Behind the Plaid

live, 'tis the way of things. But as a lover, ye are owned by none. I would only ask ye to belong to me and no other. To share your affections with me alone. Until the time we both decide to go our separate ways."

A proposition I'd never thought to receive in my entire life. Tantalizing as it was—images of his mouth trailing over my skin, his fingers massaging, his naked flesh pressed hard to mine—I couldn't bring myself to say yes. The words wouldn't come forth, no matter how hard my body strained for me to agree. To strip naked and beg him to kiss me again. I wanted this night, for there was no promise of tomorrow. But on terms? To be labeled? In my own time, no one would bat an eye at such an arrangement. But this wasn't the twenty-first century. This was an era where an unmarried woman sleeping with a man was considered to be sinful. I'd no desire to be any man's whore.

"I can see by the expression on your face what ye're thinking, love." He clasped my hip, branding me with his solid grip. "I assure ye, I'd never label ye a whore. We'll be discreet. My staff has long been loyal and with…" He trailed off, giving me the impression Gealach and its laird had a lot more to hide than what any historian knew. He appeared to choose his next words carefully. "None would dare to call ye such. They'll treat ye as a lady, a queen." Logan massaged circles around my hipbone, and I tried as hard as I could to breathe, but my lungs had ceased to function. "There is something about ye." His eyes met mine. "Something that drew me since the moment I knocked into ye."

"It's the same way for me." Oh-my-God, had I just said that out loud? What was I thinking, admitting such feelings to a man I hardly knew? It was his eyes, so deep, his very aura that made me trust him, feel comfortable with him.

He leaned down, his hot mouth pressed once more to mine, sucking the breath from my lungs and replacing it with a hypnotizing yearning. "Do ye want me, lass?"

With a deep shuddering breath, I let out yet another confession. "Yes."

CHAPTER SEVEN

Logan

To say I was shocked at the lass's answer would be an understatement. I'd fully expected her to deny me. For what reason did she have to agree? Emma wasna like the other women I bedded. They chased after me, lifting their skirts with a raise of my brow, or they were sent from the king—women whose trade was pleasure. I never seduced innocents. Though Emma had been married before, she appeared as much an innocent as the virgin lasses of Gealach.

She shook beneath my fingertips, her skin puckered despite her warmth. 'Twas too dark for me to see her eyes—the windows to a person's soul. Oddly, I craved to look into them. To decipher her true intent. And yet, hers were shuttered from me. I pulled back, a moment of doubt filling me. Hell... I'd never cared before. Never even sat back to wonder.

I stroked along her arms, paying special attention to the sensitive skin inside her elbows.

"Aye?" I asked, needing to hear once more her affirmation.

She nodded. "Yes." Her trembling hands came to the sides of my waist, pressing so lightly I could barely feel them.

The effect she had on me was potent and something I didna want to reflect on. Nay, a man in my position couldna allow a woman to have such an influence on him. I could, however, persuade her to my side. She'd said aye, that was a start.

And yet, she did not act the eager, willing lover I was used to. The women who came to my bed pounced on it. Everything about Emma was different. I found I didna want to exploit that, but to cherish it. Keep it for myself. I wanted to see her passions unleashed, to feel her grip me tight. Wanted to feel her back arch, see her mouth open in a moan, feel her legs twitch, her slick desire on my fingers, my tongue, my cock.

I kissed her again, enjoying the slight quiver of her lips, the timid way her tongue touched mine. I explored her mouth slowly, tantalizingly. Learning the curves of her lips, the line of her teeth. 'Twas a lazy kiss, with no end in sight and no need to change the pace. An exploration of each other, a way to dissipate some of her nerves and for me to gain control of whatever had unhinged me.

Emma's body, which had been strung taut, eased, her limbs loosening, her grip on my waist tightening—just the tips of her fingers increasing their pressure. Gasps rushed from her lips every so often. I was surprised at her genuine, raw reaction to my kiss and the gentle stroking of her ribs and arms. I'd not even delved into her stimulating areas and already her response jolted me.

I licked at her lips, her chin, traveling across her jawline to her ear where I whispered, "Did your husband make ye feel this way?"

'Twas bad form to bring up other lovers, but I had to know. Her natural response was so potent, 'twas almost like she was experiencing pleasure for the first time.

Emma shook her head. Although the room was only bathed in moonlight, I could make out the wideness of her eyes. Her own response frightened her. Even if she liked it, that much I could recognize.

"Dinna be afraid, lass," I whispered, keeping my gaze steady on hers, not wanting to frighten her. "Think of this as...a lesson. Let me show ye what pleasure is."

Again she nodded and an idea struck me—one I'd never deigned to entertain before. That tonight should be for her pleasure, and hers alone. I'd never simply given pleasure and expected nothing in return, but somehow I knew that seeing her melt in my arms, hearing her cry out when she crested, all of it would be enough for me...for tonight. This was what I wanted. To teach her and to master my own body in the process.

To see if I could give her what she so clearly desired and what I so deeply wanted to bestow on her.

Trailing two fingers from the top of her forehead, over her nose and chin and down her neck, I paused on the spot where her heart beat swiftly. The rapid bump against my finger increased the pace of my own. We were both embarking on a journey here. Something entirely new and different to ourselves and to each other.

"Tonight, I see to your pleasure, Emma. Will ye let me?" My voice was hoarse, a rasp through thick desire.

"Please," she answered, her voice a mirror of my own.

I nodded, pressing my lips to her pulse and sucking gently. Emma gasped, her nails digging into my skin. I hissed against her neck and lightly bit her, just a taste of a darker desire.

Slipping a finger into the knot of ribbons near her throat, I tugged until they were no longer tied.

Wanting to see her breasts revealed to me in the moonlight, I sat up. Emma's gaze connected with mine, and I was again struck with a visceral blow at the intensity of her gaze and my need to consume her. With both hands I parted the chemise as far as it would go—all the way to her navel—revealing her supple breasts and a flat belly. I took a moment to gaze upon her perfection. Her breasts rose and fell with each gasp, and then stopped—like she held it.

"Breathe, Emma," I said.

Again her chest rose and fell, her nipples hardening into tiny pink buds. I flattened a hand between her breasts, feeling her heart beat beneath it. Her skin was warm, but even here her skin dimpled with chills. I smiled. "Are ye cold?"

She shook her head.

"Then your skin prickles for me."

Emma swallowed and bit her lip.

"Tell me." I wanted to hear her say it.

"Yes."

I slid my hand over toward her breast, feeling the silky smoothness of it on my palm, her hard nipple tickling the center of it. Emma pulled a breath through her nose, her chest rising a fraction of an inch, as though she hesitated, but wanted me to cup the soft globe.

I watched the way her lips parted as I massaged her, swiping my thumb over the plump tip. I leaned down, wanting to take her gasp into my mouth, to feel her moan against my lips. Emma was a timid, lass, and I wanted to be the one to break her of it. To ignite her passion.

How could her husband not have pleasured her? A bit on the thin side, she was still perfection. Silken creamy skin. Beneath her reticence, I sensed a woman who wanted to break out. A woman who wanted to unleash the power of desire, and all I had to do was unlock her soul.

This, I was good at. Pleasure, passion, sensuality. I was a master.

With both hands stroking her breasts, I skimmed my lips down her neck, licking, teasing her flesh until she whimpered. I nuzzled her plush skin, breathing hotly on her flesh, loving the way it prickled beneath my touch. My tongue a fine point, I slid it from the underside of her breast, up to the middle, pausing just beside her nipple.

"Please," Emma whimpered.

"What do ye want, Emma?"

"I...I don't know."

I laughed softly, and flicked my tongue over her nipple and she cried out. "This? Is that what ye want?"

She arched her back. "Yes."

I grazed her nipple with my teeth, then fluttered my tongue in circles. Emma's hands came from my waist to thread through my hair. She tugged, her pants coming heavy.

I thoroughly enjoyed myself. Relishing her response and how it affected me. I felt powerful, in control. Her body was mine to manipulate, and yet, I sought only to see her pleased.

She groaned when I took my mouth away, but I didna let her forget what my tongue could do. Her hair spread out on the pillow in soft waves, but I resisted touching it. Descending onto her other nipple, this time instead of teasing her delicious flesh, I suckled it. Rolling my tongue over the soft bud. I skimmed my hands up and down her ribs, up her arms and then grabbed both of her hands in one of mine. I held them above her head. Her breath puffing out in bursts. Even my own increased. My cock surged, wanting desperately to bury itself inside her. And I didna even know how she felt, slick, tight... Oh, how I wanted to know.

But no. Not yet. If I were to delve there now, I might frighten her away from our fragile pact. Then where would I be? I had a feeling my desire to possess her would ruin me if I didna know that someday soon she would be mine. That I could make love to her whenever I wanted, hear her shout my name as she peaked, her cunny squeezing fluid from my cock.

So instead, I held her hands above her head, teased her nipples with my tongue until she moaned with uncontrolled abandon. Sliding my hands over her hips and down her thighs, I inched her chemise up, revealing the length of her slim legs — and they were flawless.

"What's this?" I asked, scooting lower to stroke her silky legs.

"Oh," she said, sounding embarrassed. "Your servants were shocked by it."

"Aye..." Holy Heavens... Her legs were bare of hair. So smooth and soft. I'd never felt a woman's legs like that, and I was all the more fascinated by it. "Were ye born this way?"

She laughed. "No. It's from shaving or wax, depending on the month."

"Wax?"

"Yes. Where I come from, it's standard to remove hair."

God's teeth. I bent down and kissed her knee, skimming my lips down to her ankle, and then nipping the bottom of her foot. "All the way up too?"

"Yes," she said, breathlessly.

I kissed my way back up her leg until I reached her thigh. Her sex was still covered by the chemise, but I couldna wait to see.

"And here, too?" With a finger I slid the fabric higher, revealing a thin strip of hair. In the darkness I couldna make out the color and wondered if it was as fiery red as her hair.

Behind the Plaid

Emma bit her lip. "Do you…" She trailed off, her voice suddenly small. I had to remember her husband didna enjoyed her—or at least in a way that was pleasurable.

"I like it, Emma." And indeed I did. I wanted to taste her, to see if it would be all the easier to slick my tongue through her cunny lips and taste her essence with barely any hair there. "I want to taste ye."

"Oh," she said again in that small voice.

"Did your husband?"

She shook her head emphatically. "No, never."

I smiled, secretly pleased that there was yet another thing I could teach her. "I'm going to."

She didna say a word, but I wanted her to. Wanted her to tell me that she wanted me to kiss her there. To taste her, make her peak on my tongue.

"Tell me ye want me to."

"Wh—what?"

"Tell me what ye want."

Her eyes widened again and she shook her head. "I don't know."

I breathed deep, smelling her desire. I'd bet my life her sex was slick with wanting.

"Ye can tell me anything, lass. I want to hear ye say it."

I placed my hand on her naked hip, gently massaging, and I bent to kiss her navel, dipping my tongue inside to swirl around. She smelled musky and sweet. "Do ye like this?" I asked, nuzzling her belly, my chin scraping on the very top of her pubic hair.

"Yes," she whispered.

I kissed her hip, my eyes catching on a dark spot, a birth mark perhaps. I'd have to examine her in the light next time. Nudging her thighs apart, I heard her gasp as her sex was revealed to me. I could barely make out the pink petals of her sex in the dim light, but the one thing I could see was that she was wet.

"Beautiful," I murmured. I kept my gaze locked on hers and cupped her sex, letting her get used to the feel of my hands on her.

She cringed and squeezed her thighs shut, while at the same time she shuddered. A contradictory reaction. Scared, and yet wanting.

"Did he hurt ye?" I asked, suddenly filled with rage for her dead husband. If he were nay already with his maker, I would've sent him there. Who could hurt a woman as docile and intriguing as her?

Emma bit her lip again and nodded. "You won't, though." Her words were infused with a confidence I'd not imagined she could own. I was extremely pleased by it.

"Nay, I never would." I kissed her lips, as if sealing that promise between us. "Open your legs, Emma."

Slowly, she parted her thighs, allowing me to slide my fingers through her hot, velvet folds. I groaned, feeling as though I'd been sent to paradise. "Ye're so wet, lass."

"Is that bad?"

I shook my head. "Nay, never bad. 'Tis the way it should be. Shows that ye desire me, that your body is ready."

"Ready for what?"

Her question was so innocent, and yet I knew she couldn't possibly be that naïve.

"Ready for me to fuck ye."

Emma gasped. "Oh."

I grinned and winked, not sure if she could see it. "Ye want me to fuck ye, dinna ye?"

She stilled, and I sensed she was too embarrassed to answer. Already I'd opened her eyes to much, and I didna want her to distance herself from me.

"Ye dinna have to say the words, lass. Your body has already given me the answer." Sweet heavens... I pushed a finger into her cunny. Tight. Her muscles clamped around me, squeezing my finger. If she'd not said she was married, I might have thought her a virgin. I was happy to think that her arse husband had a small cock.

Nudging her legs further apart, I laid between them, and put them over my shoulders. She fisted the sheets.

"Ye're going to enjoy this, lass."

But she didna answer, couldna. I took her breath away with one long swipe of my tongue. I kept my finger inside her cunny, swirled my tongue around her clit, licked every inch of her folds. Breathing in her essence, I couldna get enough of her sweet, utterly individual scent. Glorious was the only word I could think to describe it. And so delicious.

I licked her until she moaned incessantly, her head thrashing back and forth. I nudged the little bundle of nerves until she jumped. Flicked over it, around it, and then flattened my tongue to rub back and forth until she screamed. Her thighs shook, clenching tight around my head. Her cunny muscles vibrated, clenched my finger, and yet, I wouldna let her finish. Refused. I wanted her to live out this pleasure for as long as she could. To know I was the one who did this. To know that I was in control of her body.

"Logan!" she pleaded. "Please, please, please..."

I chuckled and only resumed my sensual torture. God, I loved the power of it. My cock was so hard, I was sure it'd remain that way for days. And I wouldna seek release. Nay, I preferred to wait until I could sink inside her, fuck her into the next heavenly realm.

"Now, Emma," I demanded, suckling on her pearl.

She cried out, bucking her hips, squeezing the breath from me with her legs, and yet I did not stop. I sucked until her body subsided, then I stroked lazily over the bundle of nerves with the flattened side of my tongue. With my finger still deep inside her, I felt a fresh flood of fluid. She was going to peak again.

I continued at that same lazy pace. Licking, thrusting gently with my fingers. I stroked her breast, pinched her nipple. Her breaths quickened, her moans deepened.

"Mmm... Oh!" she moaned, fisting her hands into my hair.

God, she was coming undone before my eyes. She lifted her hips in a rhythmic movement, riding my face and hand. Her passion was unleashed, and completely out of control. With the desperation of a starving man I wanted to climb on top of her and pound her through the bed.

"Logan!" she shrieked, a violent climax ripping through her. She bolted upright, using my hair as her anchor. Pain seared through my scalp from the force of her yank, but it was a welcome pain.

"Aye, lass, ride my tongue," I murmured continuing my ministrations until her trembling subsided and she flopped back on the bed, utterly spent and satiated.

I climbed atop her, pressing my hard cock between her thighs, letting her feel how much I wanted her. Thank the devil, I kept my plaid in place or else the feel of her slick and pulsing cunny against my cock would have been too much.

"Do ye feel that?"

Her eyes fluttered open, gazing into mine.

"Yes." Her voice was hoarse.

"Feel how much I want ye?"

"Yes." She tentatively put her hands on my back. Her touch light, no longer strong and demanding as she'd been moments ago.

Leaning on an elbow, I slid a hand up her arm, placed it more firmly around me. "Ye can touch me, lass. I won't bite. Well, maybe a little." I nipped at her lower lip.

"That was...Out of this world." A shadow of unexplained emotion slipped over her face, and she lowered her lids, no

Behind the Plaid

longer looking at me. "I truly enjoyed it." She shook her head as if not believing in what had happened. "I didn't think..."

"Shh..." I said, kissing her. "Dinna think of him. Erase him from your mind. Ye're here with me now."

She nodded, her eyes opening once more. "Yes. With you."

CHAPTER EIGHT

Emma

Holy shit...

This had to be a dream. A gift from God, maybe? A way to escape the misery that I'd been living with? When would I wake up? Was I already dead? One moment I'm in a cab running away from the nightmare of my life and the next moment being kissed and licked and coming so hard I thought I was going to die.

My limbs still sparked with a life I'd never experienced before. The way Logan's cock pressed against me filled me with such fear, and desperation. I was scared, yes. But he'd promised not to hurt me, and I believed him.

I shifted my hips beneath him. Wanting to feel more of the glorious pressure. He was big—bigger than big. I didn't even

Behind the Plaid

want to see. Steven had been small. The size of a finger, small. And I thanked my stars for that since even with his tiny girth it pained me when we had sex.

After being in Logan's presence less than twenty-four hours, I knew why. I was never wet with Steven. Never turned on. But just looking at Logan sent my body into a tailspin. Almost like my body sensed the sexual magnetism Logan radiated. He was powerfully sexy. He exuded sex. Hard sex. Hot sex.

And I found myself wanting *that* sex. Hard. Hot. Sweaty. More of his tongue.

That scared me, too. What was I getting myself into? I'd just left my husband and already I was sleeping with another man. Not just sleeping — fucking — well, nearly fucking. And not just any man, the most gorgeous, drop-dead sexy man I'd ever seen. I ran my hands over the rippling muscles of his back, trying to reassure myself that he was indeed alive and on top of me.

Less than twenty-four hours and I could already sense a change in myself. An awakening. A part of me that had lain dormant, never allowed to rise beyond imagination and fantasy. I'd not enjoyed sex in my marriage. True, I'd never been with a man other than Steven. But I knew what passion was. I'd read books, watched movies, seen people on the streets who shared that spark when they looked at each other. A kind that made me want to turn around and look the other way, like I was intruding on their private life.

I knew it was out there. I'd just never thought it would be something I'd experience. Ever. And I still didn't understand what this powerful man saw in me. Steven made it clear I was nothing special. Everything I did to please him only made him angrier.

What did Logan see that Steven hadn't?

I gazed into his dark eyes, the outline of his face bathed in moonlight. I traced the line of his jaw, mesmerized by how sturdy and square it was.

"Why do you...want me?" I asked, sure he could hear the fear in my voice. A nagging terror built in the pit of my stomach as he studied me. I waited for the barrage of insults.

"Ye mesmerize me, Emma."

Mesmerize? The same feeling I had about him. I was drawn to him, even though I didn't know who he was. Somehow, maybe unconsciously, I knew he could heal me. Or at least set me on the path to healing.

He pushed some of my hair off of my forehead, smoothing it down the pillow, then twirling a tendril around his finger. "Ye are beautiful. I see a strength in ye that I dinna think even ye see."

Logan sat beside me, straightened my nightgown and pulled me into his arms. He was warm, and I felt completely safe in his arms. I curled into him, resting my head against his chest and counting the steady beats of his heart.

"Ye're different than the other lasses I've met."

"Different?" I didn't like the sound of that. Different to me meant that I was a freak, unworthy, the things that Steven had pounded into my head many times.

"Aye. Deeper. There is substance to ye. But there is also a hidden passion that I want to unleash. Can ye sense it, lass? That we were meant to bring ye from your shell?"

Weird thing was, I did sense it. I nodded, trying to understand all that was happening, would happen. And yet, still there was a part of me who waited to wake up.

"Is this a dream?"

Logan laughed. "Do ye aim to flatter me?"

"I only wanted to thank you." Heat infused my cheeks as I realized how I sounded. I felt like an idiot and stiffened. Leave it to an arrogant warrior to take my words as meaning his own prowess. He was partly right in what I referred to, and I realized then he had no idea what I was talking about. How could he? Logan didn't know that I was from another time. That when I visited his castle it was with a tour guide.

Logan squeezed me a little. "Ye dinna need to be embarrassed, nor do ye need to thank me. I was only jesting, lass. I canna know what your life was like before ye arrived at Gealach, but I can promise ye that from now on, 'twill be better."

A chill stole over me. He was right. He had no idea what my life was like. His words only served as a reminder of how much we were strangers. I knew so little about him. And I'd told him nothing about myself.

"I'm getting sleepy," I said with a fake yawn, wanting to cut off the intimacy. Uncomfortable in my own skin. What sort of magical spell did this place hold over me? How was Logan able to take me out of myself? I'd barely had a moment to figure out who I was before I fell headlong into his embrace.

"Good night, lass." He didn't argue, perhaps feeling the same thing. He kissed me on the lips briefly before sliding off the bed.

I watched his dark figure walk to the door where he paused. Glancing over his shoulder, he said, "I shall see ye tomorrow night."

Then he was gone, just as swiftly as he'd come.

I buried myself beneath my blankets, still feeling chilled. I jumped between being enamored with Logan and wishing we'd never met. It wasn't that he offended me—not in the least. He'd offered to pleasure me and he'd done it, with aplomb, and wanted to come back for more. I couldn't quite put my finger on what it was. Only that I felt altered. That he made me see things in a new light. Yes, I wanted a different life. But while I was running away from my past, I wasn't sure I was ready to take on reality full force.

Reality... The word brought me back around in another circle. How could I even be sure this wasn't some figment of my imagination? Though it seemed real enough, there was always the possibility I'd had some sort of mental break.

A true yawn stretched my mouth wide. I was exhausted, my limbs heavy. Perhaps when I woke in the morning I'd find myself in a Scottish hospital, or on the ground beside the road. What the morning brought would be my reality.

I woke to the scrape of a door opening. Startled awake, really. I refused to open my eyes. That sound wasn't the noise a hospital door made. It could only mean one of two things. I was at Mrs. Lamb's B&B or I was still at Gealach.

Both of which were places I didn't want to be.

"Good morn' to ye, lass. The laird has had me bring ye a hearty meal."

When I heard those words, anticipation and excitement stole over me. A reaction wholly unexpected. I was still at Gealach. And apparently happy about it. Fine. This was reality. I was a time traveler. I was now Logan's lover. But no matter how much my body yearned for that reality, my mind couldn't help but want to get back to my own time. I couldn't stay here, not forever. It was dangerous. There wasn't modern medicine — or toilets!

They served ale or beer at breakfast didn't they? I was going to need a drink.

"Shall I draw ye a bath?"

I opened my eyes to see Agatha standing beside me. I studied her face, waiting to see the scorn and distaste, but there was none there. She looked...normal.

Pushing up on my elbows, I said, "Do people really bathe so often here?"

Behind the Plaid

My understanding was that baths were a hard commodity back in the day. Having just arrived yesterday and already being offered a second bath couldn't be usual.

Agatha wrinkled her brow. "Well, lass, his lairdship said ye may want one."

She didn't answer my question with words, but I read the meaning behind them. Agatha was aware of what went on behind closed doors, and Logan wanted me clean. I was surprised she didn't seem fazed by it, didn't shun me. I anticipated the warmth of the water and scented soaps.

My nipples hardened and between my thighs tingled, still overly sensitive from his ministrations. Traitorous body. I grumbled my thanks and pulled myself from the bed. The floor was frigid and I hissed a breath. I'd heard castles were drafty places, but jeez! I forced myself to power through the walk from the bed to the table. The maid wrapped the same plaid robe around my shoulders that she had for my first bath.

"Eat first, while I assemble the bath." Agatha left me to my breakfast.

A sweet smelling porridge, slice of ham, and thank heavens, a mug of ale.

I downed the drink first, unaccustomed to such a heavy brew. Steven rarely let me drink, thinking it was unfeminine. And the few times I did, I noted how it took the edge off. I had a definite edge that needed smoothing.

The beer was thick, dark. Even heavier than the one time I'd had a Guinness. I much preferred the Guinness, but I supposed I'd have to get used to this beer if I were to be here. I picked up the bowl, my feet now used to the floor—either that or the warmth of the alcohol that forged a warm path throughout my limbs had made it to my feet. I carried the porridge, taking a bite, to the window. Not bad for medieval oatmeal. It wasn't runny, nor was it chunky. The cook here knew just the right way to make it. Slightly sweet but not overly so. I shrugged and looked outside toward the gate.

The gate was the key. I'd been consumed by the intense allure of Gealach, my reason behind making the driver stop, but it wasn't until I reached the gate that things got weird. I shivered, staring at the stones. The spires that had been there in my time weren't there anymore. I wondered if that would be a problem. How could I get metal up there? And how could I incite a storm so lightening hit it?

I dropped the wooden spoon into the bowl, unexpectedly full.

Blowing out a breath I leaned against the cold wall and continued to stare off into the distance. It seemed an impossibility that I'd made it here, and yet, it happened. Getting back to my own time felt a hundred times more unfeasible. Tears struck my eyes and my limbs grew heavy.

Yes, I liked Logan. No, I didn't want to be stuck here. I didn't want to go back to Steven, but that didn't mean I wanted to give up modern technology and my life altogether. This wasn't my time. Seemed wrong somehow, like I'd mess up the equilibrium of time. I didn't want to be responsible for something like that. And quite frankly, I was pretty fond of deodorants and antibiotics. Hot sex didn't replace modern conveniences. Well…it didn't, did it?

I walked back to the table, set down the bowl and picked up the mug again. I drank the last of it then ambled back toward the bed, about to crawl into it, intent on sleeping the rest of the day when the door opened.

I lay down anyway, ignoring Agatha. I'd rest until she had the bath set up.

"Are ye tired?" The deep baritone of Logan's voice set every inch of me afire.

I turned my head in his direction, shocked to see him. He'd not said he'd be back until tonight.

"What are you doing here?" I asked, unable to stop the cranky tone.

Logan scowled. I bit my lip hard. I'd never use a tone like that with Steven. Just showed how much more comfortable I was with Logan—and I didn't even know him. That was dangerous.

"I mean—"

But he cut me off with a shake of his head. "Ye are tired. Your travels were hard. I kept ye up most of the night."

I nodded, accepting his excuse for me.

"Agatha says ye'll have a bath."

I swallowed and pushed myself to sitting.

"Dinna get up on my account. I rather like ye lying in bed." He grinned, his eyes sparkling with devilment.

Heat rushed to my cheeks, and the rest of my body coiled, ready for him to unhinge it.

"I will see ye this evening." He turned to go.

"Wait." I rushed to stand, coming to the front of the bed.

Logan turned slowly, a brow raised. "I'm not used to taking orders from a wench." His words were light-hearted, putting me more at ease.

"What am I supposed to do all day?"

The thought of sitting in this room waiting for him for hours and hours, all while imagining the things we'd do, would make me crazy. Already my thighs twitched, and my sex was damp, clenching.

Logan looked truly perplexed at that. "What did ye do before?"

Sat in a despondent heap pondering the various ways to end my miserable existence. I shrugged.

"I dinna care what ye do. Be of a mind to stay within the walls. 'Tis dangerous outside, and I'll not have ye impairing my day with having to chase after ye. Be in your chamber in time for the evening meal."

"All right." He was going to allow me to wander free? Do as I pleased? Not since before I was married had there been a day I could devote to myself.

Logan stepped closer, reached out and curled a length of my hair around his finger. My body instinctively swayed toward his and I suppressed a shiver.

"Even having just woken, ye are beautiful."

I smiled. How many times would he tell me that? How I craved hearing it.

"Eat though. Ye've a lovely body, but I could use a bit more flesh on your hips to grip."

Logan had no idea the extent to which his words meant to me. He *wanted* me to eat. He *wanted* me to be fleshier. He wanted *me*.

Picking up the slice of ham on my tray, he pressed it to my lips. Obediently, I opened and took a bite. His fingers lingered as he outlined their shape, and I resisted the urge to lick them. As I chewed, he leaned forward and brushed his lips over mine. It was awkward, yet so sensual, and as graceless as I felt, the art of chewing became something I wanted to master. When I swallowed, he pulled away and gave me another bite. Again, once I'd bitten it, he kissed me. This time, he slid over my chin to my neck, flicking his tongue out to scorch my flesh.

I think I could stand like this all day—eating, while he kissed me.

Logan folded his arms around me, tugging me closer so that our bodies were flush. He was easily a foot taller and all sinew. Without thinking, I put my arms around him, kneading his back. He kissed my shoulder, skimmed my collarbone with his teeth, and I moaned.

"Ye need another bite." He touched the meat to my mouth, and this time while I chewed, he knelt before me.

"What are ye doing?"

"Tasting ye." His voice was deep, sensual and my traitorous sex quivered with the thought. Lips slick with need.

He lifted the chemise over his head and buried his face between my thighs. My legs buckled and I almost choked on the meat. I chewed fast as his tongue slipped between my naked lips, scorching hot against my over-sensitized flesh.

With shaking fingers I gripped his shoulders for balance, swallowed hard, then cried out as he suckled that firing ball of nerves. Long, masculine fingers massaged up my thighs, gripping my ass, pressing me further against him. I could hardly believe it. I floated somewhere between reality and an erotic hallucination.

This man, for all his outward hardness, had dropped on his knees in front of me. My entire body trembled, blood pounded in my ears and I moaned like some exotic creature I'd never even imagined I could be.

I was on the edge. So close… And just when I was sure an orgasm would rip through me, he slowed his movements, lapping at me like my sex was melted chocolate and he a greedy connoisseur.

"Logan," I pleaded, digging my nails into his shoulders. "Please."

He slid a finger inside me, massaging inside until he hit a spot that made me jump. It was exquisite, euphoric.

"Ye want to soar?" he asked.

"Yes!"

"Let it happen," he demanded.

As if my body was already his to master, I did. I came so hard, I fell forward, gripping his back.

"Aye, that's it…" he encouraged, pumping his finger inside me, licking me with enthusiasm.

I rode out the orgasm, if possible, stronger than the ones he'd given me the night before. When the spasms subsided and

I could move again, he kissed my inner thigh and leaned back on his heels. Glancing up at me, he smiled.

"Ye taste so good, I canna help myself."

My throat tightened. "Thank you."

Logan chuckled and stood. He leaned close. I could smell myself on him, but it didn't push me away. Wasn't vulgar. In fact it turned me on, because I knew just what he did to get me all over his lips.

"Tonight, I'm going to show ye how to pleasure yourself," he said.

"What?"

He grinned again and claimed my mouth in a hot, demanding, carnal kiss. I sank against him, boneless, my body begging for more of what he could give me. When he pulled back, he nipped my lower lip, growled and cupped my sex.

"This hot little cunny is mine. But 'tis also yours and I'm going to show ye how to use it."

I swallowed hard. Unsure of myself.

"I...I don't think I can."

"Oh, ye can, and ye will."

I was so eager to please him, a fault I had to rid myself of, that I nodded. I disgusted myself with how much I wanted his lesson right now.

"Finish your meal. Have a bath. Do whatever 'tis women do. I shall see ye when the sun sets." This time when he walked away, I felt like I was being pulled with him.

I didn't want him to leave, nearly said as much before clamping my mouth shut. There was no need for Logan to know the extent of my — obsession? — with him.

How the hell had he already made a claim on me? Dominated me?

Moments later, Agatha returned with a slew of servants who set up the bath. The room was instantly warmer and steam rose from the heated water they poured into the tub.

Behind the Plaid

Agatha set up a nice little table beside the tub with soaps, a square cloth for washing and a bottle of something else.

"What's that?" I asked, coming to grasp the bottle.

"'Tis oil."

"Oil?"

"Aye. Ye have such beautiful skin. Verra soft. But taking a bath will leach some of that softness from your skin. Ye dinna want to lose your softness do ye?"

I shook my head.

"When we finish your bath, I can massage the oil into your skin."

I knew I was damned when I wished that Logan was the one to rub the oil *all* over me.

CHAPTER NINE

Emma

The bath was luxurious. I felt languid, spoiled. I wrapped the towel Agatha provided, around myself. It was woven wool, soft like cashmere. Picking up the bottle of oil, I sauntered to the bed and sat down. I'd dismissed Agatha, and before she'd left she opened the shutters and daylight streamed into the room, yellow golden streaks across the wooden floorboards and the bed.

I popped the cork on the bottle and dumped a little of the oil into my hands. The scent of mint and herbs wafted up toward my nose. Using a tiny amount, I massaged the oil onto my calf, captivated by how it made my skin feel. I tingled, like my flesh was coming alive. It reminded me of Logan and his hands and mouth.

Behind the Plaid

This was why it had been offered to me. Perhaps Agatha believed it was for my skin, but I knew better. Logan wanted me to think of him. Wanted me to remember his hot, velvet mouth and strong, massaging fingers as I rubbed this minty oil over my skin.

Well, he'd won. I couldn't stop thinking about him.

I had to get out of this room. I needed fresh air. Everywhere I looked reminded me of him. I was too raw to fall for someone else. Was I falling for him?

I shook my head and corked the oil.

No. I couldn't be falling for him already. We'd only just met. Sexuality aside, I didn't know him anymore than I knew the maids.

Someone knocked softly on the door. Was he back? I pulled the towel around myself. "Who is it?"

"Agatha, my lady."

"Come in."

Agatha entered the room with a bundle of fabrics in her arms. She shut the door then came toward the bed and began laying out the cloth. But they weren't just materials.

A beautiful gown of ivory with gold embroidery around the hem, sleeves and collar. Another one the color of heather. And a third which made me blush. Even Agatha's face had turned a little pink. The third gown was black—sheer black. I could see the coverlet beneath.

"What is all this?" I asked, wanting specifically to know about the black one.

"His lairdship wished me to bring these to ye."

Agatha unraveled another slip and some stockings.

"Which would ye like to wear today?" She eyed me wearily, and I wondered if she thought I might choose to wear the black one.

I had the urge to point to it just to tease her. But I wasn't the teasing type. Or at least I hadn't been since marrying Steven. I couldn't remember much of who I was before I met him—other than it wasn't the way I was supposed to be.

"Purple," I said.

Agatha visibly let out a breath.

"Let me assure you, that one" —I pointed to the black negligee—"you will never have to dress me in."

Agatha laughed nervously. "Come now, take off that towel."

I pushed aside my anxiousness of being nude in front of her. I would just have to get used to it as long as I was here.

My gaze kept traveling back to the flimsy black gown. I was curious about it. Wanted to touch it. Imagined myself wearing it and seeing Logan's eyes as they greedily took me in. He'd be able to see my nipples darkened against the sheer black, the strip of my pubic hair.

I swallowed hard. This was not where I wanted my mind to go.

"His lairdship didna want ye to wear a corset, and with these gowns ye won't need one."

Thank God. I'd worn a corset on my wedding day. It was heinous and I never wanted to wear one again.

"Where did he get the gowns?" I asked, wondering if there was a dressmaker with a shop in the little village. I wasn't certain how that sort of thing worked, and since I had a day to myself, I wouldn't mind doing a little window shopping.

There was a long pause before Agatha answered softly, "His lairdship has these sort of things."

"Oh," I said, trying to keep my voice even. I didn't want her to know that her answer hurt.

He had these types of things? The gowns were much too small for him to dress up in. And that could only mean one thing—he had women. More than one. Perhaps more than a dozen. He was so good at giving pleasure…

Irritation filled me. I was furious with myself for having allowed an unrealistic dream to take shape in my mind. Damn Logan. Why did he have to make me feel those things? Not only had he manipulated my body to his commands, but somehow my mind, too.

But then it fell back on me again. I was the one who let him.

I was starting to feel a little like I was going crazy. All these thoughts about Logan, sex… I hadn't even had a chance to acclimate to where I was or this era. And I'd only just left my husband. Eight long years of verbal and emotional abuse couldn't be wiped away overnight.

"Thank you, Agatha," I said when she finished dressing me and braiding my hair.

"Here ye go, lass, have a look."

She opened the large wardrobe and muscled out a floor length mirror.

"Haven't had a guest in here for a while to make use of it."

The mirror was beautiful. Etched, polished wood. The glass wasn't as clear as what I was used to, but staring at my reflection, I was stunned. Who was that staring back at me? I had a healthy glow to my cheeks. The purple in the gown brought out the color in my eyes, and my hair wasn't all crazy.

I looked away. I was changing. I could feel it on the inside, but having seen it on the outside was unexpected. I'd thought that whatever was going on inside me was a figment of my imagination. But there it was—plain as glass—I looked…happier, healthier.

"What is it like outside?" I asked, the need to escape making my skin itch.

"'Tis unusually pleasant today. Usually time of summer can be a little hot. 'Haps 'tis because ye have come to us."

"I doubt that," I murmured, refusing to believe the weather would change simply because I'd traveled through time.

"Do ye plan to go outside?"

"Yes. I want to take a walk."

Agatha nodded. "Let me fetch ye a cloak."

"But isn't it warm?"

"Indeed, but if ye are gone long and a wind picks up... His lairdship will be most displeased with me if I dinna furnish ye with a cloak."

I fought the urge to roll my eyes. Who needed a cloak in summer? "I'll wait."

His lairdship had everyone eager to do his bidding, including myself. But I was enthusiastic for a different reason—my reaction to him. Logan made me feel like to I was...special.

For the last eight years, I'd been belittled and dictated by Steven. A man I'd once looked up to as my savior. When I'd been devastated by the death of my family, not knowing who to turn to, what to do, he'd been there for me. He'd lifted me up, made me safe. Now I knew he was simply drawing me in. That he'd been looking for someone to abuse and I'd been unlucky enough to be the first woman who walked into his path.

Steven made me see how worthless I was. That if it weren't for him, I would have been on the streets. I could have died. I was *only* eighteen. What did I know of the world?

Running away from him had been the first thing I'd done for myself since the day we met. It terrified me in a way that nothing else could. Because if I failed, he was right. Part of me believed I would fail. What skills did I have to survive on my own?

I'd not even had a chance yet to try. I was already enamored with another man. A controlling one. A warrior who wanted to rule my every move.

Except he didn't. He didn't care what I did during the day as long as I remained inside the walls of Gealach. In modern times I would have seen that as the same fate Steven dealt me, but here it was different. In this era, going beyond the walls meant death or torture and Logan only sought to keep me safe.

Behind the Plaid

Was I free to go? If I wanted to bad enough, I don't think he would stop me. But I didn't want to. I wanted to stay. Needed to.

And that was what scared me more than anything.

"Your cloak, lass." Agatha handed me a wrap of soft black wool, made sure I put it on.

I followed her down the stairs, amazed by how different the castle looked in morning than it did in late afternoon. Bright light shafts pierced the dark near the windows, and fanned out touching everything with a bit of warmth that it could reach. Shadows danced along the walls and floors. Alcoves made for guards to observe outside the castle walls were dark as night, except for the brightness of their spy holes.

"Enjoy your day, my lady. I'll be about if ye find ye're in need of something. I'll have the noon meal placed in your room if ye should come back for it."

I smiled and nodded. Why did the woman keep saying "if" each time she mentioned me coming back? Did she expect me to leave? Was she hoping I would?

"Wait, Agatha," I called. "What is the date?" I hoped she didn't think me odd for asking, but I thought it would be best to ask her over Logan.

"'Tis the twenty-fourth day of June, and the year of our Lord 1542, lass."

Oh my God... I'd gone back nearly five hundred years. I nodded my thanks and Agatha left me. I had to stand a moment motionless, letting her answer sink in. At that point I'd already known that time travel was possible, but there'd been a hope in my mind that none of it was real, however much I felt for Logan. *1542.*

Frowning, I pulled the cloak tighter as if it were a barrier against the onslaught of conflicting emotions, and watched her walk away before stepping outside. The air was a little brisk for a summer morning, and I closed my eyes for a moment, breathing in the scents that surrounded Gealach. So different than present day. I could smell peat burning, horses, wood, bread baking. When the wind blew softly against my cheeks I could smell...nature. It was breathtaking, sending chills along my skin. I felt the pull of Scotland more keenly than I had before. Like I belonged here.

Opening my eyes, I descended the stairs I'd toppled down the day before. People who milled around the courtyard doing their various chores stared at me for a few moments, then glanced away. They didn't give me odd looks, just watched, and then went back to their business. It was strange. Like they expected me to be there. Or maybe they didn't expect me to be around long enough to make a difference, or to hold their interest.

With a sigh, I walked through the inner bailey, noting the thinned grass, turning a yellower shade of green with the fall. When I'd been here with Steven, there'd been a gravel path. Not now. The path was forged by trampled grass. The courtyard had a few roughly-made huts. Three walls of wood, the rooftops made of thatch and the front open. People worked inside. I was more than curious to go and see, but I didn't want to intrude, and quite frankly didn't want anyone to bother me either. A few men were making weapons, some melted metal, and others prepared chickens. All of them had small fires to keep them warm.

I stood a moment watching the men assembling swords, and when one saw me looking, he pulled a string and a leather flap came down over the opening. I was momentarily stunned by his rudeness. Had I offended him so badly by watching? Trying not to take it personally, I reminded myself that these people didn't know me. They were so inundated with enemies they had every cause to believe I was a spy. Did Logan think the same thing? Was that why he'd drawn me in so close so soon?

Behind the Plaid

A little bit of fear slid up my spine. Perhaps he was not as enamored as he would have me think.

I turned away and glanced through the archway that led down into another bailey, the line of the gate in my sights. I had to try walking through that gate. See if I felt anything, saw anything.

I took off at a steady pace, through the archway, ignoring the glances from everyone. There was no need to make friends. I wouldn't be here long. The outer courtyard was even more busy than the inner one. Chickens scattered about, dogs chased them. Children ran. Women grabbed them. People carried baskets full of things. Vegetables, fur, cloth, straw, herbs, scrolls. It was amazing to see history brought to life before my eyes.

History books and movies focused so much on war and royalty that a lot of this everyday life, the majority of history, was somehow washed away. And I was completely guilty of it. I loved the series *The Tudors*... Henry Cavill and Jonathan Rhys Meyers saved me on more than one occasion when Steven came after me. *Spartacus* was another favorite. But this was so different. So *real*. Their faces were mostly clean, but their hands were dirty. These people had been working for hours already.

Stark reality hit. This wasn't glamorous. Life was hard for most. Even Logan had to fight for his life nearly every day. My stomach knotted, the beer I'd drunk curdling the cream in my oatmeal, making it feel like a heavy lump. Head down, I continued on my way toward the gate. I didn't want to make eye contact with anyone. It was too unsettling.

At last I reached the gate, standing just three feet away. Its wooden doors were closed, a gigantic, thick board locking it in place. I looked up at the stone arch tower above me. A few guardsmen stood on the parapets that aligned with the top of the gated arch. They glanced down at me.

"Dinna go through the gate, lass," one of them said.

I nodded, annoyed that he would tell me what to do. I stepped closer.

"Mind what Angus said. 'Tis dangerous beyond the gate."

Their words were ominous. Logan had said that it was unsafe, but hearing them say it, like a chant, was unnerving. Almost like they were goading me. Like they knew where I'd come from and warned me not to go back there.

I ignored the guard and reached out my hand, feeling a tingling sensation race up my arm the closer I got to touching the stone.

"What are ye about down there?" the first guard said.

I wasn't quite sure. I'd not come down here intent on leaving immediately. Maybe just find out if it was possible, and stay to enjoy Logan's attention a little while longer.

I touched the stone, feeling a zing of exhilaration rush through me. It was a surge of energy that went through my arm, my chest, my other arm, down my legs, taking over my body. I couldn't breathe. And then just as suddenly all of that energy was sucked back through my fingertips into the stone.

That was it. Nothing else happened. I blinked several times, perhaps expecting the wooden doors to disappear and show me the city beyond these walls, or the people to vanish and I'd once again be alone.

Cringing, I looked around, noting that everything remained the same. Except for the men atop the walls. They looked down at me like I had three heads. Had they seen my reaction to touching the stone?

"Lass? Are ye all right?" This was spoken by the third guard who'd not addressed me previously.

I gasped when he turned toward me, his thin brows furrowed in a frown. He walked along the wooden planks and climbed down the stairs, coming toward me with purposeful strides. "What are ye doing?"

I swallowed hard and snatched my hand back from the stone. What was going on? His hair was fiery red, almost the same color as my own. Longer than... No. It wasn't who I thought it was. It couldn't be... Looking at this warrior's face was a painful memory of the brother I'd lost. He looked so much like Trey that I almost said his name aloud.

"I'm fine," I managed, although my voice sounded strangled.

I wobbled on my feet, feeling close to fainting.

The man smiled. If I hadn't seen Trey's body mangled after the crash, I would have sworn he'd somehow traveled through time, too. Or was it possible I hadn't actually traveled through time, that I was dead and this was my Heaven?

"Lass? Ye look pale."

I felt pale. All the blood was draining from body, making me feel light-headed. Where was I? What exactly was happening to me?

CHAPTER TEN

Logan

"Ewan, I want ye to task a few of the men with going into the village and surrounding area. I want to know if anyone saw a red-haired lass wandering around before she landed at the foot of my stairs. I need to find out more about her."

"What does she say?"

I frowned, recalling her face, filled with fear at the mention of her past. "Not much. She's timid, and the mention of her past... I didna want to push her too soon."

Ewan nodded. "I will send them out immediately. I saw the lass not long ago by the gate."

"What was she doing? I told her not to go beyond the castle walls."

Behind the Plaid

Ewan shook his head and looked confused. "She seemed mesmerized by the stones. When I confronted her she paled. Almost like she'd seen a ghost."

"I think she has a lot of those haunting her. She's a widow, with no family."

"That would explain a bit."

"Keep an eye on her for me. I need to go down to the loch and inspect the ships."

"And the prisoners? Shall I have them questioned?"

"Nay, I want to do that myself." I couldna wait to sit down with the men I had tossed into our dungeons the previous evening. After a night of cold, with no food and water, they'd best be ready to converse—although no parley would be coming their way.

Ewan nodded. "I'll see about the men then."

"We'll discuss after the noon meal."

"Aye, my laird."

Ewan left my library and I glanced out of the window toward the loch where the ships sat innocuous—not like they'd approached. Best to get my investigation over with. Collum and Tavish had been fed and warmed. I'd take them with me down to the ship before sending them back out to scout.

Just as I was leaving the library, a thought occurred to me. I turned back around and made sure the lock was set on my writing chest. I had doubts about Emma. I thought her too timid to be a spy, but all the same, if she was, I didna want her skimming through my correspondence with the king. There was no hint to the deep secret that I held, but all the same... Much information was conveyed.

I doused the candle and then locked the door, tucking the key back into place within my sporran pouch. A gift from my mother, made from the fur of a wolf I'd hunted as a child. No one need enter the library. I didna usually keep it locked as I believed those within my castle were loyal—or at the very least too scared to spy inside. But with Emma... I just didna know and I wouldna take any chances.

I spun around to see the lass staring at me. Her face was blank of emotion, but her eyes were deep and penetrating, and I could sense the torment lying just beneath the surface. What had her life been like before she came here? Was that the reason for the agony I sensed within her soul or was it the task she'd been sent here to accomplish? Was there even such a task?

"Lass, I hear ye tried to leave."

She shook her head, and I could tell from the way her eyes widened and she readily reacted that leaving was not her purpose for going to the gate.

"I only wanted to see it."

"Why?"

She shrugged and looked away. "I was curious about the stones."

"The stones?"

"Yes..." she drawled out. Judging from the way she was avoiding the subject I was positive I wouldna be getting a straight answer.

"They were cut from a quarry and brought here on carts a few years ago. I wanted a stronger gate. The one we had before was built of wood."

"So they are new?"

I nodded. "Were they not here last time ye visited?"

She shook her head. "No, I saw them."

Such a strange lass. "There were spires though." She gasped as though she hadna meant to say it.

"Spires? Atop my gate?"

She shook her head so vehemently her hair came loose in places from her braid. "I'm thinking of another place, sorry."

Emma shifted nervously, which put me on edge, making me think my suspicions of why she'd come to Gealach were warranted. And yet, there did not seem to be an evil bone in her

Behind the Plaid

body. She was more of a wounded soul that needed to be embraced, brought back to earth, soothed. For some ungodly reason, I needed to be that man. The one that lulled her back to a sense of peace.

Shaking my head slowly, I said, "Emma, I dinna know why ye came here." My throat grew tight with the strong desire to demand she tell me all, but I knew the way to draw in a wounded animal was not by making them feel threatened, but safe. "I'll not press now, but know that in time, ye must tell me. Ye can trust me. Ye are safe here."

She nodded and looked away. Almost like she'd heard those words before. Was it the wrong thing to say?

"I'm off to the wharf."

She glanced up, interest lighting her eyes.

"Would ye like to join me?"

She bit her lip, wrung her hands. "I would."

I was only going to assess the cargo. The ships were now commandeered by me, and I'd make a gift of them to the king. He'd be pleased for the added vessels in his fleet. Might even make a gift of one to me.

"Come then. I see ye have your cloak already. 'Tis windy by the loch."

"I'll be fine," she said quietly.

"'Tis good to know. A woman with a robust nature will survive well in the Highlands." Taking her by the elbow, I led her through the castle, down the damp, spiral stairs to the water gate. The heat of her body was warm beneath my fingertips. At the sudden contact, she trembled, but after a few moments seemed to calm.

"Oh, I've seen one of these before," she said, her eyes widening in surprise as we reached the iron sea gate.

I pulled the keys from within my sporran and unlocked the postern. "The water gate? Where?"

"In London."

110

"Oh, aye, the Tower."

She nodded again. Her eyes were riveted by the flow of water and the row boats that were tied to the stone walkway, awaiting myself. The gate was hidden inside a cave at the base of the loch. I'd had it built after hearing of the Tower water gate. The idea was perfect for keeping Gealach safe. Not many outside the castle knew of it and I kept it that way. By showing Emma, I was hoping to ease my concern about her possibly being a spy. Her genuine interest and surprise relieved me a great deal. A spy would have greedily taken in their surroundings and not shown such enjoyment. Well, a good one at any rate.

Overhead the stone was black with dampness. Water gathered on the pinnacles of some stones until enough accumulated to for a single drop which then fell, echoing in soft pings. The platform was stone, carved from the rocky mountain itself, as were the stairs leading down to the waterway.

We nodded to the half dozen warriors who sat watch.

"Are we getting into a boat?" she asked.

"Aye. Can ye swim?"

"Yes." She looked from side to side, nervous. "You've no safety vests."

"Safety vests?" I'd never heard of such a thing.

Again the look of panic flitted over her face. "To wear. In case we capsize. Even though I can swim, I could still be pulled under."

"I'll keep ye safe."

Her eyes locked with mine and she studied me for several moments. Her lips were pressed together as though she contemplated just that.

"Ye dinna have to come, Emma."

"I want to," she said quickly.

I got the feeling she didna want to be alone in the castle if I was not near.

Behind the Plaid

"Come, then." Again, I took her by the elbow and led her into one of the boats, our added weight making it rock. I settled her onto one of the wooden benches and the men untied the line holding it to the dock.

"Should ye like one of us to accompany ye, my laird?" Seamus, one of my guards asked.

I shook my head. "Not necessary."

The men nodded. I lifted the oars and began paddling. As we withdrew, the dimmed light of the cave turned into the brightness of a sun drenched summer. Emma closed her eyes and tilted her head, absorbing the sun. She was beautiful, innocent in that moment.

"What is it like in Washington?" I asked her.

She jerked her head toward me, eyes widening a little. "Not at all like Gealach."

"How so?"

She frowned. "There are many buildings. Seems like they've taken over whatever beauty there once was." She looked around, then down at the water. "But I will say the buildings are stunning."

"In what way?"

"They are made of stone, marble, carved." She shrugged. "The architects made constructing them an art form."

Her words were odd to me. Architect… It was a relatively new position I'd heard of. Mostly in Spain and Italy. They were constructing massive buildings. Perhaps some of the Spaniards and Italians had made it across the ocean? However impossible…

I grunted, not sure how to answer.

"We do have beautiful hiking trails, and there are still lots of places in the country that are beautiful and untouched by…civilization. But I haven't spent much time there." She hungrily eyed the mountains that crept up behind the loch, skimming the clouds. "It's very beautiful here."

"I agree, but I am also partial."

Emma smiled, her lips curling attractively, showing even white teeth. I wanted to reach across the boat, gather her in my arms and claim those lips once more. Her beauty was like none I'd ever seen before. But beyond her outward appearance, something deep down drew me closer. I wanted to consume her, be a part of her and have her be a part of me. 'Twas an odd feeling. I wanted to dominate her, and yet I wanted to hold her cradled in my arms and cherish her.

"What do ye think of Gealach Castle? Is it as grand as those ye saw in Washington?"

Her smiled dipped. "They are too different to compare. Gealach has a magical feel. A raw, electrifying power emanates from its stones. The age and wealth of history in Scotland are just..." She shrugged. "Different."

I could understand. Traveling to Edinburgh or even to the border of England and Scotland, and then north to the Isles—all those places were different, too.

We rowed the rest of the way toward the ships in silence. As we approached, Emma eyed the vessels warily.

"They are huge," she murmured.

"Aye."

"Do all Scottish ships look like this? They look almost..."

"Viking?"

"Yeah."

I nodded glancing up at one particular stern with a carved eagle jutting from it. "They were built to entice fear from those who gazed on them."

"The Vikings were a cruel lot."

My lips peeled back in a semblance of a smile. "Aye. The man who owned these galleons boasted of being a descendant of the bastards."

"Are you?"

I jerked back toward her. She eyed me curiously. Tamping down my alarm, I said, "Nay. Are ye?"

She shook her head. "Not that I know of."

I looked back up at the ships. Those who I'd put in charge of the ships were instructed to bring its cargo to the deck so I could inspect it. My men could be seen walking to and fro.

"Where is the man who owns these ships now?" she asked.

Her question was legitimate, but I studied her anyway, trying to see if she was curious or digging. "He was not on any of them. Most likely home, protected in his vast castle, whipping his slaves and beating his women."

Emma's mouth formed a shocked O. "He sounds horrid."

"He is."

Reaching the roped ladder, I tied up our boat. "Ye climb first, lass."

A flash of fear came and went from her eyes. "It's much taller than I imagined." She gripped the rope and craned her neck. "Much taller than they look."

"Have ye never climbed onto a ship?" I asked.

She shook her head.

"Then how did ye get here from across the ocean?"

Startled, she hadna expected me to question her. "A plank."

I grunted again. Washington must have had impressive docks. Our harbors were remarkable as well, and had we approached from them, a plank could have been lowered, but I preferred not to use the planks. Planks meant many men could climb aboard a ship in a quick amount of time—easier for them to escape with the ships. I wanted to make it difficult. My own ship was not even kept here at our quay, but anchored within one of the hidden alcoves Gealach Mountain provided against the loch. Just as easily reachable from the water gate as the docks—in the opposite direction.

"Well, are ye going or staying?" I asked.

"Going," she said, a tremor in her voice.

She gripped the roped rungs, her knuckles white. Tentatively, she placed a foot on the first rung and yanked herself up, placing her other foot on the next rung. She paused there, the rope ladder taut with her weight.

"Ye've got it, lass. Keep going."

"It's harder than I thought."

I chuckled. "Aye, but ye'll get it. And I'm right behind ye."

With jerky movements she grabbed the next rung, hoisted herself up another one. Her lavender gown and black cloak billowed in the wind. I'd not noticed she was wearing the gown I'd given her, the cloak having covered it. I was pleased she wore it. Her slippers were not really suitable for climbing, and flashes of her pale ankles were seen with each movement of her skirt.

"My arms are trembling," she mumbled.

"Aye, mine did the same, first time I climbed." I didna tell her that had been when I was a boy of only a few summers.

Once she'd gone up enough rungs, I grabbed the ladder.

"Whoa! What are you doing?" she cried, stilling her ascent.

"I'm climbing."

"No. You have to wait until I'm done." Her voice was shaky. Holding herself there, nearly plastered to the ship's side, instead of moving was only going to tire her out.

"Why, lass? There's plenty of room for both of us."

"You're shaking the ladder," she answered.

"I'll be still."

She shook her head.

With a deep sigh, I let out shrill whistle, which startled her even more. Several of the men came to the side of the ship.

"Calm yourself, lass. I'm only calling the men to help ye over."

"Okay," she said, her voice sounding choked.

"Help the lass when she gets to the top," I ordered.

The men nodded, eyeing Emma.

Behind the Plaid

"Go on, lass. The longer ye hang there, the more tired your arms will get." Climbing a rope ladder up the side of the ship, one's feet were useless and arms took the brunt of a body's weight.

She didna say anything, but continued her jerky climb. She didna pause again, and even found a steady rhythm. Once she reached the top, the men gripped her arms and helped her over the side. I grasped the rope and climbed, moments later reaching the top. I jumped over the side to the deck and gazed down at Emma.

"How are your arms?" I sent a teasing smile her way.

She rubbed her arms and fingers. "Fine."

I chuckled. "Ye did well for your first time."

Her hands still trembled and she looked a little shaken. "We'll have to climb down that rope, won't we?"

"Aye, lass. But not for a little while." I turned to the men, seeing the piles of crates behind them. "Is that everything?"

"Nay, laird. We've several more store rooms to go through. There are also the captain's quarters."

I nodded toward the crates. "Have ye looked inside?"

"Nay, laird."

"Let's have a look, then." I walked toward the crates, my men following, but I noted that Emma stayed behind. "Come, lass."

Biting her lip she followed, huddling close to my side. I resisted the urge to grab her hand in mine. The crates were not labeled. No discerning scents came from them. I lifted one from the top of the pile.

'Twas heavier than I thought. I placed it on the ground, pulled my *sgian dubh* from my sleeve, and used the blade to open the lid. Straw covered the contents and I wiped it away to reveal iron shackles.

I recoiled at once. 'Twas as I worried. The galleons were meant to take my people away in chains. The MacDonald would seek to imprison us. Make my people his slaves. Never. Not even over my dead, bleeding, broken body would I allow it to happen. If I had to come back from the dead as an avenging demon, I'd keep my people safe. Stealing them wouldna get him closer to Gealach's secrets.

I slammed the crate shut, completely disgusted.

"Melt the iron for weapons. Break up the crates for fire wood."

Turning to Emma, some of my anger ebbed. Our gazes locked. Unexpectedly, a sensation of being whole swept over me. I shoved it aside. There wasna time to ponder it. Wasna time to entertain it. Scotland was in trouble, and no one realized how deeply, except for me.

"Wait." Before the men went about my orders I opened the crate again and took out a set of ankle and wrist shackles.

CHAPTER ELEVEN

Emma

I watched as darkness clouded Logan's features. A shiver stole up and down my arms and I pulled my cloak tighter. The crate he'd opened held shackles, which angered him—that much I'd garnered.

Why would a ship contain crates upon crates of shackles? Such an odd thing to have on deck. I knew there were slaves throughout history, and perhaps I was being naïve to believe slavery wasn't here in Scotland. I'd heard stories of Vikings in medieval days coming to shore and taking slaves, but not of Highlanders. Yet again, I was being shown the cruelty of a world previously only romanticized.

I shuddered, imagining if those who'd held this ship had been able to capture Gealach. I might be handcuffed now, with rusted metal biting into the flesh of my wrists. Maybe even dead. I stepped a little closer to Logan, already feeling the power of his presence and how it calmed me. Made me feel safe.

"Check the rest of these crates. If they contain the same, ye know what to do with them." Logan turned from the man he'd been addressing, back to me. His gaze was steady, unreadable. "Come with me."

I followed without question. Not because I thought to take orders from him, but because there was nowhere else to go, and I didn't want to stay behind with hundreds of handcuffs and warriors I didn't know.

I trailed behind him, looking over the side and taking note of how far down it was. My arms still shook from the effort. Climbing the rope ladder had been one of the hardest things I'd ever done. Physically exerting, yes, but also the fear of falling, of my hands slipping or muscles giving out. It was terrifying, but when I finished I'd felt a sense of accomplishment, too.

I'd never been on a ship before. Funny that the first one I'd ever been on was in a different era. All the surfaces were made of sleek wood, which looked as though it'd been polished or washed just that morning. The sails were white, billowing fabric. Dark iron nails, hinges, hooks. Thick, corded ropes were coiled on the deck and tied up nearly everywhere. Against masts, against the rails, piled here and there. And barrels, too. A lot of them. I envisioned they contained the bodies of the wannabe Vikings' victims, but knew that had to be my imagination.

Tripping over a bit of rope, I righted myself with Logan looking at me over his shoulder. "Watch your step, lass. Most men would say a ship's no place for a lady."

"And you?"

"I'm not most men."

I had to agree there. Logan was nothing like any man I'd ever met. His arrogance was growing on me, and in fact, I was starting to find it charming. We went down a few stairs, more slippery than the deck and I held tight to the railing with one hand, lifting my skirts with the other.

"Where are we going?" I asked.

"To the Captain's quarters."

I'd only read about captain's quarters in novels. They seemed so romanticized, and automatically my blood rushed faster. What would we find there? Would Logan kiss me again? *There*?

A slick patch of wood caught me off guard and my feet slipped out from under me. I fell forward into Logan's back with an, "Oof." His muscles were taut, bunched and I gasped at the feel and with embarrassment at having fallen.

Logan turned around with me still clutching him. "Be careful, the decks are usually damp."

He set me upright, his large hands circling my upper arms. His gaze went from my eyes to my lips and I licked them, with both nervousness and anticipation. But he shoved me back, and turned to trudge ahead. I didn't know whether to be offended or relieved that he didn't want to kiss me.

If we'd been seen kissing by any of his men, then I would have been labeled the laird's whore. And while most probably suspected it, it wasn't a title I was readily able to accept.

I tread even more carefully along the wooden planks, which put me several feet behind him. Logan stopped and waited, his face blank as he studied me.

"What?" I asked, wanting to know his thoughts.

"'Tis nothing. This way." Logan led me up about eight stairs and toward a stately metal studded wooden door with carvings in the corners and intricate iron handles and hinges.

"Is that the captain's door? He's not inside is he?" I had the sudden image of a man gagged and strapped to a chair. While I understood Logan's need to interrogate his prisoners, that didn't mean I wanted to witness it.

"Aye, 'tis, but he is not within." His voice was filled with such coldness when he talked of his enemies.

"Why would anyone attack you?" I asked.

Logan paused with his hand on the door knob and again turned around to look at me. His eyes bored through mine and I had that odd sensation he wished to see inside my soul.

"Dinna ye know?"

I frowned and shook my head. "Should I?"

He shrugged, opened the door, and walked through without answering. What were the secrets he held? What was the appeal of Gealach to so many? Obviously, the castle was beautiful, had a lot of interesting and ornate relics, but to be attacked weekly? Seemed odd to me, for sure. Then again, I was no historian. Maybe it was normal.

I stepped through the door and gazed around the room. It was mostly as I'd imagined it. A desk nailed to the plank floor, a chair tucked beneath. A large bed, also nailed to the floor — but the bedding was not plush, nor beautiful. It looked dirty and old. A cleared table was also nailed down with four chairs around it.

Logan went straight for the desk beneath two portholes. He fumbled with the drawers, then took out a long screwdriver-looking instrument from his boot and fiddled with the locks. While he did that, I went to another table covered with maps — a dagger slicing through the old paper and into the wood of the table, just by a body of water and the word, Gealach.

There were no other places marked on the map, but a long black line from the North Sea was drawn down into Loch Ness. Gealach was very obviously the target of an attack. But I was still confused as to why, and the laird of the castle wasn't forthcoming with information. I traced my finger along the route, wondering about all the things I'd seen but didn't understand. Logan made it clear he didn't like my questions. I'd have to figure out another way to find answers.

Behind the Plaid

The way he stared at me when I asked questions was unnerving. Like he expected me to already be privy to the things I asked. And maybe if I was from this time period, I would be. Or maybe he suspected me of knowing more than I should. I tried to remember that women of this era were different than those of my own time. Inside, I groaned, wishing I'd paid more attention during history class. Even during the tour of Gealach. I'd been too preoccupied over Steven's reaction to everything instead of paying attention to my surroundings. I was always so skittish around him. Hated myself for walking on knife blades every waking moment of the last eight years.

"What are ye looking at?"

I jumped, my back hitting Logan's thick chest. I hadn't heard him come up behind me.

"A map."

Logan glared down at the map. Stepping beside me, he pulled the knife from it and rolled the map up. Another document was beneath it. This one was written in a strange language I didn't recognize. Logan rolled that up as well. He grabbed a leather satchel from beside the bed and stuffed the map and letter inside, then a wool bag of something else he must have found in the desk. I had to bite my tongue to keep from asking what it was.

If I'd been here with Steven, the urge to ask would never have taken over me. No, with my husband it was always about self-preservation. That one time I'd push him too far, he'd raise his fist instead of his voice. Why did I feel so differently about Logan? It couldn't have been simply that he'd pleasured me, or his repeatedly telling me I was safe. There was something else altogether. The way he made me feel, his presence. His aura, even.

"What?" he asked me this time, and I realized I'd been studying him, my brows creased.

"Nothing," I answered.

Logan stepped closer, his feet nudging mine. "'Tis not nothing."

"What do ye mean?"

"Ye're frowning. Tell me what ye're thinking."

I sighed. "I can't."

"Canna or willna?"

"Won't."

He raised a brow at that. "Obstinate little lass. I suggest finding the will to answer."

He didn't add in the "or else" but I could hear it all the same.

"Fine. I was just wondering what you found in the desk and what that weird letter said."

I wrung my hands, waited for the explosion, waited for him to drag me to the mast where he'd shackle me and whip me as the men of the medieval ages were known to do.

Logan just grinned. "Ye've an avid curiosity."

I nodded, cringing.

"I bet your husband didna like it."

I shook my head.

"Most men, wouldna. I shouldna. But I do. I find your interest...interesting." He traced the outline of my jaw. "But I also canna help but wonder why a lass like ye is so curious. Tell me, Emma, do ye seek to destroy me?"

I gasped. "What? No!"

He chuckled. "We'll see about that. Whatever your task is, whatever the reason ye've come here, know that I canna be fooled. Many have tried. Many have lost."

"You have it all wrong."

"Do I?"

Why did he have to be so dangerously handsome? His brows arched, eyes sparkling, lips curved and all I could think about was kissing him. Licking him. Not my usual line of thinking. It was extremely disconcerting. Logan brought out a

Behind the Plaid

side of myself that I didn't know or understand. A side that was frightening. A side that could be controlled by him, with just one look. Every time I was near him, I melted, changed. Had the overpowering urge to let him have his way with me.

A different domination than with Steven. My husband had been cruel. Logan wasn't cruel. His dominance was…sensual. And he allowed me to lead it.

"Yes, you do," I whispered, unable to find my voice beyond the racing of my heart.

I heard him drop the things he'd been holding, but I didn't look to see. I was too mesmerized by his face, the way he was looking at me. Hungrily.

Logan grasped my hips and lifted me, sitting me on the table. A burst of excitement made me hiss through my teeth. With firm pressure, his fingers slid from my hips, down my thighs to my knees. He pushed them apart. My sex was instantly wet, knowing whatever he had in mind, I would enjoy. I felt helpless, and yet, I soared. A contradiction in itself.

I chewed on my lip, but only for a second, because within the next, he'd pressed his body between my thighs and his lips to mine. Logan's kiss was possessive, hot. His tongue swept in to rub tantalizingly against mine, and he growled like he'd been waiting to feast on me for hours.

I wrapped my arms around his neck, and inched my hips closer to his, wanting to feel the hard pressure of his body against me. Logan didn't make me suffer long. Gripping his belt, he yanked it to the side, moving the fur pouch he kept at his hip out of the way. He gripped my thighs, and hauled me closer. His cock pressed against me, long, rigid, and I wanted desperately to rip at my skirts, at his kilt and let him come inside me. Even if it hurt. I was desperate for him. Desperate to feel what our joining would be like. If it was half as good as his kiss, I was in for a euphoric ride.

"I want you," I murmured against his mouth, surprised at myself.

"Oh, Emma…" he groaned. "Ye have no idea, lass."

Threading my fingers through his hair, I tugged him closer, our tongues slicking back and forth.

He pushed me back on the table, hands on my breasts. Wrenching open my cloak, he tugged the gown down so my nipples popped out. A cold wash of air hit my breasts, making me shiver, but I didn't care. I didn't want him to stop.

"Ye look beautiful in this gown," he murmured. "And out of it." He smiled, so sexy, so filled with sensual promise, my insides quivered.

Logan bent over me, cock pressed tight to my sex, and he took my nipple into his mouth, sucking gently at first and then hard. I whimpered, writhed. He ground his arousal against me, sending frissons of delicious pleasure ricocheting through me. Where he licked and sucked my breasts, shots of pleasure fired toward my clitoris, which throbbed in desperate need of climax.

I kneaded his scalp, moaned with each delicious lick, even undulated my hips with his. I was coming undone in his arms. The surrounding cabin walls seemed to close in tight, cocooning us in an equally magical embrace. Logan was bringing all of my fantasies to life. The few romances I'd been able to secretly read, the depths of the heroine's emotions, the heat of their desire for one another, it was all here on this table firing between Logan and I.

"Logan, please," I begged for it, without shame. I wanted, craved, pulsing satisfaction.

"Tell me, lass. Tell me ye need what I can give." His words were gruff against my flesh, firing another shot of pleasure to my throbbing groin.

"I need it. I need you."

He grunted, and crashed his mouth down on mine. His fingers slid up my naked thigh, pushing my gown up as he

Behind the Plaid

went. He parted the folds of my sex, slipped his fingers inside me, rubbed my clit with the pad of his thumb. I cried out, bucking my hips upward. He had the magic touch, knew how to stroke me into oblivion and we'd only just met. How was it possible? Like we were made for each other.

I was so close, right on the edge, waiting for one more aching push and I'd be soaring into ecstasy. But he stopped.

I gasped my shock as he slid his fingers from my pulsing channel, skimmed them down my thigh, gave one last smacking kiss to my breast and stood.

"Wh—what are you doing?" I asked, feeling heat fill my cheeks.

He grinned mischievously. "What's the matter, lass?"

I didn't know how to respond, could tell he was goading me.

"I… Did I do something wrong?" Noticing how his eyes roved over my exposed thighs, I pushed my dress down as I sat up.

"Ye did everything right."

"Then why did you stop?"

"'Tis part of it."

Exasperation made me push him further. Perhaps further than I should. "Part of what?"

"Part of what I'm teaching ye."

I frowned. "I don't understand."

"The more your body craves release, the better your release will be." He skimmed his lips against my cheek, his stubble scraping lightly over my skin. "I want ye to think of me all the rest of the day," he whispered against my ear. I closed my eyes and shivered. "I want your body quivering, clenching, waiting to feel me to touch ye once more."

So, he meant to torture me. Sexual torture. I squeezed my thighs together, feeling the aching pulse, wanting desperately to grab his face and shove him between my thighs.

When I opened my eyes, Logan was watching me. He chuckled. "I can almost hear your thoughts, lass. Dinna worry overmuch... The sun will set soon, and then I'll show ye how to relieve yourself."

I swallowed hard, unsure if I really wanted to make myself come. I liked it so much when he did it. To think just a few days ago, I wouldn't have even thought something like that.

Logan gripped my hand and pulled me down from the table. My legs were unsteady, my body still clenched tight with wanting.

"You have an un-canny knack for diverting my attention," I grumbled, still a little perturbed at his *lesson*.

"How so?"

"Instead of answering my questions, you laid me down on a table intent on ravishing me."

"Do ye feel ravished?"

The way the word *ravished* rolled off his tongue was so sensual, I shivered, wanted to hear him say it again.

"No."

"Ye dinna?"

I folded my arms over my chest and shook my head. "Only teased."

Logan laughed. "Then 'twas well done on my part."

I huffed a breath, realizing I wasn't going to win this argument, and then my face flamed with heat because I was arguing with a man about whether or not he'd finish seeing to my sexual appetite. Traveling back in time had apparently completely stripped me of all morals and decency.

And, I didn't give a shit. When I figured out how to get through that gate and back to my own time—and part of me was starting to question whether or not I wanted to return—Logan wasn't coming with me, but his lessons were and I could start all over again.

Behind the Plaid

If that was the case, I needed these lessons. Needed the confidence he'd somehow slowly begun to build within me. Logan made me feel strong, desired...worth it.

Logan chuckled and tapped my nose. "Ye know I can practically read your thoughts."

I winged a haughty brow. "Then what am I thinking?"

"How much ye want me to lick your hot little cunny and how much that disturbs ye." He pressed me up against a wall, pushed my arms up over my head. "Am I right?"

I couldn't do anything but nod my head in agreement.

"Well, I wouldna want to disappoint ye." With that, he dropped to his knees and pressed his face against my skirts. Thrusting my dress up around my hips, the heat of his mouth found my sweet spot. He blew hotly, nuzzled me until my legs shook and my cries filled the room. Not once did his tongue touch me. "Dinna peak, lass."

How unfair that he was ordering me not to finish—I was so damn close. I gasped in air, could barely breathe.

"Oh, please, let me..."

"Tonight, not now." And again, he backed away. But this time I was in an even worse state. I was so wet, my desire dripped down my thighs. So close to coming that my clit pulsed and fired off little twinges of pleasure. If I moved, I might come. If he looked at me in that possessive way, I was sure to break apart. But I didn't, not even when he looked at me like he would devour me. My body obeyed his demand.

"How do ye feel now, lass?" he asked, leaning close enough for me to feel his hot breath on my cheek. I closed my eyes in silent surrender.

"Worse."

He laughed and then kissed me. "Even better."

CHAPTER TWELVE

Emma

When we left the captain's quarters, I prayed I didn't look like I felt—a hot, horny mess. I followed Logan from room to room as he checked for hidden doorways and safes. He broke into more chests and desks, each time finding at least one thing he found worthy enough to tuck into the leather satchel he carried on his shoulder.

The mystery of Gealach was intoxicating. My curiosity overflowed, but I kept my questions to myself. When we got back to Gealach, maybe I could somehow seduce him into telling me.

Only thing was, that idea was likely to get me into trouble. Logan wasn't the type to be tricked and already he was suspicious of me.

"Are ye ready to head back?" he asked after giving last minute instructions to his men.

I nodded.

"Do ye want me to go first?"

"In case I fall, you can fish me out of the loch?" I asked with a smile.

"I wasna going to put it that way, lass, but in a word, aye."

"Sounds like a plan." I ducked my head, trying to hide my face.

Logan tossed the leather satchel into the waiting boat below, then swung over the rail. His muscles rippled and my eyes were glued to his nude legs, and the flash of muscular thighs his kilt afforded me. No wonder women loved men in kilts. Maybe I should have gone first and then I could have seen *everything* as he climbed down the ladder.

I wanted to groan. What the hell? I needed to get away from him. Needed something else to distract myself with. As soon as we got back to Gealach I would find Agatha. I needed to ask her about the man I'd seen by the gate. Had to find out who he was, where he came from. He was just about the same age my brother would have been had he lived. I knew it wasn't possible, he couldn't be the same... But if there were such a thing as time-travel, or reincarnation, or something, maybe a part of the man was Trey. Ordinarily, I would have thought it was a long shot—but *I* had traveled through time. Anything was possible.

Fairies and elves could be real. The black hole in the middle of the ocean, maybe it really did strand people on deserted islands. Who the hell knew, certainly not me. The world was unquestionably altered. What I thought I'd known, believed in, was not the same anymore. I was no longer the same woman.

"Lass?" I jerked up, realizing I'd been completely consumed by my thoughts. One of Logan's men held out his hand to me, which I took, glad that touching him didn't create the same sensations that touching Logan did.

He lifted me easily over the side and didn't let go until I was comfortable enough to climb down. However rough and violent these Highlanders were in battle, they were extremely gentle to me, and I hoped to their own women.

Descending wasn't nearly as hard as climbing. I suppose gravity was on my side, pulling me down. Logan gripped my waist when I was close and lifted me into the boat.

"Did ye like the galleon?" he asked.

"Yes." I liked the ship. I liked what he did to me on the ship. I liked learning to climb the rope, learning a little more about myself and even Logan. "Do you have a lot of enemies?"

He frowned and pulled the oars from their slots. "A man does not like to admit such a thing. My enemies are the enemies of a ghost." His words were so ominous.

"Really?"

The oars splashed into the water, spraying a little onto my hands that rested on the rims of the boat.

"I've never done anything but what my king asked of me."

I realized then, Logan was never going to answer my questions. He would dance around them. I'd have to get better at this game of riddle-speak or I'd be forever lost.

"Well, that's a shame," I responded, staring up at the mountains. Snow topped the tips. A killer ski slope, if I were interested. Which I wasn't. The first time I went skiing, I fell the entire way down the hill. Rolled like a snowball. I refused to go up again, telling my family I'd wait in the lodge with a hot steaming cup of cocoa. They tried to tell me it wasn't that bad, that most people fell the first few times. I listened for a moment, thinking they had a point until a girl flew past us, fell and sliced her head open on someone else's skis. That was it for me. I prayed that there wasn't any reason for Logan to require that I ski. Nowhere that we were forced to go. Did Highlanders ski?

"Where are ye?"

"Huh?" I turned away from the mountains to find Logan staring at me.

"Ye were lost in thought."

I nodded, not wanting to divulge my memories. We might have connected on a physical level, even some deeper unexplained soul level, but I wasn't ready to share all of myself. Not yet. Not when there was a chance I'd end up back in my own time, and with a broken heart for having lost him.

Logan chuckled, stopped the boat. We rocked gently in the water, and I gazed down into its dark depths wondering if the Loch Ness monster was a thing of truth and if Logan had ever seen it.

"I'll not take us back," he threatened.

I raised my eyebrow at him and smirked. "Your stubbornness won't make me tell you what I'm thinking."

"'Haps the thought of Nessie will."

"I'd wondered if the rumors of a monster in your waters were true."

"Aye, they are."

"Have you seen it with your own eyes?" I asked.

Logan's grin widened. Why did he have to be so devilishly handsome *and* frustrating?

"Mayhap I have."

Folding my arms across my chest, I said, "I'd like to hear about it."

"All right, lass." He set the oars back in the boat and leaned back, his legs spread out before him.

My sex still pulsed with the memory of his touch, and the way he was laid out before me made me want to climb on top and let him show me how to have my way with him. But I remained rooted to the bench, forcing myself to concentrate on his words, not his crotch.

"When I was a boy, I stood on the edge of the loch tossing stones." He nodded his head toward the shore where a sandy beach spread between the loch and a wall of stone. "I was mad at my father, flinging those rocks like I wanted to take off someone's head, when out of the water rose a being that stopped the breath in my lungs. I couldna scream. Couldna move."

"What did it look like?"

"Black as night. A neck as long as a warrior's body. Yellow, slitted eyes like a snake. Sharp teeth."

I rubbed my arms, looking at the water in a whole new light. "Sounds terrifying. How old were you?"

He shrugged. "Maybe five summers."

"So young. Were you all alone out here?"

"As the laird's son, I shouldna have been, but I snuck away."

I smiled. "You strike me as a child who often disobeyed the rules."

Logan laughed and picked up the oars again, stroking them smoothly through the water. I wondered if he was nervous about a repeat visit from Nessie.

"I was mischievous, for certain. What about ye? Were ye a troublesome lass or did ye do everything your mother and father bade ye?"

I swallowed, frowning. Memories of my parents' faces floated in my mind. Their smiles, hugs, voices… All of it was slowly fading away. I wanted to grasp those recollections and pull them toward me, hold on to them forever. At least back in my own time I had their pictures hidden in the lining of my suitcase where Steven couldn't take them from me. But here, all I had were the images in my mind. "I was good to them." My voice wavered and I grew angry at myself for having showed some emotion. I didn't want to share that part of myself.

Behind the Plaid

With Logan, I was someone new. A reinvention of myself. If I were to tell him all of my past, he might use it against me as Steven had. As soon as the thought entered my mind I battered it away. Logan was nothing like Steven.

"I miss my family," I whispered, half hoping he wouldn't hear me.

Logan nodded, his eyes connecting with mine. "I miss mine, too, lass."

The silence stretched between us, but while we didn't speak, our souls melded more firmly together, or at least it felt that way. I drowned within the depths of his dark eyes, yearned to climb into his lap.

"Ye've a painful past, I can see that, lass." Although it was a statement of fact, it was also an invitation to divulge.

I simply nodded. I wasn't ready. Wasn't sure I'd ever be. "Sometimes I wish I couldn't remember it."

"We all have our secrets," he murmured, gazing off in the distance.

Logan was right. We do all have our secrets, and I wanted more than anything to know what his were. What made him the man he was today? But I would first have to open up all the way myself. Asking him to give me his secrets and not returning the courtesy was just wrong.

The sounds of the water lapping against the boat and the oars dipping and churning were soothing. But it was colder on the water. A breeze blew lightly, the kind that seeped into each gap in my clothing, winding its way inside to knife its chill against my exposed skin. I had a feeling it had more to do with my emotional state than the weather. Letting go of the rim which I'd been clutching, I huddled deeper into my cloak and hoped that Agatha had kept the fire going in my room.

"What will you do now?" I asked, staring at the looming towers of Gealach.

"There is much to be done."

I resisted the urge to roll my eyes. "Can I help?"

"I dinna think ye'll want any part of what I have to do."

His words were ominous and sent a deeper chill inside my bones than the loch's winds.

"Oh," I murmured. The lightness of day dimmed as our boat floated into the cave.

Logan tossed a rope to the guards on the platform who pulled us in and tied the boat to a post.

He held out his hand to me, and as usual, when I placed mine in his a spark seemed to fill the space between us. Pulling me to my feet, Logan wrapped his hands around my waist and effortlessly lifted me onto the dock. I moved aside as he agilely leapt up beside me. I could watch him move all day. Everything he did was smooth, controlled, powerful.

Logan nodded to his men and led me through the iron gate and back up the stone stairs.

"Are ye hungry?" he asked.

What for, I wanted to ask, but kept my lips tight to any cheeky phrases. "Yes."

"Agatha has most likely set out your noon meal in your chamber."

Disappointment sank in. I wanted to eat with Logan. Didn't want him to leave me, even if it was only for a few more hours.

"Come, I'll escort ye."

I'd grown accustomed to his fingers on my elbow. Liked the way he touched the small of my back when guiding me this way and that. Maybe it was okay to let a man be the dominant force in the room, if he wasn't overbearing and cruel. I found that I liked the way Logan treated me—most of the time.

"When I come for ye tonight," he said in a low voice, "I want ye to wear the black gown."

An image of the sheer fabric lying on my bed came to mind. And with it, Agatha's words on Logan's many women. My

Behind the Plaid

stomach did a flip and I bit my lip, trying to keep myself from asking what I so badly wanted to.

"How many others have worn it before me?" Too late, the words slipped out.

He didn't answer for a few moments, and he stiffened a little. "Does it matter?"

I pulled away and turned to face him. I clenched my jaw in an effort to stop my lip from quivering. I couldn't speak—feared speaking. I was most certainly feeling jealousy, but was uncertain how far I could go in asking Logan about my place, his feelings. I didn't want to make him mad, but I also needed answers for myself. Didn't want to lose myself again. This world was so much different than my previous world. Balancing on a ledge, I never knew quite how to react.

Logan crossed his arms over his chest, muscles bulging. He narrowed his eyes as he stared at me, but it wasn't a glare, more like he was confused and trying to find the answer on my face.

"Ye have to have known ye are nay the only woman I've taken to bed," he said.

His words stung, making me feel stupid for even bringing the topic up.

"I... I know that." I wanted to swipe my hands through my hair, but being in a braid, that was impossible. Mortification sunk deep. I wanted to run the other way, but there was no escape from this place. Not yet, at least. "But I won't wear another woman's cast-offs."

"They are not another woman's cast-offs as ye say."

"But another woman has worn the gown?"

"Another woman wore the gown that ye have on now, lass. What is your point?"

My skin crawled. Definitely jealousy. How many others had he touched the way he touched me while wearing this same gown? I wanted my own things. My own memories.

"I dinna know how it is in Washington, but here, in Scotland, women share clothes. Fabric is expensive—not that I dinna have the funds for it—but why should I throw away each piece just because more than one woman wore it? They are not wearing it now."

Steven would have labeled me a whore. It was harder said than done to get his nagging voice out of my head. What was I doing? What did I hope to accomplish by becoming Logan's lover?

My throat tightened. The walls felt like they were closing in around me—and not like the comforting cocoon on the ship. This was dark, drowning. I was so confused. Embarrassed. I'd not had a moment yet to let Logan, this new world and my place in it, sink in. The things he said, they made sense. He gave a super reasonable explanation. Especially since crafting clothing took so much effort in his time – no malls to run out and get something new. And I *liked* what we did together, the way he made me feel. But self-preservation was ringing its ugly head. I was falling deeper than I should and afraid I'd get hurt.

I shook my head, whispered, "I don't know if I can do this." And that was the truth. I didn't know.

Logan's face fell, the first signs of emotion I'd seen in him toward me today that weren't of a sexual nature.

"We'll discuss it over the evening meal," he answered.

I shook my head. "No."

"Nay?" he asked, this time his scowl was fierce and directed at me.

I squared my shoulders, lifted my chin. As Steven's wife, I would have backed down. Allowed him to bully me into a corner, submitted to his will because he demanded it. I refused to be that Emma anymore. I wouldn't let a man tower over me and command my life as though I were a puppet. One thing Logan had taught me over the last couple of days was that while he was a commanding man, I had a choice. I could make a choice.

In my own era, a woman sleeping with a man was nothing. Common, no one would blink an eye. Here, it meant something completely different. Sex was seen as something different, sacred. What I was doing was a sin and sins were punishable. I would be shunned by those who saw it that way. Even eventually by Logan. I was wearing his previous lovers' cast offs. Someday, another woman would be wearing them, too.

"I can't allow you to use me the way you've used others. I'm not that type of woman."

He stepped closer, his heat enveloping me. "What type of woman are ye, Emma?" he asked.

His voice, the Scottish burr, his overwhelming presence, all had the power to affect me in the greatest of ways. I wanted to sink against him, melt into the floor, climb all over him. But I had to remain strong. Had to stand my ground.

"Not that kind."

"What is *that* kind?"

"I'm not a whore."

"I never said ye were."

"I won't be made into one."

"I've no desire to make ye into a whore, Emma."

I was fast losing ground. His words were designed to make me cave to his will. To let him continue down the path he was leading me. And they made so much damn sense.

"I have pride," I managed. "And respect for myself."

"So do I." He moved even closer, his thighs brushing against mine, our mouths only an inch apart.

Stay strong, I chanted to myself. I took a step back, but he only followed me. I stepped back again, my butt hitting hard stone. I flattened my palms against it, looking for strength in the immovable wall, wishing I possessed the magic to sink into it.

"You can't have me," I muttered.

Logan grinned. "I've already had ye."

"You can't have my soul." I don't know why I chose that word—soul—but I felt like that was what he was after, like I was losing myself to him.

A flicker of doubt flashed in his eyes. "I only want this." His hand cupped my sex and I squirmed against the intense pleasure of his touch.

"You can't have that either."

"Ye've already given it to me. It's mine."

I shook my head.

"Go to your room, Emma. We'll discuss this further over the evening meal."

"No," I said weakly. Why was I starting to cave? I couldn't let the physical feelings he brought out in me take over my mind, my sanity.

"Aye," he whispered against my ear, nipping the lobe. "Oh, aye."

Logan ground his hips against mine, and of their own volition, my hips ground back.

"See? Ye do want me. Your body does." He skimmed his lips over my jaw, stopping by my lips. "Your mind does, too."

I shook my head, feeling the wall scrape my scalp.

"I've never wanted a woman, like I want ye," he murmured. "There may have been others in this gown, in the other ones, too, but none of them compare to ye. None of them do to me what ye do. None of them have possessed me so wholly."

I was speechless. I affected him that much? *Wholly?*

Power curled in my belly and spiraled outward. He was just as moved by our connection. Bound to me in some strange, out of this world way.

His mouth slid over mine, sealing in any response I might have had. I resisted touching him, kissing him back, but only for

Behind the Plaid

a few moments. I was consumed by him. I let myself melt against him, just as I'd fought not to do.

CHAPTER THIRTEEN

Logan

Raking my hands through my hair, I backed away from Emma, even though her bemused expression made me want to whip her lavender skirts up around her hips and devour her on the stone floor.

How could she say nay to me?

Why was I so disturbed by it?

"I shall see ye this evening." I stormed down the corridor without looking back.

The way she moved me was too much. Never before had a woman consumed me as much as Emma. Never had a woman made me want to bend down on one knee and offer her the world. And it all made no sense. I barely knew her. But the pull was there. A bond that seemed to hold us together.

Behind the Plaid

Ballocks! I didna need the distraction. Not now.

I blew out a breath and made my way down three flights to the dungeons. Questioning the prisoners would be a good distraction. The dungeon was dark, dank and smelled of piss and blood. Only a few torches were lit in the sconces. Moans echoed off the stones. My men nodded to me.

"Bring me the ship captains," I ordered and entered one of our interrogation cells.

The floor was dirt-packed, the stone walls damp. There was no window in this place as it was carved from the earth. Two torches lit the room and a battered chair and bucket sat in the corner. The room was cold, and puffs of my breath showed before my lips.

A few moments later the men returned with four shackled prisoners. Two of the ships had belonged to the Sutherlands who'd trailed the MacDonalds on their way to Gealach. Their captains had met with Ewan on the beach and after a short discussion, had been sent back up the North Sea with a bag of gold for their laird.

My warriors shoved the shackled captains to their knees. Each sported various MacDonald plaids, and all of them glowered at me like I was the devil. One even had the ballocks to spit on the ground near my feet. I walked a line in front of them, ignoring the insult.

"Who sent ye?" I asked, knowing the answer already.

None of them spoke.

"Why are ye here?"

Again, not a word. I stopped at the second man, stared down at him. There was fear in his eyes but also obstinance.

"Ye've the look of the MacDonald," I said, a cruel smile splitting my lips.

The man's throat bobbed, he blinked, but said nothing. I had a fair idea that the prisoner before me was a direct relation of my enemy. They shared the same shape of eye, and hawkish nose.

"Think ye that he'll send a ransom should I demand one?"

The man's eyes widened ever so slightly.

I nodded to the guard holding him in place, and he tightened his grip on the man's arms, bringing them up enough to cause discomfort.

"Mayhap I should remove the arms that steered ye here." Taking the dirk from its sheath at my hip, I scraped it over his shoulder, slicing the fabric of his dirty shirt, but not his skin. "This is *my* castle. No one will take it from me."

The prisoner on the far end snickered. "Not for long."

I laughed at that. "Strong words from a man at my mercy. Ye shall be the first to die."

"I fear not death, only the wrath of my laird," he said proudly, even though he trembled.

"Then I shall be sure to send him after ye in hell," I answered. Nodding to the guard holding the mouthy one, he yanked him upward to standing.

"Any last words?" I asked, holding the dirk at his neck. The vein in the man's thick neck throbbed, ready for me to slice into it.

"Not to ye, ye bastard."

"Wait!" the MacDonald relation shouted.

I didna pull the dirk from the man's neck but I did turn my head enough to eye the prisoner on his knees who looked up at me with pleading eyes.

"I'll talk to ye, if ye let these men go."

I shook my head. "Not going to happen."

"At least put them back in their cells."

Again, I shook my head. "I dinna negotiate with prisoners. As Laird of Gealach, guardian of the loch in his majesty's name, I have the authority to kill all ye and your men without questioning ye first. Dinna think 'tis courtesy I give ye. I want information."

I could see the struggle on the man's face. His lips thinned, eyes looking from the other three captains, to the floor and then back to me.

"If I give ye the information ye want, what will ye do with us? How do I know ye willna kill us anyway?"

I shrugged, liking the power I held over them. "Ye dinna know." My ploy was two-fold. A man who has nothing to lose, has no reason to speak. A man who fears for his life may be forced to lie to live. A man who knows not, speaks the truth.

"Tell me your name," I demanded.

The man swallowed, his eyes glued to the dirt-packed floor for several moments, then raised his gaze to mine. A fierceness in it proved he was indeed of some importance.

"I am Allan."

I narrowed my eyes. "Allan o' the Wisp?" The bastard was known for setting fires to cottages in every village he raided and for violently plundering women. I was more than glad to have him in my custody.

At the mention of his name, Allan's lips twitched, but he didna confirm it. "Allan of the Orkney Isles. Cousin to the MacDonald."

My suspicions in his connection to my gravest enemy were true.

"Tell me what I want to know."

"I dinna presume to guess what ye must know."

I backhanded him for that. The crack of skin against bone echoed eerily in the room. Allan's head snapped to the side with the force of my blow. Just because he was a notorious villain did not mean I would tolerate his inflated sense of self-worth. Allan wiped a trickle of blood from his lip onto his shoulder and glared up at me.

"My cousin would not be pleased to see how ye treat me."

I laughed heartily at that. "Then why did he not come here himself? Why send ye? Dinna be a fool, Allan of the Orkney Isles. MacDonald is well aware that I would have captured ye."

Allan smiled then, cruelly. "Are ye so sure that was not his plan?"

MacDonald was a tricky bastard, there was no telling what his plan was or if Allan simply wanted to put fear in me. "Ye tempt with your words, Allan, but who is the one in shackles?"

I nodded down at him and the guard holding him tightened his grip, causing Allan to yelp in pain.

I hoped my men were already melting the iron shackles I'd found on the ships. With the sword forged from the pool of metal, I vowed to slice through MacDonald's heart.

"Tell me your purpose. I'll not ask again." I pressed the tip of the dirk harder into the bare flesh of his shoulder, nicking it.

"I came to capture your people."

"And?"

"No other purpose. Our galleons were to carry your clan back to the Isles for the MacDonald's pleasure."

"And me?"

"Ye were to be left here."

I raised a questioning brow, digging just a little harder with my knife. Allan yelped.

"I wasna to do anything to ye. The MacDonald says he already has that taken care of."

"How?"

Allan shook his head, pain etched around his eyes. He appeared to be telling the truth. "I know not, only that he said we were nay to harm ye, that he'd already made sure of your death."

"Why does your master want Gealach?"

"Gealach is Scotland. The MacDonald will rule. Our bastard king has no place—"

Behind the Plaid

I stopped him short with my fist slamming into his chin. No man would talk about my sovereign that way.

"Lock them back up. Dinna open their cells without my permission—I dinna care if they are killing each other."

Allan's words pointed toward Emma. I'd wondered at her purpose for coming here, so timely, so convenient. She was sent by the MacDonald to seduce me, to murder me. There was no other reasonable explanation. Had she somehow poisoned me? Was there a way for a woman to put poison on her lips or her sex so that I lapped it up like a lust driven lad and then fell into her embrace? When would she strike out at me?

The facts must be laid before me, but I couldna see them. Something wasna right. Emma was no killer—or else she was very good. And her cunny had been as sweet as a ripened fruit, no poison on either set of her lips.

Exiting the cell, I was more uneasy than when I'd entered. I went straight to my library and penned a letter to the king, to the Sutherland laird and several other allies informing them of the MacDonald's intent and his latest attack. I kept the fact that there was an assassin in my midst to myself. I'd have to be extra careful.

Leaning back in my chair, I pulled a flask of whisky from my desk, popped the cork and took a deep draw. Ever since the day of my father's death... the visit from the king... my life had been irrevocably changed. Violence had taken on a new level. Buried twenty feet below the castle was a treasure even I was not privy to the contents of. Buried in my heart were the secrets of my true blood line and a deep-seated pain at having been rejected.

I had honor. More than any man I knew. I wouldna bow to the danger, let it pass me by and take all I knew, plunging me in to the dark. I had a duty. A duty to my country. A duty to my king. A duty to my dead parents. A duty to my blood.

Honor. Duty. The two words I repeated to myself a hundred times a day. That was why I must remain strong. An indomitable force.

I took another long sip, swirling it on my tongue, and leaned my head back against the wooden headrest. My hearth was empty—I preferred it that way. A chill always helped me to think, to focus.

If anyone were to find out the truth, to steal the treasure, the entire realm would explode in unrest. The dark secrets I guarded over were world changing. Questioning the prisoners only made it more apparent that the Lairds of the Isles, MacDonald in particular, were out to tear my hold from Gealach. The king was unaware how deep the unrest was within Scotland.

But thoughts of Emma kept crowding my mind. The obvious facts about her appearance, made even more plain by Allan, and then the way I actually felt. In my heart I didna want her to be an assassin, didna believe it could be true. Foolish, aye. Disturbed by political intrigue from dawn to dusk, I found myself looking forward to being in her presence, when I could lose myself in teaching her all there was to know about passion and pleasure.

With her, this world of treachery disappeared and I could be myself. Lose the façade of a man I created in the face of all that had been laid before me. With Emma, I could be the man I was destined to be.

But then I must also wonder why wasna I good enough to be the man I was born to be? Why was I thrust aside? Why was I not ever brought back into the fold?

I wanted harmony, peace. A desire almost laughable if it weren't a need so intense within me. Emma seemed to bring that to me—despite my fears of her coming here. I was tormented by my dark past, by the secrets I harbored. Only she could set me free.

Behind the Plaid

A rapid knock jarred me from my thoughts and Ewan entered the library.

"My laird, there is something ye need to see."

"What is it?" I shoved to my feet and corked the flask of whisky.

"The devil Allan wasna lying."

I barreled through the door, following Ewan to the great hall. When I entered, a half-dozen of my men surrounded another who'd been forced to his knees.

The colors of his plaid were the first clue, but even without it, his face was plainly seen. Hawk nose, eyes as black as the devil, skin wrinkled and scarred from a lifetime of battling for the place he'd set up for himself—a position made from the blood and loss of others. Even held in such a powerless position on his knees, the bastard looked to have instilled fear in a few of my men. "MacDonald."

"Ye've taken my galleons," the man said indignantly. "And my men."

I fingered the sword at my hip. "And now ye."

MacDonald laughed. An evil sound. "Ye'll need to give them back or suffer the wrath of the king."

"I have orders from the king to take them."

MacDonald shook his head, a smile, that didna quite reach his eyes, cruelly splitting his lips. "And I've a missive ordering ye to return them to me."

"A forgery."

MacDonald only smiled wider. "Nay, man. Your king wants me to be happy."

Why in bloody hell would the king want that? Then I remembered the missive I'd sent yesterday informing my liege that MacDonald was after the crown wouldna have reached his ears yet. I had to stall.

"I will nay return them to ye until I hear from the king himself. Ye're not a man to be trusted."

"Oh, come now, Logan Grant. Isn't it time we shook hands? Perhaps ye'd like to marry one of my daughters and create a powerful alliance?" The man's words were said softly, but underlying them was a malicious intimation.

The thought of marrying one of MacDonald's daughters, being forever twined with my enemy, was abhorrent. "I'd rather take nap in a wildcat den. Or eat an entire hemlock plant."

"Both of which could be arranged." The moment the words were out of his mouth, each of my men drew their swords, pointing them at MacDonald's thick throat.

"As can your death. I can make it quick. Burn your body before anyone missed ye. Then what? I'd still have your ships, your men—and your daughters."

"Ye, bastard," MacDonald said through gritted teeth. "Go ahead, kill me. There are many that know I'm here. If I go missing ye'll be the first one they come after."

"Ye dinna understand," I said, walking closer. I raised my arms and turned, making him look around the room. "Do ye see this castle? Do ye see me? I *am* the protector of Scotland. Ye are a threat. No one will look twice in my direction if I were to kill ye." I stopped just short of a foot away, took out my sword and pressed it against his shoulder so the blade touched his neck. "One swipe and your head will roll."

"Ye canna hide behind the king forever. If I dinna unlock your secrets, then someone else will."

"Let them come. Let them all come," I said quietly, my voice laced with danger.

There was a flash of fear in MacDonald's eyes, but the man quickly covered it with scorn. "Ye're a fool then."

"Not as foolish as ye. Ye'll never be King of the Isles, King of Scotland. Not as long as I live."

"Then I pray ye die soon."

"Take him to his quarters—our *special* guest quarters."

Behind the Plaid

Two men gripped MacDonald by his shoulders and wrenched him to his feet. Straw from the floor clung to his plaid at the knees.

"Oh, before ye go, MacDonald," I said casually, as though we'd just finished a friendly chat. "I've a gift for ye."

I murmured orders to Ewan who returned moments later with the shackles.

"I believe these are yours. Did ye not want your things returned to ye?" I sneered and nodded for the guards to restrain the bastard with his own manacles. "Have a pleasant night."

He sputtered and cursed my name loudly as he was dragged from the great hall, irons scraping over the floor.

The calming effect of my earlier dram of whisky was starting to wear of. I craved Emma. But this had to be finished first.

"Where was he found?" I asked the remaining men.

Gordon stepped forward. "We found him skulking around the beach. Must have slipped off one of the vessels and disappeared before we got to them. He was trying to climb the cliff when we spotted him. He was heavily armed."

I nodded, wondering if he'd heard of my evening swims and hoped to catch me unawares. I almost wished the men had left him there so I would have had an excuse to kill him once and for all.

My king had never heeded my warnings, always believing the honeyed words of a man who swore fealty but then betrayed him behind closed doors. Perhaps now, he would realize that I'd spoken the truth, that MacDonald was a threat that needed to be dealt with.

"Did he say anything?"

Gordon smiled. "Besides cursing my name and threatening to rape my mother?"

I shook my head. "Sounds like him."

"He's a ballock sucking maggot."

"I couldna agree with ye more. Gratitude, men. Each of ye get an extra flask of whisky from the store room. Ye've done well this eve."

While the men enjoyed the sweet tang of honeyed whisky, and MacDonald enjoyed the bite of metal around his ankles and wrists, I would partake in teaching a lesson in pleasure to a nymph. Watch her mouth open in a silent plea as I showed her the decadence that could be had from the touch of one's own hand.

And lose myself in the softness of her embrace.

CHAPTER FOURTEEN

Emma

I paced the length of my chamber, unnerved by my latest encounter with Logan. I couldn't think when he was around, couldn't concentrate on the things I'd vowed I would and wouldn't do. When he was with me, nothing else mattered. My fingertips were numb with cold and I stopped pacing for a moment to kneel before the fire. I stared into the flames as I warmed my hands.

Never had I felt this way before about a man or myself. Certainly, *Steven* never pulled such feelings from me. If anything I wished I'd never met him…

I could still picture standing on those stone steps outside of the local community college. My first day of school. My first day in the real world without anyone to turn to. Aunt Sheila had come to help get me through the summer, take me to therapy. But she had her own issues and soon was back in rehab. As much as she wanted to be there for me, she couldn't. Since I was eighteen, I was legally able to live on my own. My family's house was paid for. There was enough insurance money for me to get by on for a few years. I didn't have to worry about bills.

But I was utterly alone. Afraid. Isolated.

I stared up at those tall campus buildings wondering how I could ever step foot inside. Doing so meant moving on with my life, and I wasn't ready to do that.

Then Steven had touched my arm, asked me if I knew where to find the advisor building. He was older. Mature. A man. I pointed toward the brick building that housed all the campus advisors, the ones who'd helped me figure out I wanted to get a degree in nutrition.

I was coming out of my first class at the same time he must have left the office because I ran into him again. He asked if I wanted to have lunch, his treat. I laughed when he took me to the campus cafeteria. I ordered a Cobb salad and ate barely any of it, munching on a few of the croutons.

He asked me why I didn't drink diet soda since most girls were normally worried about the sugar in soda. I told him I was worried about the lack of sugar and I didn't want to poison myself. Steven seemed charmed by me, and I was merely looking for someone older to guide me, maybe another father figure.

He came by the campus often—his company hired interns year round. We exchanged numbers and it became routine that when he visited, he took me to lunch. Eventually, lunch morphed into dinner.

After a few months, I felt close to him, and when he offered to marry me, to help me get into a great nutrition program at the local university, I took him up on the offer. I was lost. And I thought I'd found myself with Steven. My friends had gone

Behind the Plaid

away to college, and I'd pushed most of them away besides. My family was gone. I had no one to confer with about it. Looking back, I realized Steven took advantage of that.

He wooed me, made me feel special, but once the marriage license was signed, the thin gold band on my finger, my parent's house sold, my money joined with his, Steven's true self came out. The first time he berated me, I could remember like it was only a moment ago. I shivered and huddled closer to the fire, the bitter memories needing to be had, if only to remind me of what I'd run away from.

I came home from school, thrilled for having gotten an A on an exam I'd studied all through the night for. Steven stood just inside his house—it was never mine—hands on his hips and a scowl on his face that scared me half to death. My parents were kind people, calm. When they were mad, there was a discussion, not the pure hatred that came off my husband in waves—the man I thought was going to keep me safe was actually the one frightening me.

I'd left my cup of coffee on the table that morning. One of his cats knocked it over and it shattered. The cat had cut its paw and tracked blood throughout the house. He was so furious, he broke another cup, throwing it so close to my head, a breeze fanned my cheek as it whizzed by. He forced me to the ground and made me scrub the floors of the entire house on my hands and knees. Afterward, he raped me for the first time.

Tears trekked down my face, and I hugged my knees close, feeling the pain all over again. Once that jar had been opened, Steven never closed it again. I was trapped. Tortured. Too mortified to ask anyone for help. Too young and scared to know that I could.

The door burst open with such force the fire actually flickered. I fell back as I turned with a start to see Logan filling door's expanse. His features were etched with concern as he raked my face with his gaze, noting the tears on my cheeks.

He stormed forward, lifted me into his arms and demanded, "What's happened? Who hurt ye?"

I shook my head and swiped away the tears, feeling the heat of embarrassment filling my cheeks.

"Nothing. No one."

"Dinna lie to me, lass. I swear, I'll slice through anyone who's hurt ye." His passion for my protection was incredible. So much so, I couldn't quite believe it.

"Memories, Logan," I managed to say, still rocked by his need to harm anyone who wounded me.

His eyes shuttered then, as though he too knew how much memories could affect a soul. "Demons more like," he said.

I nodded and he carried me to chair, sitting down and settling me on his lap.

"I wish I could take away your demons." Logan used the pads of his thumbs to wipe at the tears I'd missed. Then he licked those thumbs. My lips parted on a sigh. "I would, ye know."

"I know." I'm uncertain how I was aware of his conviction, but deep inside, in my gut, I could feel it. Logan was a good man. A strong man. A different sort of man.

"Mayhap that is one reason I'm so…drawn to ye," he whispered. "Ye make my demons vanish when I touch ye, a small reprieve for a man with so many. All I want to do is destroy yours." His hands stroked up and down my arms, and I softened in his embrace.

I wasn't cold or stiff. I sank against his comfort, absorbed it.

"You do more than you know," I said.

"I've an ear if ye want to tell me." His words were softly said as he nuzzled my cheek with his nose.

"I know."

"Want me to tell ye something?"

I nodded, liking the idea of learning more about the man who exuded mystery.

"I am the guardian of Scotland."

He said it so seriously I hadn't the heart to tell him he'd already made that clear, so I just nodded.

"Ye dinna understand. I am *the* guardian."

"You're right. I don't." I was confused by his words, and the way he stroked his hands over my spine wasn't making it any easier to concentrate.

"The king has entrusted in me not only a treasure but a secret."

"Don't all leaders trust their men with their secrets?" I asked, placing my hands on his chest, feeling his heart beat beneath my fingertips. The light of the fire flickered in his eyes.

"Some. But not a secret like this one."

"Do you want to tell me what it is?"

He nodded. "But I canna. If I were to ever tell anyone, ye would be it. I know not why, but I would."

"But if you told me you'd have to kill me?"

Deadly serious, he nodded. "And I would also die."

Holy shit. What kind of secrets did he have? The kind that really would end in death? Of all places... I had to fall here. With him. But I knew if I had a chance to choose where I went, I would always come back to Logan.

"No matter what your secrets, you can trust me." I stroked his hair away from his forehead.

"I still canna tell ye."

"Please don't. I want to live." Saying those words, my chest swelled with emotion. I did want to live. Before coming here, whether I lived or died wouldn't have mattered to me.

But it was almost like Gealach Castle was a fortress surrounding me so that I could find my reason to live and Logan was the one who led me there.

"Now, I've told ye something about me. 'Tis your turn to share."

I refrained from mentioning he hadn't exactly told me anything. "My parents and brother died just before my eighteenth birthday."

"Ye had a brother?" His eyes widened. "I had a brother, too."

"How did your brother die?"

"He..." Logan shook his head. "He's always with me."

I smiled wanly. "That is a good way to look at it. I guess I always feel like my brother is with me, too."

"How did he pass?" Logan asked.

Realizing Logan would have no idea what a plane was, and I'd probably sound insane trying to explain it, I simply said, "An accident while they traveled. They were killed instantly."

"I'm sorry to hear of it. How did ye survive?"

I looked down at my hands on his broad chest. He was so much larger than me, and again I was stunned with how safe I felt around him. Not like when I'd met Steven, when I'd been looking for someone to guide me. This was different. "I wasn't with them."

"Where were ye?"

"At home." My brother was a brilliant soccer player. His team had made it to an international championship game, and while they all trekked off to Brazil, I stayed home because of friends. We had a couple of spring break events planned and I didn't want to miss it. When the crash happened...my friends, they all kept going, and I didn't. I'd wished I'd been on that plane.

"Do ye ever feel..." He stopped and looked toward the window.

I looked there, too, noting that inside of a golden slice of light cutting through the thin opening, it was dusk. Night was falling. "What?"

He looked back at me, his gaze intense, eyes strained. "Do ye ever feel like ye can change the way the world progresses?"

Swallowing back my denial, I thought on his question. "Before reaching, Gealach…no. I wouldn't have. Now…" How could I say that I had changed the world already, mine at least?

"What is it about ye?" he asked. His gaze searched my face, and instead of shutting him out, I let him see inside. Let him see my pain, my angst, my desire for him, for a new life.

I flattened my hand to his face. "I don't know, Logan."

"Me either."

The intensity of the moment proved a little much for me. I climbed from his lap. "Can I get you some wine? Agatha left me a nice spread, I've barely touched."

Logan glanced toward the table laden with meats, pies and a jug of wine. He nodded.

"Maybe that's the problem," he chuckled. "Neither of us has had enough wine this eve."

"Your world…mine…they are both filled with stress, I think." Logan came to stand beside me and I poured a cup and handed it to him. "Wine can help take the edge off."

Logan grabbed a hunk of unknown meat and popped it into his mouth. "I agree," he said as he chewed. He wrinkled his nose. "Agatha has given ye mutton."

"Is that what it is? Sheep?"

He nodded.

"I don't care for sheep," I said, feeling actually quite sad about it. Sheep were cute little creatures that children sang about in nursery rhymes, not something I wanted to see on my plate.

"I dinna care for it either."

"What do you like?" I asked, taking a sip of the wine I'd poured myself.

"Whisky," he said with a mischievous grin.

"To eat?" I asked with an answering smile.

"Besides the cleft between your thighs?" he said gruffly.

I drained the cup of wine and poured more. "Yes, besides that." How could he turn a conversation about eating sheep into one of carnal pleasure? The wine coursed into my belly and straight through my veins making me feel warm, light. Just like the beer I'd had, the wine was more potent. Only one more glass, I told myself, or else I'd pass out cold.

"I like pastries. I confess a weakness for sweets."

I reached for one of the fruit pastries on the table. Its crust was flaky, and sugared apples with a hint of spice filled the center.

"It just so happens that I have a pastry right here." I took an exaggerated bite, chewing the delicious, melt-in-your-mouth apples. Once again I was a little stunned at the way he brought out a side of myself I'd not known existed. How was it possible I was two different people wrapped up inside one mind?

"Ye little tease," he growled, lunging for me.

I leapt out of his way and ran to the opposite side of the room. Logan laughed and barreled toward me. I hopped up onto the bed to get out of his way, and just when I thought I was going to make it to the other side, he grabbed me around the waist and hauled me backward against his chest.

"I believe ye've a treat for me," he said against my ear, licking the lobe.

I murmured, "Yes," and closed my eyes.

"Give me a bite."

I held the pastry over my shoulder, prepared for him to take a bite, but he turned me around instead. Opening my eyes, I watched him dip his head to nuzzle between my breasts.

"The best treat of the day," he declared.

I laughed and gasped while he softly bit my hardened nipples through my gown—the lavender one. I'd not the balls to dress in the sheer black one.

"Now, for my sweet." He flattened me to the bed, and instantly my sex was drenched, quivering, waiting. Logan sprawled on top of me, his hips settling between my parted thighs. Only this time, he did grab the pastry from my hands and shoved the entire thing into his mouth. "Mmm... So good."

I laughed and shoved against his shoulder. "Now who is the tease?" I asked.

He grinned and licked the syrup from his lips. "I never promised anything other than eating that treat."

"Not true," I admonished, then bit my lip.

"Ah, but ye're right. I did promise ye a lesson."

I bent my knees and lifted my hips. This was the kind of lesson I wanted, a deep, thrusting, hip pounding, thigh clenching, air gasping, shrieking, sexual lesson.

"Not yet, lass... Tonight I want to teach ye how to pleasure yourself."

"And I want to pleasure you."

He shook his head and grinned in the overpowering way he had that said he was the one in control and knew exactly what he was doing. With a wink, he whispered, "Prepare to be satisfied."

CHAPTER FIFTEEN

Emma

Oh. My. Gods.

I gulped, trying not to be as shocked by his words as I was turned on. What could he teach me? My nipples tingled, belly quivered, sex clenched.

"I am," I answered, feeling heat sear my cheeks.

"Are ye?" Logan trailed his lips from the inside of my knee up the middle of my thigh.

I swallowed. My legs shook. Logan stroked over my thighs, spread them wider, pushed my skirts up to my hips so my sex was fully exposed. He gazed on my exposed flesh, his pupils dilating, nostrils flaring. I could tell he liked what he saw. I wanted him to forget his lesson of teaching me to pleasure myself and instead pleasure me himself. I wanted to feel his tongue slicking over my heated flesh.

"Ye are exquisite," he said softly, his words empowering me. He could say it a million times and I'd always be amazed hearing praise from his lips.

"Touch me," I pleaded, a little surprised at the words forming from my own throat. I'd never begged for anyone's caress. And yet, if he didn't touch me soon I might collapse from the pressure building inside me.

Logan loomed above me, swept down and captured my lips. He took complete control of my mouth, his tongue delving inside to own mine. I wrapped my arms around his neck, arched my back to feel my breasts scrape across his chest. Lifted my hips, feeling the pressure of his organ brushing mine. Not enough pressure. I wanted to feel the weight of him pushing me into the bed. But he teased me. Kissed me hard, but kept his body light above me. I gasped, moaned, grazed my nails down his back. So overcome with desire, need, that I felt out of control. His will was my command.

Anything he wanted.

"Take me," I said breathlessly.

"In time." Logan pulled away with languid ease. His mouth slid over my chin, down my neck, where he dipped his tongue onto the space at the base of my throat. "Now for your lesson."

Logan leaned back on his heels, his eyes once more riveted between my thighs. I was dripping wet, could feel the hot slickness slipping down to my buttocks. He must have seen it too. Licking his lips, he said, "Take off your gown."

I didn't say anything, only lifted my butt to pull the gown over my hips completely, then sat up. I untied the gown's bodice, trying to remember exactly how the maids had put me into it. My fingers trembled and Logan made no move to help me. Instead he intently watched, though I sensed an urgency in him. This was a test as much for him as it was for me. For him a trial in control and for me an experiment in pushing aside my fears, letting myself go. Eventually, I finished the task, and tossed the fabric aside. I sat quivering in a thin chemise, my skin on fire.

Logan traced his finger over my neck, down my chest to the ribbons tying the chemise. With his thumb and forefinger he tugged a ribbon. The ties easily unraveled and my chemise fell open exposing the swells of my breasts. Logan hissed a breath. "This too needs to go."

I nodded and pulled it up over my head. The chill of the room caressed my skin. But at the same time, my skin was flushed. I shuddered. Logan reached behind me, fluffed the pillows, then gently pushed against my shoulders.

"Lay back."

His gaze raked over me, stopping briefly at the small tattoo on my hip. His eyes narrowed and he reached out, touched the mark.

"What's this?" he asked.

"A tattoo."

"I've not seen this before. Ye're…marked."

The way he said it, the way his maids had reacted, sent a ripple of fear up my spine. "I asked for it."

His brows raised. "Why?"

I shrugged. "When I was young. I had a fascination with Celtic history. My family…" If I said too much, he'd think I was crazy. As it was, people with marks like this were often seen as witches, or marked by the devil. "I just liked it."

Logan's eyes blazed with earnest interest, and something flashed in his eyes that looked like pride, but I couldn't truly tell. He glanced away and climbed from the bed and walked to fire, stoking it, building the flames like I wished he would do to me. Just watching him at the task, the way his body moved so fluidly, the way it was second nature for him to do things for others, did stoke my desire. But as much as I wanted him, the

Behind the Plaid

thought of pleasuring myself frightened me. I wasn't opposed to masturbating. Surely, most girls practiced touching themselves. Steven had not allowed me to have a vibrator or anything of the kind, but that didn't mean I did not touch myself when he wasn't home. In the shower. The relief of pressure, the pleasure would often take me away for at least those few minutes.

Logan turned around, his gaze raking hotly over my nude form. He wanted to watch me. A man of his caliber had probably pleasured hundreds of women and I wasn't naïve enough to believe that I wasn't the first one he would have commanded to touch herself. What if I did it wrong? There was every possibility that I wouldn't touch myself in the way he wanted, make the right sounds, faces. I was worried about him observing me in one of the most intimate acts a person could perform. Self pleasure.

There was no backing out. No running. Logan stalked the bed, a grin of awareness playing on his lips. Again I was struck with awe. How was it possible that he'd taken an interest in me? That I'd come here? Traveling through time I could have fallen anywhere, could be stuck in a dungeon, could have been killed. And yet, I was lying naked in bed with the most handsome, arousing man gazing at me like I was the most important, desirous woman.

That was how I felt. Feminine. Wanted. Needed.

"Emma," he said, coming closer. "Touch your breast."

I obediently placed my hand on my breast, not giving in to the embarrassment that pushed to the surface. It was a battle. My breathing quickened, my chest rising and falling. My hardened nipple pressed to the middle of my palm.

"The other one, too."

I did as he said, even taking the initiative to knead them. I gasped, surprised with how much I enjoyed it. I'd never played with my breasts before. Never needed to. But with Logan gazing at me, eyes filled with wickedness, hot sensation whipped through me, and an erotic pull tugged at my core with each stroke.

"Pinch your nipples," he said, his knees knocking into the mattress.

I did it. Cried out with the shock of it.

"Ye liked that?" he asked, grinning wide. "Do it again."

I rolled my nipples between my fingers, surprised that it felt better with every second that passed. Logan sat down on the bed beside me, placing his warm hand on my thigh. He leaned forward, nuzzled my breasts and when I moved to pull my hands away, he shook his head.

"No. Dinna stop." As I played with my nipples, his stroked his tongue over my fingers, licking between them. The tip of his tongue seared the flesh of my breast. He teased, taunted. Flicked his tongue over my nipple. And I kneaded, plucked, gasped. My entire body sang with pleasure. My toes curled, legs shook. I wanted him sitting between my thighs, not on the side.

Logan went back and forth from breast to breast with his mouth. He held himself up with one hand, the other massaged my thigh. I writhed beneath his touch and my own, not thinking it could get any better than it was. But then it did. He removed his hand from my thigh, took one of my hands and slid it down over my belly. Goosebumps followed the path, igniting my skin to a fever pitch. Sweat trickled along my brow, beaded above my upper lip, gathered along my spine. The room was warm, but it was Logan's touch that had me blazing hot.

He leaned up, his eyelids heavy. "Your body is beautiful. And 'tis yours."

"I want it to be yours."

Logan grinned and winked. "But first it must be yours." He swirled his fingers around my navel. "A woman's belly is so sensitive. The slightest touch can set her to quivering."

I exhaled as he lightly stroked and tickled my skin. Nipples ached for him to touch them.

"When ye touch yourself... Dinna think to only touch your cunny." He cupped my sex and my hips bucked, leaping me a good couple inches from the mattress.

"I won't be able to touch myself the way you do," I said, my voice shaky.

"Try it." He removed his hands.

Tentatively I put my hands on my belly. I quivered at my own touch. Gently I stroked up and down, scraped my nails lightly, and blew out a slow breath.

"That's it, lass," he crooned. "Dinna forget your hips, thighs." His fingers moved over my hips, swirling circles on the way to my thighs.

I followed his path, running the backs of my nails over my hips, then sinking my fingers into the muscles of my thighs. My head fell back in pleasure. I'd never thought to touch myself anywhere but between my legs. If touching my breasts and receiving pleasure was a surprise, then gaining bliss from stroking my own hips and thighs was a complete shock.

"Ye should love your body. Worship it. Make love to it." Logan was deadly serious, his words spoken softly but firmly and his brogue stroking a path over my mind just as his fingers stroked over my body.

Kissing his way up my neck to my lips, he breathed the words, "Touch your cunny."

I shuddered deeply. The way he talked dirty to me, the images that floated in my mind, his breath tickling my skin, took the wind from me. He kissed me, taking possession of my mouth. I couldn't think for a moment. Logan surrounded me claiming even my soul. His tongue stroked, teased, and it was all I could do to stay conscious.

"Emma... Touch your cunny," he demanded.

I slipped my fingers between my thighs. I was drenched, hot. Liquid slicked on my fingertips, my skin pulsed, my clit throbbed.

"Oh, God," I gasped.

Logan sucked my lower lip into his mouth. "Oh, aye," he murmured back.

His fingers followed mine, slipping together in my juices as I stroked my lips, rubbing my clit in a little circle. Arrows of pleasure shot outward making me shake and yet I was boneless. Logan had started something inside me I wasn't strong enough to stop. Had no interest in stopping whatever roller coaster we'd jumped on. I was hurtling through the air, exhilaration filling my blood. Adrenaline pumping. We were on a riveting ride that I never wanted to end.

My hips bucked upward. I wanted him inside me so bad. And then I knew a way to get at least part of him there. I skimmed a hand between my lips to my opening. Naturally, Logan followed. I pushed his finger inside me, with my pointer finger. Filling myself with both of us. A low guttural moan escaped me, answered by his feral growl. That was so freaking hot. My entire body shook and pulsed. Fiery zings blasted from my core, shimmering outward, bringing me so close to the edge. The pleasure was unimaginable, delicious, addictive. I didn't want it to end, and yet, I was on the brink of shattering. My sex tightened around our fingers. I was going to come.

"Hold on, lass, not yet," Logan whispered against my ear.

But then he bit my lobe, tugging on it and sending another frisson of fierce wanting to radiate through me. My hips rocked back and forth as I actively fucked our fingers. God, I was so hot, so desperate for release and yet didn't want to disappoint him, never wanted it to end.

Logan slipped his finger from inside me. I whimpered my protest. Tugging on my lobe, he pushed my middle finger inside me, then my ring finger so I filled myself with three, stretching. The tremors inside me quickened, spiraling me into another realm. I was so close. So very close.

"Oh, Logan, I never—" I gasped unable to finish as he manipulated my hand so that my fingers pushed in an out. He captured a nipple between his teeth, applying gentle pressure. I couldn't think. Couldn't breathe.

"There's no such thing as never." His voice vibrated against my breast as he sucked and teethed.

"I want to come." Somehow I managed to say it, even as my breath hitched.

"Come where?" he asked, his mouth traveling south, tongue dipping into my navel.

"T-to orgasm."

"Orgasm?"

Were the terms not in use? I didn't know. Wouldn't have. Couldn't even contemplate.

"Finish me," I demanded.

Logan chuckled.

"Finish yourself." With his command, he bit my hip, let go of my hand.

I didn't still. I listened. Drove my fingers deep. In and out. Used my other hand to rub my clit. Circle, circle, circle. My cheeks where hot. Blood pumped loud in my ears. Logan moved between my thighs, dipped low. Then his tongue flicked over my clit, between my fingers, as I stroked myself. That was all it took. I shattered. Exploded. Back arched, hips thrust up. Fingers moving at a furious pace. Died and gone to heaven. I shrieked. Called out his name.

"Aye, that's it, come for me." He spread my thighs wide, his tongue pushing into my slit to tease my fingers. "Good, God, lass, ye taste so good."

The tremors of my orgasm did not subside, they only built. I was going to come again.

"Again," I moaned.

"Aye, again," he answered.

Once more I pulsed, juices slicking around my fingers, body pulsating in its own magical rhythm. Logan lapped at me, flicked his tongue, made my orgasm even stronger.

"Yes!" I cried.

His hands pressed to the inside of my thighs, he licked me until it was painful, my over-sensitized flesh unable to take anymore.

"Stop, please," I whispered, my fingers trapped beneath his face.

Logan chuckled and tilted up to look at me. "Had enough, already?"

I smiled. "I can't seem to get enough of you." I couldn't believe the words actually came out of my mouth.

"Then why did ye tell me to stop?"

"I—I..." I didn't know what to say.

"I'm only teasing ye, lass." Logan gently pulled my hands away from between my thighs. Licked my fingers clean. "Ye did verra well. Verra, verra well. Watching your face as ye moaned, pleasure clouding your eyes. My fingers inside ye. Your fingers inside ye... Och," he sighed. "I have fallen under your spell."

With him kneeling between my thighs, I hooked my legs behind him. "I want to pleasure you, too."

"That will come in time."

"Why not now?" I pouted, leaned up on an elbow and stroked my hand down his chest, feeling his muscles rippled. I gripped his belt. "Just a little bit?" God, I'd never been so forward, but the way he made me feel...was powerful. Like I could do anything, be this woman who was desired and wanted in return.

Logan gripped my wrist, stilling my movements. His jaw muscle flexed. "Not now."

"You don't desire my touch?" I had thought he was only playing hard to get, but doubts which used to fill my mind once

Behind the Plaid

more took over. Perhaps that wasn't it at all. Perhaps he just didn't want me to touch him, pleasure him. Maybe he didn't think I could. And he might be right. I'd not pleasured a man before, and Steven was plenty derogatory in his comments regarding my skill.

Logan growled, his grip on my wrist tightening. He shoved my hand low, filling my palm with his rigid flesh. I wanted to flip up his kilt and touch his hot skin. He was huge. Hard. I swore I could feel him pulsing. Feel the blood rushing to his cock, filling him. "Ye, I think I dinna desire ye? Feel my desire."

"I can feel it." My voice was shaky.

"What do ye feel?"

"I feel your…"

"Say it."

I'd never said the word aloud. At least not to a man. "I feel your cock."

"Is it hard?"

I nodded.

"Say it."

"Your cock is hard."

"Hard for ye, Emma. Because I want ye. I want ye so bad, I canna breathe without your name on my lips. Your face floating behind my eyes." His gaze locked on mine, grave. He told the truth, and it was a truth that rocked me to the core.

"Then why?" I asked, holding his stare, wanting but not daring to stroke him.

"Because." I could sense he struggled with something inside.

If only I had the skill to pull it from him. "Tell me." This time I squeezed him. He hissed, his eyes rolling a little and his cock jumped in my hand. My cunny, as he called it, quivered and sparks of need flared once more.

"Because, Emma, ye are not ready yet." Logan pulled away, his face clouding. He stepped off the bed.

I'd heard his words, and there might have been some credence to it, but there was so much more behind them. *Logan wasn't ready*. That was what kept him from making love to me. I knew he was controlling. Knew he had dark secrets. But looking at him now as he walked away from me, I had the deep realization that I was not the only one who needed healing. Logan did too. And I was bringing that healing. By having me here, by connecting with me, by giving me lessons in pleasure and building me up inside, he was also healing himself.

My eyes widened, and I sat up, legs crossed, arms over my breasts. "Logan, wait. Don't leave."

He turned around, the darkness in his eyes heavy. He had much on his mind. "I have to."

I couldn't hold him here. He needed to exorcise his demons as I'd obviously rocked something deep in his soul. "When will I see you again?" I hoped I didn't sound desperate. I didn't want him to leave even if I understood it. I already felt colder with him halfway to the door.

Logan came back to me, stroked my cheek and pressed a tender kiss to my lips. "I'll be back soon."

I nodded, leaned into his touch. Turned my head to kiss his palm. He would return to me soon. Whether that meant in the middle of the night while I slept, in the morning to share sloppy porridge, or for dinner, I didn't know. And I didn't want to ask. Afraid he might push me away.

"Sweet dreams, fair Emma."

CHAPTER SIXTEEN

Logan

The door to Emma's chamber closed with a quiet click, but even still, the sound seemed to echo throughout the long stone corridor. Leaning my forehead against the cold hard wall, I closed my eyes and took a deep breath. Fists clenched tight, I resisted the urge to punch the wall. Control. Had to regain control. Cock hard as stone, I wanted nothing more than to rip off her door, storm back inside and take her like she'd begged me to.

Ballocks, but 'twas hard not to give in. The way she pleaded, the way she opened up to me. I raked a hand through my hair and blew out a breath. No woman had ever affected me like Emma. No woman captivated me more. And no woman had ever made me feel like I might die if I didna sink inside her, hear her scream with pleasure as her cunny clenched my cock tight.

I glanced from one end of the corridor to the other. Only a few sconces were lit, enough to light a walker's path, but dark enough that a body could hide within the shadows. The way I liked it. Since I knew every inch of this castle like the back of my hand, if a shadow stood too long or bulky, I'd take notice.

I fiddled with the dirk at my hip. Though I doubted anyone hid in hopes of gaining me alone, part of me hoped they did. A good fight would help dissipate some of the torment that filled my blood. I crept the twenty-three steps it took to get to my own chamber, paused outside the door. I wasna ready for bed. Knew that all I'd end up doing inside was pacing the room, punching the pillow and then somehow talking myself into returning to Emma's chamber.

I would eventually make it there. Of that I knew. In time, when she was fully prepared. When I was ready to relinquish control. For certes, I would break when my cock finally sank home.

MacDonald. I could let out some of my frustrations on the bastard. Make him suffer like I did. At the bottom of the stairs, two guards nodded to me. I inclined my head but said nothing, intent on my path to the dungeon.

"My laird."

Ewan.

I stood immobile, but didna turn around. He would only seek to stop me. I should wait for the king's missive. There was every possibility that His Majesty, in his *infinite* wisdom, would side with my enemy. In that case, I would be left with little options. I protected the king. I sheltered his secrets, my secrets. If he wanted them exposed, I had little choice but to obey.

Ewan came to stand in front of me, lowered his head in deference, then met my gaze. "Where are ye headed?"

"To the water gate."

Ewan raised a skeptical brown. "The water gate?"

"Do ye question me, lad?"

Ewan shook his head, a flash of knowing in his eyes. The man probably had a good idea that I was not only lying, but wouldna be swayed.

"I merely thought to accompany ye."

"I need no company."

"Then mayhap ye'd like a little hand on hand?"

Now it was my turn to raise a brow. "'Tis the middle of the night."

"Aye, and ye're not in your bed, and I not in mine. Couldna sleep and I assume 'tis the same for ye. Let us vent our frustrations with a few well laid punches." Ewan smiled and wiggled his brows.

"Ye pose a verra enticing proposition, lad." Ewan was my second. My conscience. I trusted him. I should let him drag me away from my true purpose. But the truth was, I couldna. MacDonald had made it closer than he'd ever come before. He was smart. Aye, more so than most. But the fact that he had would only put a false sense of confidence inside my other enemies. "I canna. If ye're only going to pester me, then come along."

"Where are ye going?"

"Where have ye been trying to keep me from?"

"I was afraid of that. The man's been silent as the dead since ye put him down there."

"Has anyone checked to see that he still breathes?"

Ewan nodded, and turned to walk with me. "Aye. He stands at the cell door as if awaiting someone."

"Me." My skin chilled. MacDonald was far too confident.

We walked the rest of the way in silence. The guards opened the heavy dungeon doors without a word and let us pass. I took a torch from the wall and descended the slick, stone stairs, the air instantly musty and filled with the scents of blood, excrement and death.

Each time I descended, the hand of the devil gripped tightly to the small of my back. Sweat trickled down each bone in my spine and beaded on my brow. My chest grew taut, and it was a labor to breathe. The sense of doom lay heavy and thick in the air, and must be the cause of my reaction. More potent tonight than any other, I could only surmise it was because my greatest enemy lay shackled only a few yards away.

"Is that ye, Grant? I can smell ye." MacDonald's voice echoed throughout the dungeon, bouncing off the walls and then dying flat, almost as if he'd never spoken. Only the ghosts of my mind playing tricks on me.

The man couldna smell me either, though for moment I swore he could. My revulsion of this place was strong. Faint memories danced on the edges of my consciousness, wanting to push forward. They were old, mayhap from when I was only a little older than a bairn. Screaming. Lots of screaming. Darkness. The smell. This smell. Fear. A terror that shook me to my very soul, made me question all I knew and threatened to never let me return.

Grinding my teeth, I forged ahead, refusing to let those distant recollections come to the surface. I didna want to know. Had kept them dark and buried. To bring them out now, before I faced MacDonald would only give him more weaponry and make me less quick-witted.

We rounded a corner and came to the barred cell where MacDonald stood. The smug expression on his face and slight nod of his head as he looked me up and down was nearly enough to make me run the man through.

"So, 'twas ye." MacDonald leaned forward, took a long leisurely sniff, but before he could do more than chuckle, I jabbed him in the nose with my fist. A cracking sound shattered the still air. MacDonald cried out, gripped his nose and took a

Behind the Plaid

few stumbling steps backward. Not a full out punch, but sufficient to sting, make him bleed.

The man ought to know his place inside *my* dungeon. He attempted to play a game of minds, but I was in no mood. Forgetting he was wearing shackles the man tripped and fell flat on his bastard arse. I didna laugh, nor flinch, merely stared him down. He was nay the only one who could be intimidating.

"Ye'll pay for that, Grant," he seethed through his teeth, using his shirt to wipe at the blood trickling in a steady flow from his nostrils.

"How?" I glanced around with raised hands in question. "Who is going to punish me?"

"Your king."

"Is he not your king as well?"

MacDonald sneered. "Ye already know that answer."

"And so why do ye think he will punish me for hurting his enemy?"

"Maybe he *wants* me to take his place."

I roared a laugh, while on the inside his words hit a chord. Was it possible that my king would seek for MacDonald to take my place? Why?

"Ye're an even bigger fool than I thought, MacDonald. If that's the case, 'haps he wanted ye to believe it. Thought ye'd end up here and knew I'd make sure ye never left."

MacDonald's face paled visibly. The bastard hadna thought of that even though it'd only take me less than a minute to surmise as much.

"His Majesty is a strategist," MacDonald drawled, pushing himself awkwardly to his feet. He approached the bars, blood staining his nose, lips and chin. The metal shackles clinked as he moved. He reached up and gripped the bars, his fingers wrapping slowly around each rung just like I imagined he wished to wrap them around my neck. The man leaned close, his smile widening, madness bright in his eyes. "He wants us both left guessing. Dinna think ye've won. I guarantee this war has only just begun."

I leaned close too, our breaths mingling. "I hope that thought helps ye to sleep better as ye curl up with the rats."

MacDonald laughed. "And who do ye curl up with, Grant? Is she a bonny lass? Supple and sweet? How can ye be sure she willna stab ye in the throat while ye slumber, sated, your cock limp?"

Because I willna sleep beside her. I smiled, baring my teeth. "Sleep is for the dead. Pleasant dreams."

I didna wait for his response. Turned my back on the man and walked back the way I'd come, Ewan following. MacDonald called after me, yelling vulgar things meant to intimidate, but what I realized with our short visit was, the man was overconfident. Almost so much so that 'twould appear false.

I'd posted guards by the end of the short corridor where MacDonald was held, and there I stopped. "Dinna let anyone near him. He is too confident. Dinna lose your sight on him."

The guards nodded.

We ascended the winding stairs and when we reached the top, I gave similar instructions to the men, adding that no one went down unless expressly ordered by me or Ewan.

"Double the guard," I told Ewan.

"Aye, my laird. And what about the battlements?"

"Double them."

Ewan nodded and headed toward the barracks to issue orders. Rather than heading back to my chamber, I spoke with the men who reported nothing untoward. A slitted window graced the wall beside the dungeon door. For most, gazing out that thin opening was the last light they ever saw. The moon was high in the sky with wispy white clouds floating on the black inky surface of the sky. Had to be nearing two in the morning.

Behind the Plaid

Dawn would crest the horizon within hours and the castle would slowly come to life. There was much to be done on the morrow. I prayed the king would return a message to me, but it was almost too soon to hope. Would most likely be several more days.

All the better for MacDonald to stew within the depths of Gealach's own Hell.

When Ewan returned with more guards, I took my leave. The shadows danced all around, threatening to unearth fiendish spirits that would pull the demons from my mind. The only things that suppressed the demons were whisky and women. Whisky dulled the mind and I had no interest in any other woman than Emma.

I passed her door on the way toward my bedchamber and stopped, backing up the few feet to stand before it. Pressing my ear to the door, all was quiet within. I half-hoped she'd been waiting for my footsteps, would call me inside to tend her once more. But 'twas ridiculous. The lass had been spent, almost asleep when I left her sated. A lesson well-learned, the shock and pleasure on her face something I'd never forget. I was drawing a part of her out she'd never thought to have encompassed. Some may say I was ruining her. But how could I be ruining someone who wanted it? Who needed it?

Emma was broken like me. Needed healing. The best way I knew to heal us both was through touch. Her appearance on the steps of Gealach seemed almost like a gift from God. But how could that be possible when I questioned His existence. For if He were a real entity, why would He not have given me my birthright?

Forcing myself away from her door, I quickened my pace until I reached my own bedchamber, and then rushed within. 'Twas dark, and I used a torch from the corridor to light a candle before barring the door. All appeared the way I'd left it. The maids had left a flask of whisky on the table, a small favor they did each night, knowing the drink would help chase away my nightmares.

I asked my king about God once, why He would see me to where I am instead of what was rightfully mine. His answer was the one I turned to whenever doubts began crowding in. I am here at Gealach for a reason. Scotland needs me here. Needs my strength. That somehow the Father in Heaven knew I would be better placed as guardian.

'Twas the only thing I could believe in. Had to hold onto it, for there was no changing places.

After a quick check about my chamber to make sure no enemies lurked, I disrobed with haste, tucking my dagger beneath my pillow and sword beneath my bed. I fell heavily onto the mattress, one arm folded beneath my head, the other holding the flask of whisky to my lips.

Bare naked, I'd not lit a fire in my room. Told the maids never to do so since there was no telling when I would return. The cool night air wafted through the windows, and should have chilled my skin. But my gaze was locked on the secret panel that led into Emma's room. My skin was burning hot. Cock raging hard and jutting from my body like a sword seeking its victim.

A shudder passed through me and a drop of moisture beaded the tip of my cock. I refused to pleasure myself. I was saving release for Emma. And once I went there, it would be beyond paradise. I continued to stare at her door, imagining what lesson I would teach her next. Had to fling the coverlet over my waist to hide my incessant erection. I craved her; would have been better off strapped to the bed to keep me grounded. And that gave me an idea.

Another lesson… A lesson in trust. I blew out a hot breath imagining Emma tied to the bed as I ravished her. 'Twas too soon to introduce that. Too soon. For all her passion, she appeared so innocent.

Behind the Plaid

And her husband had not been kind. Just thinking on it brought rage to fuel my blood. The bastard. How could he have treated her any way but with gentle kindness? A woman was to be valued, and a wife cherished. If I had a wife, I would seek only to please her. Albeit, she would also have to obey me. To be my wife, a woman would be placed in grave danger. I am hunted. And so she would be as well. She'd be used against me in any way an enemy could find.

Yet another reason why my arrangement with Emma had to be kept secret. And why I couldn't allow myself to…care. The latter was a feat proving harder than imagined. I did care for her. I cared for her safety foremost. But the demons that haunted her… We appeared to have similar damaged souls and I hoped in helping to release her ghosts, I could release some of my own. There were those that would be with me forever, and only death would give me solace from them.

I took a long pull from the flask, feeling the beginnings of drowsiness creep into my eyes. Blinking lasted longer.

I tossed the flask to the floor, extinguished the candle and was cast into darkness. I welcomed it. The whisky had done its job by dulling my senses and sleep seemed like it may come easy tonight.

"Goodnight, Emma," I said to the secret door.

Tomorrow I would treat Emma with kindness. Ignite in her a gentle pleasure. Show her that not all men are evil. That she could trust me, open up to me. I wanted to know more about her.

I would give her another lesson. And in so doing, escape from myself.

CHAPTER SEVENTEEN

Emma

Muscles hurt in places I didn't even know existed. Deep, internal muscles that had never been used screamed their protest as I stretched out on the bed, and tossed back the covers. Logan was not only changing me mentally, but physically. He was my first thought in the morning and my last thought at night. I wondered if he'd wanted it to be that way. Made intoxicating love to me knowing he'd be forever ingrained in my mind.

Logan. Even his name was full of brawn and sexuality.

With a snort of disgust I shoved myself from bed and trudged to the window, opening it to the morning sunshine. As if on cue, a knock came at the door. I hoped, well, more than hoped, it was Logan. Instead several maids entered, and young men followed with a wooden tub.

Behind the Plaid

"His lairdship thought ye might like a bath this morning."

I nodded, watching as they set up the tub, the linens, and then bucket after bucket of water was poured in. While the tub was prepared, the maids made the bed and tidied the room. At last, the males left, and four maids remained. Would I ever get used to them washing me?

"My lady," Agatha said, wringing her hands in her apron. "His lairdship had us bring wax and a blade."

My eyes widened. They'd never waxed a woman before—nor shaved her—and the thought of them anywhere near my nether region and legs brought cold sweats and fear to me faster than Steven ever had.

"Will ye show us how 'tis done?"

I nodded. The maids set up beeswax candles on the table. The blade glistening beside a bottle of oil.

"We brought the best wax."

The maids looked as nervous as I felt. My legs were feeling a bit prickly, and could use a shave. Starting on them was the best choice before I let them near my privates. I just prayed my legs didn't get a hack job.

"I'll bathe first. It works best if the pores are open."

"Pores, my lady?" Agatha asked.

"Yes, the place where your hair comes from. The warm water helps to open them a little which will make taking the hair off that much easier."

Agatha and the other maids nodded and stepped forward to help me undress. Considering I was in a nightgown only, it didn't take long. With my face hot with embarrassment, I slipped into the tub and tried to relax as they washed my hair and scrubbed my arms, hands, shoulders, breasts, belly, legs, even my tender sex.

"Should ye get out of the water for the waxing and shaving?"

I nodded and stood, holding my hands to the side as I was instructed while the maids dried me off.

Grabbing the clean linen chemise they set out, I slipped it over my head, feeling less exposed and then settled myself on the bed.

"Let us shave my legs first. Have you ever used a blade to shave before?" I winced.

Agatha nodded. "Aye, I've shaved a man's face with it."

"Okay. Hand me the oil." I spread the oil over my legs and stared with trepidation at the blade. I'd never used a knife to shave, and was more than scared. "My razor doesn't look like yours, can you show me how you used it?"

"Aye, my lady." Agatha placed the blade at an angle on my shin and scraped slowly upward. I was shocked that none of my skin came with it, and instead she gathered oil and hair.

"Well, done, Agatha!" I smiled at her and waited for her to finish the task. The other maids looked on with awe, each citing that they wished to try it next on themselves. I'd started a fad.

"Now, we shall wax ye." Agatha handed the blade to a maid who took it to the bath and rinsed it.

I cringed. It hurt like hell to get your crotch waxed.

"Light the candles," I said, hoping this wouldn't be too painful. The women at the salon used a special beeswax. Was it too much to hope it was the same type of beeswax? Probably.

"What should we do first, my lady?" Agatha and the maids each brought a lit candle toward the bed.

This was going to hurt like hell. "Drip a bit of the wax on my finger, I want to see how hot it is." I leaned up on an elbow and held out my hand.

Agatha's brow was furrowed, lips thinned as she dripped the wax onto my finger tip. A slight sting, but then it dried immediately, no pain. Not as bad as I thought. Much like when I went to the salon. Seeing how the wax dried instantly, there would be no need for linen strips. Instead, the other maids would have to rip the dried wax off — and with it my hair.

"Agatha, you drip the wax, and you ladies, pull it off."

The other maids nodded, their faces full of concern as they set down their candles on the side table. If I weren't so nervous for how this would end, I'd laugh. Here I was, five hundred years in the past, lying on a castle bed, nearly nude, and about to be waxed by a bunch of medieval maids who'd never even heard of the task before. Just wild. And so fantastical. I'd never have believed it myself, except the memories of Logan's touch, his whispered words, the deep pull between us…they were tangible and potent.

"It may be best if you climb onto the bed Agatha, so the maids have more room." I patted the space beside my legs, trying to get them all to feel more comfortable. Even if I wasn't entirely. Best to get it done.

Agatha nodded, lifted her skirts and scooted on her knees to the place beside my legs. The candle trembled in Agatha's hand, bits of wax spilling onto the linen I'd spread. She held it over pubic bone and tilted so hot wax poured onto my skin. I bit my lip at the instant hot sting, but it quickly cooled. She dripped more in a line. But it wasn't a thick enough layer. There had to be a better way to do this…

The maids pulled the dried wax off — which also stung — leaving a thin, small strip of stinging, hairless labia.

"We'll be at this all day if we aren't more efficient," I mumbled.

"I'm sorry, my lady," Agatha said, the maids following suit.

"No, no, it isn't your fault. I think when you pour, I'll smooth it out immediately before it dries to cover a bigger area." I motioned for her to pour and when she did, I smoothed the wax while it was still soft, feeling the pull on my tender flesh. The wax stuck a little to my fingers, but dried thicker. The maids waited several seconds and then yanked the hard wax off.

"Ow!" I cried out, unsure I could handle anymore.

"Lass, I can see ye hesitating. And believe me, I wouldna want it done myself, but the laird…"

If Logan wanted it, how could I deny him? Steven had never cared about it, but Logan… God, he'd been enamored, loved the silky feel of my lips as he plunged a finger inside or licked me like a melting ice cream cone. I nodded, spread my thighs and waited for the next hot drop.

Agatha held the hot wax above me. I closed my eyes.

"Open your eyes, my lady. I'll need ye to make sure we do this right, else we'll be at this all day," she teased.

"We promise not to hurt ye," the other maids said quietly, the first time they'd spoken to me today.

I opened my eyes and peered up at them. They looked ever more nervous than when we'd done the first strip, and rightly so. This was my vagina! I almost laughed aloud. The stories these ladies would tell, if they could, of how they'd poured candle wax on the laird's lover's privates and then ripped off her hair. Sounded more like a punishment than a cosmetic remedy.

"Let's get his over with," I muttered. Then held up my hands. "Wait!"

The maids startled and looked at me with wide eyes.

"Give me a sip of something strong."

Agatha chuckled a little, and pointed to the shorter of the two maids. "Get her the wine."

A jug of wine sat on a sideboard table, and the maid poured a healthy portion into the waiting pewter cup. I guzzled it like I'd been crawling through the hottest desert. The potent, thick wine went straight to my veins—as if it bypassed my stomach altogether. I was warmer, lighter, gigglier.

"All right, I'm ready."

Behind the Plaid

Agatha didn't wait for me to stop her again. She poured the wax on the inside of my thigh, close to my lips, and I smoothed it out. The maids waited for it to harden, then yanked.

"Ow!" I cried out, then laughed. Good God, it hurt!

The maids tittered nervously, but I waved for them to continue. We did the inside of my thighs, then moved inward to the lips — the hardest part. Agatha moved slower, dripping less wax, most likely knowing it was more painful on the lips than on the thigh. We moved up to what had been a racing stripe of hair. I wondered if Logan would like it completely bare. A sexy surprise.

"Wax all of it," I instructed. And props to the maids, not one of them raised a brow. Another quarter of an hour later and we were done. I stared down at the juncture of my thighs. Bare, red. And wet. Just thinking of Logan's reaction when we saw me, my sex dripped with need and clenched, waiting to be filled.

I snapped my thighs closed, my face probably as red as my vag. "I'm hungry." I tried for nonchalant, but my voice came out a little squeaky. Had they noticed the moisture growing between my folds? Lord, I hoped not. I yanked the gown over my legs. "Will you help me dress so I can eat?"

"Aye, my lady. Brenda, see to her meal." Agatha climbed from the bed. "Keira, get the lads to come and take away the bath."

The other maids left the room, and Agatha went to the wardrobe, throwing open the doors. "Should ye like to wear the ivory gown today?"

I nodded, not having much choice. I'd worn the lavender one the day before and I wasn't quite ready to wear the sheer black. But I would force myself to wear it tonight. When Logan saw me dressed in it, my sex clean of hair, I hoped he'd fall to his knees and press his hot, velvet tongue inside me. I shivered, and rubbed my arms, pretending I was cold and not just full of craving for the laird of this dark castle.

Agatha dressed me, and offered sage advice about a half-lemon to be inserted inside me before Logan came to visit. She'd put a bowl of them and a tiny knife on the table, and I bit my lip. How many times did he plan on visiting? I was grateful for her caution and her remedy, which she showed me how to use and since he would be coming to me soon, I let it be. With Steven, I'd never wanted to be a mother. This was not the time nor the place to decide otherwise.

Agatha slipped an ivory gown over my head, embroidered with gold thistles around the hem, sleeves and neck. The gown scooped low, showing off the tops of my breasts. It was made of soft wool, a versatile fabric that would keep me warm in the winter, but still let the light breeze coming from the windows touch my skin. She slipped on my shoes, and I felt beautiful. Almost like a princess. Though I was far from it. But that didn't matter. Logan treated me more gently, and with more kindness than any other man. He made me feel special. I would miss him terribly when I figured out how to get back to my own time. Enough so that it made me waffle on whether or not I should keep looking. Deep down, I knew that I couldn't stay here. It wasn't right. Would mess with the balance of the world, wouldn't it? I had to look at my time here, with Logan, as a time to heal, and a time to grow. A time to live and be...cherished. And that was how it was with Logan. Like he cherished me.

I would let Fate lead me. Decide when it was the right time for me to leave this place. For now, I wanted to enjoy it.

By then, my hair had dried. Agatha started to braid it, but I stayed her hand. Something about this castle made it so my hair wasn't so frizzy and actually curled in nice, tamed tendrils. I was starting to like the look of it.

"Leave it down. Logan likes it this way."

Agatha nodded, then moved around the room picking up miscellaneous items and putting them in place.

I walked toward the window, and gazed outside. The sun shone on everything, lighting the trees and grass to vibrant greens. Sheep dotted the countryside. In the fields beyond the walls, crops grew in abundance, and in others, wild flowers grew with colorful abandon. Smoke curled from the chimneys in the village beyond, and, taking in a deep breath, calm washed over me. This place felt like home. A disturbing thought considering it could never be mine. Even if I weren't to get back to my time—a thought I didn't want to entertain—this place couldn't be my home. As much as Logan made me feel cherished, he was the type of man that women clamored for.

He'd probably had more than one in his bed before I fell at his feet. He himself had confessed there were many lovers in his past. I wasn't naïve enough to believe that I was going to be the last one. I was his woman right now. The one he wanted to spend time with now. Not forever. I had to remember that, because every time I saw him, I fell deeper in…

In… I didn't know what. It couldn't be love. Could it? I didn't even know what love was. Steven messed me up so bad inside, I wasn't sure I'd ever be normal again. But the gifts Logan gave me —confidence, the ability to trust again—those were gifts that would forever change me, and already were.

I stared up at the cloudless sky, wanted to take a walk after I ate breakfast and hoped that Logan would let me.

As beautiful as it was, and as much as I wanted to feel the sun on my face, glad for it. Sun meant no storm. Storm meant no ability to test out the gate and traveling forward to my own time. If there were a storm, I would be hard pressed not to see if the gate held some magic—even if I did want to stay.

I found myself praying the good weather lasted, as much as I prayed Logan would let me take a walk in those fields full of bright purple and red flowers.

My thoughts were interrupted as servants filed into the room. Some dismantled the bath and took it while others set up a feast on my table. A feast. Why did they all think I ate so much?

I walked toward the succulent scents, my stomach growling. I'd never eaten as much as I did since arriving. The table was full of different foods, and the scents made my mouth water. Fruit, tarts, hardboiled eggs, freshly baked bread, sautéed vegetables, and a fish that looked a lot like salmon. Thank goodness.

"Will the laird be joining me?" I asked Agatha while she poured me another cup of wine.

"Nay, my lady. He has gone out to hunt."

"Hunt?"

"Aye, my lady."

"What is he hunting?"

Agatha glanced at me with eyes that said I asked too much. Gave the impression that he was hunting men and not dinner. I waved my hand, letting her off the hook in answering me, and took a big bite of a sugary blueberry tart. "Delicious," I mumbled around a mouthful.

The maid smiled. "I shall tell Cook ye said as much."

I nodded and used a napkin to wipe some of the syrup from my lips. "I was hoping to go for a walk this morning. Will that be possible?"

Agatha swallowed. "Within the walls."

I frowned, disappointed in her answer. "I wanted to walk in the fields."

"Ye'll have to consult with the laird about that."

"But you said yourself, he is not here."

Agatha nodded, and I felt suddenly trapped, like a prisoner.

"'Tis for your own safety. Outside the walls is not safe for anyone."

Behind the Plaid

"Then shall I say prayers for those who live in the village?" My reply came out a little haughty and I felt instantly bad for it.

"They are well guarded, my lady."

"Is it possible for me to have a guard?"

Agatha sighed and set down the jug of wine. "My lady, if 'twere up to me, I'd give ye an escort and go with ye myself to the fields. The flowers are beautiful, aye. But it isn't up to me. The laird would have my head. He's gone out, but his second, Ewan is here. Shall I send him up for ye to discuss it with him?"

My blood ran cold. Ewan, who so resembled my brother. I nodded, feeling the bite of blueberry tart like a thick lump in my belly. I swallowed, but it didn't help. I was suddenly no longer hungry. I leaned back in the chair, trying to think of what I would say to Ewan. Wishing I could ask if he was Trey without sounding like a complete lunatic.

"As ye say, my lady." Agatha left the room, motioning everyone else to leave as well.

With the room empty, I could hear my heart pounding, echoing off the walls. The stones were closing in on me, vibrating with a heartbeat of their own. I took a gulp of wine, but it didn't make me feel better. If anything I was feeling a little nauseous.

All I could do was wait for Ewan to arrive. Had to distract myself. I counted the oranges in a bowl. Five. But who the hell cared?

A light tapping startled me and I jumped in my seat, the wooden legs scraping on the floor. "Co—come in," I said, then cleared my throat.

The door opened and Ewan stepped inside. Again, all the air whooshed from my lungs. He was so like my brother, so shockingly similar I couldn't stop staring.

"Agatha mentioned ye wanted a word, my lady?" He didn't step past the doorway and I wondered if that was a rule set by Logan, or if he felt that uncomfortable around me.

"I wanted to take a walk in the fields, but Agatha told me I wasn't allowed to without Logan's permission."

"Aye, my lady. His lairdship wishes for ye to remain within the walls."

I swallowed around the lump in my throat. "You look so much like my brother."

CHAPTER EIGHTEEN

Emma

Ewan looked startled by my comment, his eyes widening a little as he crossed his arms over his broad chest.

"I'm sorry—" I took a gulp of wine.

Ewan waved away my apologies and stepped a little further into the room. He studied it, but his face showed nothing of his thoughts, and I felt stupid for having brought up his appearance.

"Ye dinna have to apologize, I only hope ye didna think your brother horribly ugly." He grinned, humor dancing in his eyes.

"Not terribly so."

"Then I take it as a compliment."

"As you should. I loved my brother dearly." I bit my lip, hoping he didn't think I was insinuating in any way that I loved him.

"I will endeavor to treat ye as a sister then."

Oh, thank goodness. My breath came out in puff and I didn't realize I'd been holding it. "Thank you."

"Where is your brother?" he asked.

"Dead." I ran a hand through my hair, trembling fingers snagging on a knot. I wrenched them out, embarrassment filling my cheeks.

He nodded as though death were nothing here. But I'd noticed that. With so much war, disease, and capital punishment, death was normal. Death wasn't distasteful, it was a natural part of life. Church and God were revered and worshiped, and Heaven seen as a better place. Death was bred in the people as a daily occurrence, whereas in my time, death is feared, death was not accepted and people couldn't handle the loss of life. They feared there was no Heaven.

I tried to ignore it. To think that my parents and brother were not somewhere in the clouds living in eternal bliss was…unthinkable. To acknowledge there might be a void was…terrifying.

I had to think of something else, because now I had imaginary images of my family crashing, hurting, screaming, drowning. Their bodies were never recovered and it was unknown exactly when or how they died, and my mind went numb examining one painful scenario after another. I'd be in bed for the rest of the day crying, sick to my stomach, if I didn't stop.

I stood suddenly, the chair wobbling behind me. I whirled around to stop it, putting it rightfully back on the floor.

"I need some air. I wanted to walk where the flowers are. Since the laird doesn't want me beyond the walls alone, will you escort me?"

Behind the Plaid

Ewan's glance returned to mine and he lifted a brow. "I never said he ordered ye not to be out there alone. I said he didna want ye out there."

I took brisk steps toward the staunch, rule-following warrior and put my hands together in prayer before my chest. "Please, I am begging you."

Ewan's throat constricted as he swallowed. I could see in his face that he struggled with an answer. No doubt he wanted to please both me and Logan.

"My lady, I am—"

"Please!" I gripped his arm, then quickly yanked my hand back. His skin was warm, muscles just as taut as Logan's. So different than Trey who'd been lanky, long. His legs had been thick with muscle, but his arms weren't like this.

"All right. But ye must stay by my side and follow all orders."

Relief and happiness struck all at once and I clapped my hands back together as a rush of excitement wound its way through me. "I will, I swear!"

"Stay put. I'll need to gather a guard."

"Is it really so dangerous out there?"

"Have ye truly no idea?"

I shook my head. Not sure I wanted to. "I was here the day you were ambushed. And I saw the ship."

"Then that should be enough to tell ye, my lady. Gealach is hunted." Logan turned on his heel and left the room, shutting the door behind him. No one left doors open in this castle. I wondered if it was due to drafts or for another reason. Like keeping everything hidden and secret.

This place was full of closed doors.

Ewan was the second person to mention hunting today. Gealach was hunted and their laird was out hunting. I felt completely naïve. There was so much I didn't understand, so much that I didn't consider. There were no police to be called if a criminal harmed someone, stole something, or if murderers climbed the walls. The men within the castle were the police. It was enough to almost make me reconsider my need for the fresh outdoors.

Almost.

I'd spent the better part of the last eight years in fear. I wasn't going to do that here. I refused. Fear had no place in my life anymore. I would use caution. I would be aware of my surroundings and the things I said and did, but I couldn't hide. If I was going to be stuck here for who knew how long, I had to make do and live like I'd be here forever.

The awkwardness of seeing Trey's likeness gone, I picked up one of the oranges from the table and peeled it, popping a juicy wedge into my mouth. I walked to the window and leaned against the alcove, eating my orange and studying the landscape. All seemed so peaceful. Not like the dangerous terrain I knew it to be. It was deceiving.

Logan's face flashed before my eyes. He was the only normal part of this remarkable existence I found myself in. And he was nowhere near ordinary. He was incredible. Took me aloft, but kept me grounded at the same time. I wished I could take him with me when I left, whenever that may be.

The door opened and I turned to Agatha. "My lady, Sir Ewan awaits ye in the great hall."

"All right." I ate the last bit of orange and followed Agatha out of my room. She shut the door behind us and then led me down the hallway.

The castle was ridiculously vast, with so many twists and turns. If I didn't have her to guide me, I never would have made it to the great hall. I probably should go exploring later. But honestly, I was a little scared of the castle. Even in broad daylight it was dark. And with all the warnings of enemies and such, I was afraid of being jumped in a darkened corridor, however silly. Logan had a dungeon. Filled with prisoners, I was sure. If any were to escape...

A shiver wound its way up my arms to the base of my neck, and I clamped my teeth to keep them from chattering.

"Are ye all right, my lady?" Agatha asked.

"Fine. Thank you."

Agatha accepted my answer without question and led the rest of the way to the great hall. The sight before me had me gasping with a sudden dread. I actually pressed my hand to my chest and gasped. Ewan stood, strapped from head to toe in weaponry and at least two dozen warriors stood behind him, dressed similarly. All wore white linen, billowy shirts and plaid kilts, similar shades of red and green like Logan's. The sight was impressive and terrifying. After several moments, I was able to catch my breath and slow my pulse. They weren't going to attack me. My guess was, these men were meant to protect me.

"Sir Ewan, is all this necessary?" I asked, moving closer and eyeing all the indifferent expressions behind him. The men stared at the wall above my head.

Unnerving.

"Aye, my lady. The laird would not be happy with less."

I blinked a few times. My walk with a couple dozen warriors would most likely not be as peaceful and refreshing as I thought.

"Well, then, let's go," I mumbled. I waited for Ewan to pass me, but he stood still. I gave him a questioning glance and he smiled.

"We'll follow behind ye, my lady. Ye'll hardly notice we're there."

I doubted that and gave him a look that said as much. He only smiled and waited. If that was the way it was going to be...

I turned away from the men and headed toward the wide wooden doors that I'd come through a few days before. The day my life had changed irrevocably. Stepping outside, I paused a moment on the stairs and let the sun coat me in its warmth. I closed my eyes, tilted my head and breathed in the scents of Gealach. Salt water, peat smoke, hay. The air was different in this time than in my own. Unmarred by pollution.

I made my way through the courtyard toward the gates. I paused, touching the stone and waiting for that painful spark to hit my fingers. Again nothing happened. I stepped under, waiting beneath it. Nothing. And so I passed through, relief filling me. The men behind me were indeed so quiet, I actually checked to see if they were still there, a part of me wondering if they'd disappear into thin air once I left the gate.

But they were behind me. Bored expressions and all. Except Ewan. He looked serious as he scanned all around them, one hand on the sword at his hip. His stance reminded me how dangerous it was for us to have passed beneath the gate. And it made me wonder how many visitors like myself had found their path to Gealach. Was Ewan one of them? Did he remember being Trey or was it all some sick fantasy I was making up in my head—guilt at not being on that plane finally taking away my rationality?

I was going to go crazy if I kept it up. He wasn't Trey. I just had to keep repeating that in my mind. All of this…it was just a holding ground. I was only passing through.

I turned away from him and walked over the bridge, my shoes sinking into the lush grasses, short here, but growing in length with the beautiful flowers. Wild, untamed. A true picture of tempestuous splendor. A gentle breeze glided over my skin and rustled my hair, cooling me from the summer sun. The scents were luscious, and I breathed them in deep, glad I'd never been one to have allergies to pollen. The field would be a nightmare for anyone who had. Behind me, clinks of metal faded into the background, and I held out my hands as I walked, letting the tall grass tickle my palms.

Behind the Plaid

I'd seen wildflowers growing like this in abundance along the side of the highway, but never up close. I crouched in the middle of it, the flowers at eye level, and a hummingbird buzzed by, its wings going a million miles a minute. It paused, its little beak poking at a flower. His wings beat so fast I could barely see them, and he looked like he was hovering. I smiled, never having taken the time to appreciate such beauty in nature. Life flew by, and most of the time I was stuck inside my own head, my own fears. But sitting surrounded by flowers and watching that hummingbird, I realized I spent entirely too much time thinking about myself, and I needed to spend more time just enjoying the world around me. Appreciating the life I still had.

The hummingbird flew off toward another flower. I watched him until he disappeared, and then I picked flowers. A fresh bouquet in my room would brighten up the darkness of it. Reds, purples, whites, even grasses, I gathered in a huge bundle. When I had more than one hand could hold and I had to fist them together to keep it within my grasp, I turned back to Ewan.

"We can go."

He nodded and waited for me to lead the way back toward the gate. But I was stopped by a thunderous noise. It shook the earth and sent fear skittering up and down my spine. I dropped all of the flowers, hands out to the side. No one else appeared at all bothered by the noise. Was it possible it was the time warp? Was I the only one who could feel and hear it?

Seconds later, Logan came pounding into view atop a magnificent horse, several dozen men behind him. He pulled up short on the reins and glared down at me like I was his worst enemy.

"What are ye doing outside the gate?" he asked.

"I was..." I glanced down at the spilled flowers, bent to gather them. "Picking flowers, my laird."

"Ye are never to leave the gate." His voice was harsh and sent chills over my skin.

He'd never been so harsh to me before, and instant images of Steven passed through my mind. Luring me in with kindness only to prove he was brutal. I suppose I should have known. The harsh realities of this world would not allow him to be so gentle-hearted. I glanced up, knowing my pain and disappointment showed on my face.

Logan frowned, and his eyes pleaded with me for something. Forgiveness? I looked away. I had no intention of playing mind games.

"Lass, come here." His tone hadn't lost its edge, and demanded compliance.

If there was one thing I'd learned since meeting Logan, it was that he was a control freak. Had to be the one governing every moment. Didn't like when things happened that he wasn't expecting.

I wished I could pretend to ignore him, but given we were surrounded by sixty warriors, I chose not to make a scene. Perhaps in private, I could help him to overcome his need to dominate. I approached Logan's black beast of a horse with caution. The thing was at least a foot taller than me, and towering above the animal was Logan himself.

His dark hair was wild from his ride, giving him a rough, sexy look that made my insides quiver. Even his scowl excited me. His lips were still full, kissable, even in a frown. I wanted to climb atop his horse and kiss his ire away, but managed to keep myself on the ground. I did, however, send him a gaze that said as much. Logan's eyes widened slightly, pupils dilating with desire, jaw clenched—the only visceral response I noted.

"Aye, my laird?" I kept my voice deliberately low. We might be surrounded by sixty men, but there was no need for all one-hundred twenty ears to hear what we discussed.

Logan took the hint and leaned over his horse so that he was closer to me. The natural scent of the horse and leather invaded my senses. "I asked ye to stay within the gates. 'Tis dangerous out here."

"I'm aware of your instructions, but it was so beautiful, I couldn't resist. Ewan thought you'd be mad, but I insisted." I bit my lip. "I have guards, is it so bad?"

He nodded. "'Tis not safe, no matter how many ye have with ye. But I can understand being drawn to something beautiful. Something irresistible." His gaze traveled over me as though he were stripping me bare.

My body reacted immediately, obeying his silent demands. My nipples were hard and aching, thighs squeezed tightly closed to keep them from trembling, and my sex... God, it quivered and was as slick as Loch Ness.

I couldn't be the only one reacting. For sure his eyes showed he wanted me, but I wanted him to feel it just as keenly as I did. I reached out, tentatively, and placed my hand on his shin. Anything higher would have been unseemly. His muscles flexed beneath my touch. I didn't linger, though I wanted to. To do so would be to break the pact we'd made to keep our arrangement secret.

"Ye'll have to be punished, lass, for disobeying me." He spoke loudly, harshly, yet his eyes were tender.

I didn't know whether to be afraid for my life, or to run back to my room and eagerly wait for whatever punishment he deemed fit to dole out. A few appreciative grunts came from the men. I wondered if Ewan was one of them, but I refused to look at anyone but Logan.

"Ye put my men in danger. Ye made them disobey my instructions."

"Please," I said with a shake of my head. "Please don't punish them. It was my idea. I forced their hands."

Logan frowned, and raised a brow, but said nothing.

"Go back to your chamber. Know that as a guest in my home, ye will be expected to follow my edicts from now on."

I swallowed back tears. I was humiliated. Nodding, I turned, head down and rushed back under the gate, through the door of the castle, up the stairs and to my chamber. Magically in my state, I was able to find my way without getting lost.

I rushed to the bed and threw myself down. Frustrated. Angry. Embarrassed. Hotter than hell. His domineering turned me on faster than his kiss, and that fact disturbed me.

The door to my chamber slammed open and I sat up with a start. Logan took up the expanse of the doorway. He crooked a finger and I leapt to do his bidding. He shut the door with force and stalked toward me, meeting me halfway.

"Your punishment is about to commence."

My breath caught and I gazed into his bottomless eyes. Consumed by him. He gripped the back of my neck and hauled me forward, his lips crashing on mine in a cruel, sensual kiss. I immediately opened. Wanting him. Wanting this. Taking it.

Logan gripped my rear hard with both hands and lifted me into the air. I wrapped my legs around his waist. His mouth didn't leave mine as he devoured me. Would he finally make love to me? Was that to be my punishment?

He tossed me onto the bed and crawled up the length of my body as I tried to catch my bearings. I couldn't think straight. My mind was jumbled and interlaced with the overwhelming sensations and expectations he wrought on me.

"Wh-what is my punishment?" He couldn't rape me. I wanted him. Between my thighs was so wet, it dribbled into the crack of my ass.

"Ye will pleasure me, and me alone."

CHAPTER NINETEEN

Logan

My plan to treat Emma with kindness blew out like a tiny fire in a storm when I saw her standing in the middle of the field. Fear drove a pike straight through my chest. What the hell was she doing outside the castle walls? Was she leaving me?

Those fears should have been alleviated by seeing my men with her. Ewan was my most trusted guard. But rationality evaporated and all I could think of was getting to her. Taking her back inside and ravishing her. Forcing her to stay with me, even though I really wanted her to *want* to be with me.

Her smile upon seeing me had made my chest constrict, another problem. Desire was fine. But fear, happiness, needing her, those were feelings I wasna truly willing to accept, and yet they'd swept inside me and taken me hostage. And I did have to punish her. The men needed to see that a visitor, let alone a female, couldna overrule me. There were enough traitors in our midst. The last thing I needed was for word to swirl in their degenerate ears and then have to deal with the consequences of not humiliating Emma.

No one had to know what my punishment entailed. They just had to know I was doling it out. By the Saints, I was going to enjoy this punishment.

I pinned Emma to the bed, straddling her ribs and restraining her arms to her sides. She looked up at me eagerly, licking her lips and trembling beneath me. The lass was going to like her penance just as much as I did.

My cock was hard as stone, had been since she'd graced the front stairs of Gealach. I ripped my shirt off, not caring that the torn fabric couldna be repaired. I was hot, so damn hot, and I wanted her to see my skin, wanted to watch her eyes dilate as she took me in. I wasna disappointed. Emma could not hide her reactions from me. She was hungry for me, and she squirmed, trying to wriggle free so she could touch me.

I laughed and shook my head.

"Nay, Emma. Ye canna touch." I unhooked my belt, slid the leather over her cheekbones, snapped it together in the air and watched her gasp, but I tossed it aside. I'd tan her hide another day. Today I had something else entirely in mind. With the removal of my belt, my plaid started to unravel. I removed it from my hips and tossed that too, the fabric rustling as it descended to the floor. Naked, save for my boots, my cock rested full, hard on her chest. I wanted her naked, too.

I pulled the *sgian dubh* from my boot, slid it flat side over her chest to the fabric of her bodice, and then cut.

Emma gasped. "What are you doing?"

"Undressing ye." I slit the gown down to her waist and wrenched the fabric open. I put the knife back in my boot, and resisted the urge to groan when my cock rested on her hot flesh. Much better.

Again she licked her lips, eyes wide and riveted to my shaft. She wanted it as much as I did.

"Did ye hear what I said about your punishment?" I asked.

She nodded.

"Tell me."

"I will pleasure you and you alone."

I grinned and nodded. "Ye canna touch yourself either, lass. And ye canna touch me." I leaned close, tugging on her lip with my teeth, and then I kissed her, hard, demanding, tongue thrusting. She gasped and writhed just from a kiss and I could smell her desire. Already she was ready for me. Wanted me. One of the things I liked about her so much—her raw, passionate response. Emma had been so timid when she first arrived, but I'd unleashed the true nature of her being. Set her free, and now she was mine to play with. And in turn, she wreaked havoc with my bearing.

I pulled away, leaving her panting. A drop of moisture beaded the tip of my cock. "Have ye ever sucked a man, Emma?"

I'd waited so long for her to touch me. To make love to her. This would be the ultimate test. To have my cock inside her mouth, to force myself to wait until the last possible minute before I came. To not enter her slick, hot cunny. I hardly ever let a woman finish me with her mouth, I liked to come when I was pounding away, her legs wrapped around my hips. But with Emma, everything was different, a challenge.

Emma nodded, fear flashing in her eyes. I hated to see her scared. I wanted her willing, eager.

"Your husband?" I asked.

She nodded. I need not to have asked the question. He was the only man she could have been with and the one who'd brought fear into her beautiful eyes.

"I am nay your husband," I said, surprised by how gruff my voice sounded.

Emma's gaze flew to my cock and her mouth parted. A fresh surge of yearning made me even harder, and it was an effort not to press the tip to her luscious lips.

"I know you aren't. I trust you," she whispered, eyes darting back up to mine. The fear was gone, replaced with anticipation.

I smiled, stroked a hand over her cheek, my thumb over her bottom lip. Her breath was warm on my fingers, lip soft. I groaned and lifted up on my knees, my cock so close to her mouth. Another hot pulse of longing.

"I want ye to suck me." My eyes grew heavy as I watched her. Waited for her agreement. I would never do anything she didna want to.

Emma smiled, shyly at first, and then full on wickedly. "I've dreamed of doing just that since the first time you put your mouth on me."

A shiver stole up my spine. "Open your mouth."

She licked her lips and then opened her mouth. I dipped the tip inside, feeling the heat of her scorching tongue flick over my bead of moisture. She wrapped her lips around me and sucked me in further, then I withdrew. In this position, Emma was helpless. She couldn't bob up and down, I was the one who set the pace, and it was a test of trust for her and test of control for me, because I could go deep and fast, choking her. Neither of us wanted that. But the thing we each struggled with, the thing that drove us, this was what this was about.

Her punishment. And my pleasure.

I moved slow, flexing forward and pulling back. Hard, so bloody hard. Her mouth was exquisite, her suction divine, and I felt close to exploding every time she swirled her delicate tongue around the head, up and down the sides.

Emma was a natural at sucking cock, and I told her so. "God, lass," I moaned, guttural and deep. "Just like that. Suck it hard."

Lifting her head she drew me in even deeper, telling me with her actions that I was going too slow, but I refused to pick up the pace. I couldn't risk hurting her, letting myself get so out of control that I fucked the breath from her. This was about control, and even though the slide of her velvet tongue had me clamping my jaw so hard, I was likely to not be able to move it tomorrow, I didna care.

I gripped the top of the headboard, wood digging into my fingers and palm. My thighs shook from the effort to slide in and out of her mouth at a slow pace. Beneath me, she trembled, had somehow maneuvered her hands enough to grip my calves. Her nails dug deep as she clenched onto me. But she followed the rules and didna touch herself. Around my cock she moaned while she sucked, enjoying this excruciating torture as much as I did.

No doubt her cunny was drenched, slick as a loch and pulsing, clenching for me to do something to relieve her, bring her to fruition. But I wouldna. That was the ultimate punishment. I was going to leave her wanting, craving, and demand she not satisfy herself. I wanted to know that with each step she took, each pulse of her hot little pleasure nub, she thought of me and what I could do. And tonight, I would come back, and make sure she climaxed until she could no longer see straight.

Thinking of my plans, of her reaction, I unintentionally increased my pace. Not too much, but enough of a fraction that Emma went wild and sucked me deeper, swirled that tongue with even more enthusiasm. I was close. My sac tightened, cock grew longer, and intense pleasure gripped me at the base of my spine. I needed to gentle the pace.

"Slow down, lass," I groaned, forehead hitting the headboard. I closed my eyes, sucked in air. I had to calm down or it would be over in seconds.

Thank God, she held back, lapping at me languidly. My flesh felt heavy, and sparks of pleasure fired from every inch. I wasna sure how much longer I could hold on. Testament to how much of my control evaporated when I was around her. My hands dug into the headboard. Boots dug into the bed. Hips ground at a tortuously slow pace. I wanted to yank my cock from her mouth, spread her thighs wide and drive inside her slick, tight sheath. Pound my way to heaven and take her there with me.

I started to shake all over, my groans loud as perspiration trickled along my spine and temples. The sweat was cold where it slid down my overheated flesh. With each thrust forward, Emma managed to wriggle her arms a little freer and damn if she didna grip her slim fingers to my arse. Her nails dug in, pulling me closer. My cock buried into the back of her throat and she groaned, vibrating my entire insides. A twinge of heated sensation. I was so damn close.

With her encouragement, I thrust a little faster, not harder, but faster, hips pumping forward. Her suction was perfect. There was no going back. Not now. It appeared the only one of us who passed this test was Emma. I was full on losing the upper hand. And she was full on trusting me.

I shook the headboard in an effort to gain some control, but it didna work. I was no match for her greedy, naughty mouth. She only drew me in deeper, licking me into oblivion.

Overwhelming sensation took hold, radiating throughout all of my limbs and the force and power of it centering in my cock. My mind went blank to everything save the pleasure she gave me, and the explosion that rocked me the center of the Highlands and back. A roar left my lips that shook the room, and Emma's grip on my arse tightened. She sucked every last drop from me, murmuring encouraging words around my cock.

When had she become the temptress? I suppose the moment I let her take the lead in our little game. It was supposed to be about my control, and her punishment, but instead I think she disciplined me by taking my power away. I'd never lost command like that. Never had a climax that made me lose my mind. Only with Emma.

I didna like having the feeling as much as I enjoyed experiencing it.

A total contradiction.

Pulling my cock from her mouth, I stood on shaky legs from the bed. Hands on my hips, I looked up to the ceiling, taking long breaths and trying to slow my racing heart. Stop my limbs from shaking. Looking over, seeing the cut of her gown, her soft breasts exposed with tightened nipples, swollen red lips, my cock grew back to life.

I couldna get enough.

Emma smiled slowly. "I like your idea of punishment."

I stalked toward her, slipped my hand up her skirts until my fingers met the treasured slickness I knew was there. "Nay, Emma, this is your punishment." I drove my fingers inside her, reveling in her parted lips, seductive moan and rocking hips. "Ye seek climax."

She nodded.

"But ye must wait." And I had to taste her.

I flipped her gown up, and she spread her thighs without me having to tell her, proof of her eagerness for me to taste her flesh. She was slick and clean, not a speck of hair on her pink lips. God's teeth… I held my breath as I stared at the beauty of her bare cunny, and then I glanced back up.

"Do you like it?" she asked. Doubt danced in her eyes.

"Verra much," I growled, then brought my mouth down on her heat. Her soft lips met mine, and I delved my tongue inside to find her little nub of pleasure, reached my hand up to tweak her hardened nipples as I lapped at her cream. Her moans were loud, and gasps aplenty.

Her thighs quivered, and her hands dug into my hair, tugging, nails scraping. She was close. Already on the verge when I first licked her. Only a few more laps and she'd be breaking apart. That was her punishment.

I pulled away, her sex gleaming with a mixture of her own juice and my mouth. Her eyes were dark, lips pouty.

"This is your punishment, Emma." I yanked her gown down, swooped down to kiss her mouth. "I want ye just on the verge of coming. I want ye to think about me and my cock the rest of today. I want ye to think about what I'm going to do to ye tonight. Dinna touch yourself like I showed ye how. I want ye in this room, thinking, slick and hot and waiting for me."

She whimpered, and bit her lower lip. "Don't make me wait."

I laughed wickedly and gazed into her eyes. "But, lass, I told ye, ye needed to be punished for putting my men in danger." I slid the backs of my fingertips down between the valley of her breasts toward her navel. Emma clamped her thighs tight, the expression on her face one of exquisite, passion-filled torture. "Dinna fash, the punishment will be well worth it. That I promise."

I loomed over her again, kissing her languidly, then I whispered, "Your mouth is temptation itself. No one's ever made me come so hard. No one, Emma."

Before I said too much, confessed how much she'd made me lose control, I slipped from the room.

CHAPTER TWENTY

Emma

A swift chill surrounded me, even though my skin was hotter than fire. There were no flames in the hearth. Understandable, given we reserved resources, and it wasn't cold outside. But that didn't seem to keep the chill from sweeping its way along the stone walls and planked floors. And I no longer had the warmth of Logan's body encompassing me. In fact I was quite exposed.

I sat up and gripped my gown, trying to close it, but the moment my arms brushed over my hard nipples I shuddered. If anything, they grew harder, and I massaged them, imagining his tongue flicking over each one before he drew them into his mouth. What had he done to me?

I was obsessed with him. He dominated my mind. My every waking and breathing thought.

My lips were swollen, tingling and between my thighs, sparks of need fired. I squeezed my legs tightly together, but that set off another round of spasms and I quickly opened them wide with a gasp. I was dripping wet, and with no underwear, the slickness slid its way down my thighs. I used the gown to mop some of it up, and enjoyed that slight touch a little too much. Logan had told me not to touch myself, even though I was so close to coming I was sure the slightest thing would set me off.

I stood, walked briskly to the window and opened the shutters. I let the summer breeze cover my bare breasts hoping it would help calm the fire inside me, but all I could think of was Logan's huge shaft thrusting into my mouth. The way his hot tongue had snaked over my clit and how much I wanted to come.

Tonight. He was going to make me wait until then.

I had to do something to distract myself. And I couldn't go traipsing around the castle in my torn gown, exposing my too small breasts to those in sight. I closed the shutters and stripped quickly, finding the lavender gown I'd worn the day before. Tonight I was going to wear the black sheer gown. I'd already made him come—for the first time—but tonight I wanted him to want me as desperately as I wanted him.

Logan's dick was everything I'd dreamed of. Long, smooth as velvet, thick and lined on the top with a prominent vein. The head was a lush bulb and I'd loved flicking my tongue over it. He tasted sweet and salty. Not sour like Steven. And he'd been gentle. He'd taken his time, hadn't wanted to hurt me. The few times my husband had forced me to put my mouth on him, it had been a cruel game of shove and choke. He'd not tasted good and I'd cried through the whole thing.

When Logan straddled me, pinned my arms down and his big erection had stood ready for me to devour, while fear crossed my mind for a split-second, the overwhelming need had been to pleasure him. I wanted him to experience the same sensations I did when he licked and suckled me. At last he was giving me the opportunity to pleasure him. A task I'd wanted since the moment we'd laid eyes on each other.

Logan's reactions were raw, masculine and controlled power. Until the end when his body had shook and the moans that came from his throat were enough to bring me to the brink of orgasm.

Without realizing it, my fingers had pressed against the apex of my thighs, and my knees buckled, the heat and pleasure was so intense.

No. I couldn't. As much as I wanted to, I'd given Logan my word. And while in my time period the important of one's word and honor appeared to have declined, here in Logan's, a person's word was their everything. There was no telling how long I'd be here, even if I was starting to feel like I wanted to stay. As long as this was my world, I needed to abide by their rules.

The funny thing was, in my own time period, I'd become timid. Allowed people, not just Steven, to walk all over me. Even the woman at the grocery store who charged me twice for a can of soup and refused to take the second charge off. But in Logan's era, I'd somehow developed a bit of confidence. Going against the rules and insisting Ewan take me out. Allowing Logan to see my body, to pleasure me and in return I was pleasuring him. I was changing.

And I thought it was for the better. No, I knew it was for the better. I was becoming the real me. The me who'd been suppressed and not permitted to breathe was disappearing. Logan had somehow chipped away at the barrier that surrounded me, and my new self was trying to escape through the crack, be born again and bask in the light of freedom.

Oddly enough, this medieval castle, this place and time where women were most oppressed was the very same place I began to find independence.

My body was still on fire, and every way that I moved, the fabric rubbed against me in a tantalizing way. I kind of wished I had one of the maids' coarser gowns so the softness of this one didn't remind me of the way Logan's hands stroked over me.

I shook my head, hoping to get thoughts of his perfectly formed body out of my mind. I needed a distraction big time. Logan wouldn't be back until after nightfall—several hours at least. Maybe it was time I went exploring. I didn't know my way around the castle and if I was going to be confined to it for who knew how long, it was probably best to figure it out.

I stepped into the hallway, feeling a breeze as it wound its way around my ankles. The entire building was like that. Drafty and cold. And it was summer. I could tell already I wasn't going to like it here in the winter. I'd probably spend most of my days curled up before a huge fire covered in a dozen blankets drinking whatever hot drinks they had. That was, if I remained here. If that were the case, I wondered if they had any books and what types were published. I loved to read, a pastime Steven wasn't too pleased with. I frowned. The asshole wasn't really too pleased with anything.

Looking from side to side, I noted there was no one in sight, and I was half surprised to see that Logan hadn't planted a guard at my door. I dragged in a deep breath. It was such an odd feeling to be alone. To realize I didn't have to worry about Steven. If anything, my worries now were simplified and mostly had to do with pleasure. I shook my head and bit my lip. Very odd.

I closed my door behind me. To the right was the stairs and I'd never traveled to the left. What better way to start exploring than to go where I'd not gone before. I lifted my skirt and tip-toed. I don't know why I tip-toed, my steps weren't heavy or

Behind the Plaid

loud, but it seemed like exploring was a sneaky business. I had to press my lips together to keep from laughing at myself. Several paces away, there was a door. I pressed my ear to the panels and listened. There was no sound from within. I tried the handle.

Locked.

Why would there be a locked door?

But a quick search throughout the rest of the floor and the one below revealed many locked doors. By the time I'd gotten to the great hall, I'd discovered nothing save for that Gealach was full of secrets and I wasn't privy to any of them.

I peeked into the great hall and found that it too was mostly empty. A few servants were dusting and one wiped vigorously at the large table that went clear from one side of the room to another. They glanced at me, but then went about their tasks, ignoring my presence. Fine by me, I didn't want to explain what my purpose was and have it get back to Logan that instead of staying in my room I'd gone out poking my nose where he probably didn't think it belonged. I walked through the great hall, head held high, skirts lifted in my hands to avoid stepping on them, until I reached the back wall where a door led down several steps and toward some decadent smells.

My stomach rumbled and the room I entered was none other than the kitchen. An extremely busy kitchen. Servants ran here and there. Chopped, kneaded, stirred, turned. All covered in something—flour, spices, grease, sweat. No one looked at me. They didn't have time to turn their attention away from their tasks. The scents were so succulent, I actually licked my lips. I'd never seen a working kitchen before. Not even in a modern day restaurant. It was amazing to see how they worked as a team. Some sort of small chickens roasted on spits, and large roasts of meat, too. Loaves of bread were baking, and cauldrons bubbled. The people of Gealach ate like kings. This was why each evening platters upon platters were placed on my table.

I did mean to ask why they ate their large meal at the end of the day. I'd always been taught that in the middle ages the largest meal was eaten around noon. But not here. At Gealach it was almost as though food was an afterthought during the day, and in the evening became a necessity.

I slipped through the kitchen, or almost did.

"My lady?"

Agatha's voice stopped me in my tracks. Slowly, I turned around to face her, hoped she wouldn't insist on taking me back to my room.

"Hello," I said with a cheerful smile.

"Are ye hungry, my lady?" she asked, but before I could answer, she grabbed a pastry of some sort off a platter and shoved it into my hands. It was hot, but smelled so sugary and cinnamony sweet. "This ought to tide ye over until later. Go on now. If ye need me I'll be down here, but the staff here has much to do."

I tried not to laugh as I was shuffled out of the kitchens, back into the great hall, a steaming treat in my hand. I held it up to my nose and took a deep breath. Definitely worth venturing into the kitchens, even if I was kicked back out.

The servants who'd been cleaning were no longer in the great hall and so as I took tiny bites of the addictive apple pastry—and remembered Logan tackling me to the bed for the last bite of one—I studied all the tapestries, amazed by the handiwork of those who'd created them.

The threads were thick and soft-looking. Beautiful colors. I didn't even realize they had such good quality dyes in this time period. Rich blues, reds, golds, greens, brown, black. Colors that brought the images to life. Great battle scenes with horses and swords and blood. A scene with a king handing a knight a gift. A beautiful lady by the water. Two massive wolfhounds giving chase to an equally large deer. Ships firing cannons upon the sea. A tapestry of Gealach. They all told tales of this place and

Behind the Plaid

its people, its ancestors. I wished Logan was here so he could tell me what each of them meant.

Loud voices and footsteps came from the front of the castle. Male voices, with low timbres that shook my insides. My trust in Logan didn't erase nearly a decade of fear. I trusted Ewan, too. But none of the others. I simply didn't know them well enough. It would be a long time before I felt completely safe around strangers—males especially. Besides, I'd heard plenty of rumors about men raping anything with a skirt back in the day. Their voices grew closer, their heavy feet pounding on the floor. My throat constricted, hands grew slick. It was all familiar to me. The same reaction when Steven used to walked through the front door.

Maybe it would be worth asking Logan for some self-defense lessons. But before I could contemplate another thought, it became apparent the men were headed for the great hall when I'd been hoping they would go somewhere else.

Not wanting to be seen munching on my treat, I clambered to hide behind one of the massive tapestries, grateful their length swept nearly to the floor. The last of the pastry was shoved into my mouth as I plastered myself to the wall, hands pressed against the stone, feet at a plié angle so as not to peek beneath the tapestry.

"I dinna care. The bastard is going to pay for what he's done." It was Logan's voice. His words scared me straight to the bone, but the timbre, the brogue caressed over my body like a lover's touch. Brought to mind the wicked things he whispered in my ears and against my sensitive flesh. Sweet relief forced me to let out the breath I'd held. Though it was him, I stayed hidden. It would be pretty awkward if I came out from behind the tapestry at that point.

"My laird, I am in full agreement, but we should wait until the king's missive arrives." *Ewan.*

There was a great huff of breath and something slammed down. "That vile arse killed one of my guards. In my castle! Right beneath my nose! He must be punished."

I bit my lip to keep from gasping. There'd been a murder within the walls? Who was it they spoke of? Chills crept over my arms. A dead body. A murderer creeping about. Gealach had seemed a dangerous place from outside the walls. Romantic and passionate from within. But now...

Silence met Logan's words. *Punished...* I knew he meant it in a completely different way than how he'd punished me. But still, my sex clenched, growing damp even in the danger of the situation.

"He has not escaped. If the guard came too close it was his own fault." Ewan's voice was filled with reason, yet, his words sent another chill over me.

Escaped. So the murderer was a prisoner. While part of me was relieved to hear the murderer hadn't escaped... The other part of me was filled with fear. If he could kill a guard, wasn't it only a matter of time before he did manage to escape? Where was the dungeon? Assuming Gealach had dungeons. Yes, yes, I remembered it did. Down a flight of stairs... But I couldn't for the life of me remember where the dungeons were when I'd toured. All I recalled was Steven saying maybe he should put a dungeon in our house, and I'd nearly fainted for fear he'd make it happen. I'd be chained up in the basement for the rest of my life.

Was it the man who'd sent the ship full of shackles? I closed my eyes, wishing I could sink into the wall and pretend I wasn't hearing this. I'd been living in a fantasy since arriving at Gealach.

A heated, torrential fantasy. As if in answer, my nipples hardened.

CHAPTER TWENTY-ONE

Emma

Logan and Ewan discussed the man in the dungeon for what seemed like hours but in reality was probably only ten minutes or longer. Their voices grew hushed as they made their plans, and my limbs grew numb as I made every effort to shove myself into the wall.

And then my fingers pushed a little harder and the wall gave way. A silent give, a whisper of sound. And I bit my lip hard enough to draw blood, sure that Logan would have heard the noise or sensed that something had changed. But he didn't. Or he pretended not to. I couldn't be sure. We'd developed a sixth sense when it came to each other. Bleeding lip and trembling fingers, I pushed further against the stone which had given way, feeling a cool rush of air flutter my sleeve.

A secret door? Once the stone pressed as far as it was willing to go, I stopped and waited. Sure that by now Logan would have noticed something. Anything. I imagined the tapestry I hid behind, whipping aside as he tore it from the iron hinges it hung from. The hinges rattling within the stones it'd been drilled into. Plaster, wood and candles falling and crashing around me. Logan gripping me by the hair and dragging me up to my room.

Would he ever do something so hurtful to me? So violent? He may torture me with pleasure, swat me playfully on my ass, but would he really hurt me like Steven had?

A resounding *No* echoed in my ears and I was instantly ashamed for even thinking he would do something like that. Logan was worlds apart from Steven. A better man by far. Superior in all things. I hoped that at some point my mind wouldn't automatically go there; instead, I could think more positively, especially where Logan was concerned.

I could see his stormy eyes in my mind, locked on me, studying me. Deep emotion, possession filled those eyes when he looked at me. Not violence. My thoughts were interrupted by the sounds of the men's boots fading away. Probably to go deal with their murderer in the dungeons. I hoped that Logan would listen to Ewan. If he was supposed to be waiting for a message from the king, that would be the best thing. I would never profess to be an expert, but these were violent times and I knew I wasn't wrong in remembering that lords who ignored their kings were often beheaded for it.

Logan was passionate, but calculating. I didn't think he'd act on a whim, could control himself even if in a rage.

I turned around to examine the stone wall, darker back here behind the tapestry. Indeed one stone was pressed a good four inches into the wall. I reached in and patted around, meeting dust and crumbling rock, but then my finger fell into a crevice and caught on an iron hook of some sort. I tugged, felt a release

Behind the Plaid

from the hook and another soundless whoosh of air—hard enough it blew my hair—as the wall sank in completely. A three feet wide by seven feet tall doorway.

My mouth fell open. Secret passageways were the stuff of fairy tales, and here I was seeing a stone wall sink in on itself in the shape of a door. Gealach had many locked normal doors, never had I suspected I'd find an unlocked false door. I listened carefully for voices or footsteps and upon hearing none I pressed both hands to the stones and pushed. The door swung in on itself revealing a darkened stair leading down. Shadows crept from inside the secret passage, threatening to take my sanity down to unknown depths. Where did it lead? To the dungeon? Not a place I wanted to go. Ever. Especially not in the dark.

I pulled the stone door closed, amazed by its heavy power and the ability it had to make me shiver in fear. I didn't believe in ghosts necessarily, but I did believe in nightmares. That passage swelled with them. Closing the door, I felt rather than heard the iron hook clink closed and then the stone which had initially pressed in on itself sucked back into place. Once again the door was concealed by the wall, and I would probably never find it again. Perfectly obscure.

Wiping the sweat that somehow managed to bead on my upper lip when I wasn't paying attention, I backed away from the wall and out from behind the tapestry. My eyes were riveted on the one I'd chosen to duck behind. The image of a great king, a heavily jeweled gold crown upon his head, bestowing a gift to knight who knelt at his feet. A wooden box with a large golden lock and gilded corners. The knight was covered in regalia, a beautiful red and green plaid, a gleaming sword on his back and another at his hips. Even from the woven wool I could see the way his boots were meant to shine. A wealthy knight. The king looked familiar. An image I'd seen in history books, or perhaps on my visits to the castle. I couldn't recall if this particular tapestry had hung in the hall when I visited, but it captured my attention now.

A powerful message that those who occupied Gealach were allies of the king and vice versa. A message that would sink through the hearts of anyone who dared to step into this hall with a nefarious purpose. A shiver stole over me, and I was quick to rub my arms. But even the heat created by the friction did not warm me.

The king has entrusted in me not only a treasure but a secret. Logan's words rang in my memory. He was guardian to Scotland but also to a gift the king had given him. Was Logan the kneeling knight? It didn't look like him. Logan had dark hair and this knight's hair was made to look reddish brown. Who then was it? Had someone else guarded a treasure before Logan?

I glanced down at the floor, my eyes skimming toward the place where my feet had been safely hidden behind the tapestry. The secret door was conveniently placed behind a tapestry showing the king giving a gift. Did that passage lead to the treasure Logan spoke of? If I summoned the courage and descended those stairs would I see a great glittering treasure? What was in that sleek box with the gold lock? Did it even look like that?

"Emma."

I whirled around, coming face to face with Logan. Tall, powerful. He stood in the center of the room, commanding even the air to bend. I opened my mouth to issue some excuse as to why I was in the great hall instead of my room, but the only thing that came out was a breath of air.

"Do ye like the tapestry?" He stalked closer, making me feel like I was his prey.

I turned back to look at the vibrant tones of wool and nodded.

"What do ye see?"

He stood beside me, his heat enveloping me, taking away the chills I'd had before only to replace them with wicked shudders along my spine.

"A king giving a gift."

He chuckled. "Aye, that is true. But what do ye really see?"

I stared once more, trying to figure out a way to say what I saw that wouldn't have Logan dragging me down to share a cell with the murderer in the dungeon.

"I see... secrets."

A large hand flattened to the base of my spine, his thumb rubbing gently over a single vertebra.

"Me, too. Do ye know who the vassal is?"

I shook my head, sinking closer to his side. Torrid heat licked its way up and down my legs, slicking between my thighs. Just his light touch did that to me.

"'Tis supposed to be my sire."

"Your father?" I couldn't truly see a resemblance. Maybe the arch of the brow. The size of the man.

Logan pressed a finger to my chin, tilting my face toward his. "Aye. And that is a gift that needed protection." His eyes glittered into mine.

I glanced around to make sure we were alone and then whispered, "Is it the treasure you told me of?"

Logan shrugged. "'Haps." But he didn't say anymore and I was too scared to press him. "How long have ye been here?"

"Not long."

He grinned, a lopsided curve of his lips. "Liar."

So he had seen me hiding. I squared my shoulders. "I never lie."

He leaned close, his firm, warm lips brushing the shell of my ear. A violent shiver raged throughout my body. "Are ye looking for another punishment?"

I swallowed hard. *Yes. No.* I just wanted him to touch me.

"Tell me what ye heard?" he said, his tongue flicking over my earlobe before his teeth took its place. "I can sense when ye're near."

I whimpered, then managed to say, "A murderer."

"Naughty, lass, listening in on others." He swept me up into his arms, oblivious to his surroundings, and thank goodness there was no one to witness him storming up the stairs, his hold on me commanding and gentle at the same time. Logan's mouth claimed mine in a thoroughly brutal and arousing kiss.

He slammed open the door to a chamber that was not my own, and just as quickly slammed it shut.

"Ye are safe with me. Ye know that, aye?"

I nodded, taking in the stark masculinity of his room, the magnificent bed, easily twice the size of my own, and had matching etchings on the four posts. Intricate details.

Logan placed me down beside the bed. "I willna cut this gown," he murmured as he kissed the nape of my neck and slowly untied the bodice. I shivered, sighed, reached out to touch him but he batted my hands away. My gown fell in a puddle at my feet and my chemise, he slipped off my shoulders, allowing it to fall, too. I was naked. I shivered, nipples hardening to aching points, but I wasn't cold.

I was hotter than hell and wanted desperately to wrap my legs around this huge hunk of Highlander and let him have his way with me. Thank goodness for the lemon still in place.

Logan was slow in his seduction, trailing kisses along the nape of my neck over my shoulders, bringing my arm up to kiss me from my wrist to the inside of my elbow. I shifted on my feet unable to stand still. Moisture pooled between my quivering thighs. I clenched in torment, waiting for him to stroke me.

"I've never brought a woman to my chamber before," he confessed. His tongue flicked out to run around the edge of pink surrounding my nipple. "Not one, until ye, Emma. They've all been bedded in the chamber beside this one."

I could hardly concentrate on his words, the depth of their meaning, when he drew my nipple into his mouth. I cried out, wanting so badly for this to have happened for hours. This time, he didn't stop me from pushing my hands into his hair, holding his mouth hostage to my breast.

"Do ye understand, Emma?"

I nodded, knowing that I couldn't be the only one who'd experienced the changes to my heart. "I'm yours," I murmured, and managed to back up until my thighs hit the bed. I scooted onto his mattress, legs apart and beckoned him to me. "Take me, Logan."

His eyes riveted between my thighs, taking in what I offered. Barren of hair, I knew he'd see the slick juices of my desire covering my sex, probably could see it seeping out as my yearning only grew the longer he stared.

"Aye. Mine."

He stood between my legs, his brawny thighs pushing mine further apart. I ran my hands down the length of his corded torso, feeling the muscles flex beneath his shirt. But I didn't have to ask him to take it off. Logan literally ripped his shirt away, tearing it down the center, revealing the lines of his chest from his collarbone to his navel. The hottest thing I'd ever seen. A man so eager for my touch, so eager to get himself inside me, that he was tearing his clothes away. I gripped his belt, but he pushed my hands away and shook his head.

"Lie back."

I did as he demanded, and watched with wide, hungry eyes as he slowly unhooked his belt, letting the leather fall to the bed. His plaid unraveled, falling to the floor and revealing the gloriously thick length of his cock. I licked my lips, eager for another taste. If he wanted me to suck him first, I'd do it any day. My thoughts must have been visible because he shook his head, a wicked grin playing at his lips.

"Not this time, lass."

He slid his large palms over my naked hips, my ribs and then turned me so my head rested on his pillows.

"Put your arms over your head."

Without question, I did what he asked, lifting my arms above my head on the pillows, my chest arched, breasts quivering with each rapid intake of breath. He knelt between my thighs and picked up his leather belt. My mind was a whirl of thoughts. What was he going to do with that belt?

Logan slid the cold leather over the skin of my belly, my trembling thighs. Images of him turning me over and smacking the belt onto my bare ass came to mind. And worried me, too. I knew some people used belts and paddles as a means of pleasure, but I wasn't sure I was in that place yet. If anyone were to introduce me to that side of life, it would be Logan though. I truly did trust him with my body. With my life. He wasn't cruel to me. Genuine concern for my well-being, whether it be sexually or safety or peace of mind, he had an earnest interest in. My heart constricted.

With a wicked grin he loomed above me, took hold of my hands and pulled the leather around my wrists.

"Ever been bound?" he asked, a flash of concern entering his eyes.

I shook my head. "Never." And God held me, I shivered with anticipation as the cool belt tightened, holding my wrists captive.

Logan attached the other end of his belt to the head board, and tilting my head to look up behind me, I could see there was a hook there. Meant for this. I returned my gaze to his and raised a brow.

Behind the Plaid

He winked. "Never used that hook before in this room either. Been wanting to since the moment I saw ye shiver in my arms."

I may have worn the same gown as another woman, but I was a first for him here, in this room, doing such forbidden things. My stomach did a little flip. I was tied to the bed of this domineering Highlander, a man whose very presence sent my body to weeping. A man who made me feel whole.

Again my heart constricted. The feelings I had for Logan...they were intense. Tangible and frightening. I'd never had them before for anyone. Not even a portion of them for Steven.

I was...completely falling for him.

But then Logan's lips were on my neck, his hands everywhere, stroking, teasing. And I was whimpering, crying out, struggling against the leather with my need to touch him back. Logan only laughed and teased me all the more. His tongue swept over my hip, teased at the folds of my bare sex, flicked in unhurried strokes over my clit, then slid back up over my belly to my breasts. "Ye taste like sweet lemons," he murmured and I laughed.

If I thought walking around all day overwhelmed by the need to make love was punishment, this was true torture. He might as well have tied me to the rack and stretched me until my limbs pulled from their sockets. I cried out. I writhed. I hooked my legs around his hips and tried to tug him closer. All my efforts only spurred him on.

Logan lifted my legs and gave a playful slap to my ass. First one cheek, and then the other. Where his hand hit, stung, but it was a pleasurable sting, made all the more so when he pressed his lips and tongue to the spot.

"Please," I pleaded, my clit throbbing. "Please."

"I love to hear ye beg," Logan murmured against my ear. He spread my thighs, and pressed me into the bed, his cock pushed hard against my belly. Lower... I wanted him to move lower.

I squirmed, trying to move him into just the right spot. No luck. If he wanted to hear me beg for it, I would... I'd never talked dirty to a man in my life. Never imagined I would, but desperate times called for desperate measures.

"I want your cock inside me," I whispered.

Logan groaned, slid his hands beneath my ass and lifted me a little as he knelt back on his heels. "Say it louder."

I opened my eyes, not realizing they'd been squeezed closed. Logan's gaze was pure hunger. Whatever timidity I'd been oozing flitted away. Corded muscles. Broad shoulders. Flat, muscled belly. Thick cock. My legs spread, knees hooked over his elbows.

"Fuck me." The words came from my mouth, utterly confident.

Logan grinned slowly, a hungry, hot grin that made me want to push him back and climb on top. I yanked at the leather holding me tight to the bed.

"I dinna take orders from feisty little lasses," Logan growled. He lifted my hips higher, his biceps bunching deliciously and pressed his firm lips to my clit.

I groaned, head falling backward, rolling from side to side.

He plundered my flesh, tongue stabbing inside me, sucking hard on my clit, and I just couldn't take it anymore. I'd been waiting hours and hours and... I screamed. Yanked hard at the strap of leather. Thrust my hips higher against his face. I came so hard my entire body convulsed and my brain shut down. I floated into a cloud of pure, raw, unadulterated ecstasy, and even when I was still reeling, my body still shuddering, Logan took his mouth from my center and thrust his cock deep and hard.

"Logan!" I shrieked, the muscles of my sex clenching hard around his thick invasion.

Behind the Plaid

"Och, lass. Ye're so damn tight." His fingers dug hard into my buttocks.

He kept still for a long time, until I squeezed and clenched around him, rolled my hips in an effort to grind my pelvis into his. Shockwaves rocked me, and I was so close to coming again, I couldn't form a coherent thought. Moans and whimpers escaped my mouth when I wasn't biting hard at my lip.

Logan muttered an expletive, gripped me tighter and then pulled out. His head rolled back and he groaned as he drove back inside. He was long, thick and filled me so completely, with each move a bit of a sting mixed with pleasure. Logan's moans were feral, carnal and the way the veins in his neck stood out from his skin as he strained was so damn hot.

"Faster," I gasped.

He only slowed down. "Och, lass, ye must learn. This is my domain and ye're to submit to me."

I don't know why, but hearing him say the words, knowing he controlled whether I came or not, even if it was by my own hands, I desired him more than ever. I *wanted* to be his submissive. I wanted him to dominate me.

"Yes, Logan."

He lifted my leg so my calf was flush with his face, and lightly bit my skin. "Is this what ye want?" He pumped his hips back and forth, wild and vigorous. Just the way I wanted. But when my eyes met his, I realized the way he worked me, the way he fucked me, it wasn't wild at all, he was completely in control, giving me what he knew I wanted—and with that realization and the demand in his eyes that I come, my body shattered.

Logan barely gave me time to recover before he slid from inside me and lifted my hips again, burying his face between my thighs. Pleasure mixed with pain as his scorching tongue caressed my overstimulated clit.

"Stop," I begged.

"Nay."

I writhed, yanked at my restraints, and beyond all of that I *felt* — deeply in my soul, not just between my thighs.

"I'm yours. Now and forever," I moaned on a sob, the pleasure was so intense. Another orgasm ripped me apart, bringing tears to my eyes. And still he didn't stop. Just kept working his mouth on me until I thought I'd die.

"That's right," he growled. "Mine." Logan put me down, spread my thighs wide and came over me, his weight pressing me into the mattress.

I was surrounded by his masculine, spicy scent just as I surrounded him with my legs. He drove inside me, and I could feel him trembling, knew he too was close to the edge. I hooked my feet together on his buttocks and used whatever strength I had left in my boneless body to buck with each of his thrusts.

"Mine," he moaned against my throat, his teeth grazing my skin. "Now." He bit my earlobe, slammed his pelvis so hard into mine I thought I the bed would collapse. "And." The wooden headboard rattled and smacked into the stone wall again and again. "Forever." He roared, pounding harder and harder, until I was screaming once more, so close to fainting, and something hot seared my insides.

I love you, I thought. *Love you, love you.*

CHAPTER TWENTY-TWO

Logan

Thoroughly sated, Emma fell into a deep sleep, and I watched her for a time, studying every line of her face, the curve of her chin and earlobe, the way a tiny contented sigh slipped from her plush lips as she slept. Her long, wild hair was in disarray, spread in red flaming waves over the pillow. She lay on her side, her hip covered by a corner of the coverlet, an arm draped over her breasts, one rose-colored nipple peeking through.

The woman had the most magnificent, long legs. While she'd told me she found her knees to be knobby, I found them endearing, each and every curve of cartilage. Her toes poked out from beneath the coverlet, elegant-looking. She slept so peacefully she could have been unraveled from one of the tapestries hanging throughout the castle. Ethereal in her beauty. Untouchable.

Comparable to Venus having descended from the Heavens and draping herself across my wicked bed.

I knew at that moment I had to leave the room or somehow take her back to her own without rousing her.

I was behaving like a love struck lad and Highlanders, especially brutal ones responsible for the carefully guarded secrets of a country, did not wonder at the softness and color of a woman's hair. Or the way her lashes spread over her cheeks. Nay, I should be wrapping that glorious hair around my wrists and forcing her to wake so I could pound her through the mattress once more.

Aye. Leaving the room was the best idea. I pulled a new linen shirt from the wardrobe, tossing my torn one into the hamper for the maids to either attempt a botched sewing job or shred it for use as cleaning rags. There wasna an item in the castle not used, reused, and reused some more. With resources scarce enough as it was, no one wasted anything.

After rolling on my plaid, I realized my belt still hung on the head board. I'd left it hanging there like a trophy. Emma had so willingly lifted her hands, letting me bind her. Allowed me to torture her body until she broke apart again and again. My cock hardened, my free swinging plaid suddenly constrictive.

Trying hard not to look at Emma, since all I wanted to do was crawl back into the bed and surround her with warmth and carnal stroking, I ripped the belt from the hook, jammed it around my hips, grabbed my boots and stomped from the room. I shut the door quietly so I wouldna wake her and bent down to lace my boots praying no one saw me and gave me a questioning, if guarded, glance. No one, save Ewan, would dare ask why I was doing so.

Behind the Plaid

Laces finished, I melted into the shadows of the corridor, letting the inky blackness of night make me invisible. A cloak of shadows. The place I felt safest. After all, everything about me was shrouded in shades of grey and black, why not make my body disappear within it.

Ewan awaited me in my library as he did most evenings. But this time he looked anxious.

"What is it?"

"A missive."

"From the king?"

"Aye."

A rolled parchment sat in the center of my immaculately clean desk. I was not one to leave a mess. Not because I was an overly clean person—although I liked fresh smelling sheets as well as the next man—but because if I left something out that happened to catch the eye of the wrong person it would only make a curious man dangerous. Therefore, all business was concluded and put away before leaving any room. Most chambers were locked, some because they held secrets and some to deflect.

The most blatant of secrets were often left out in the open, no one the wiser and no one believing that I would be so bold. But the reason for that boldness was precisely that—no one would notice.

Except Emma. She was the only one who'd stared up at the tapestry, who'd looked like she was dissecting it. I had another idea of why she did though. And it had to do with me. Her interest in me. An equally growing interest I returned.

Ballocks! Interest was too mild a word. She intoxicated me. I was becoming infatuated with her. *Cock and ballocks...* not becoming—I *was* infatuated.

I cleared my throat and walked around to sit in my chair, forcing myself to remain indifferent. A missive from the king. News about his decision regarding my bitter enemy. For a moment, I stared at the Great Seal of the Realm. King James V. A mounted knight with his sword, loyal hound at his side. My sovereign's seal. With the tip of my thumb nail, I cracked the blood-colored wax. The parchment paper crinkled loudly as I unrolled it. Ewan shifted on his feet. The candle flickered. Seemed my attention was on everything save the contents of that missive.

Letting out a silent long breath, I forced my eyes to absorb his words.

Guardian of Scotland, Blood of my Blood,

Let me assure you that your messenger has arrived safely within my walls and that I have reviewed your missive with the gravest of hearts and given great consideration to your recommendations regarding Laird MacDonald.

I do believe it is in the best interest of Scotland and this realm, for you to return Laird MacDonald to his ship and have his galleon returned to the Isle of the North — alive. I shall keep the remainder of his vessels as a gift. In this time of turmoil, we must not make enemies with anyone — even those we deem to be our adversaries. The plain truth is that MacDonald has many allies, as many as he has enemies.

Leave his men to rot within your walls, a safeguard if needed or prisoners to parlay with. Keep a close eye. Allan has been known to escape many a prison.

Pure rage filled me, and for a moment I slammed the parchment down, couldna read another word. MacDonald would go free. Not just *free* — but with a goddamned ship. I was going to send my would-be assassin back into the world fully supplied with all he needed to kill me. He could sneak back into Gealach, or pay an easily turned servant, to release his men. Then we'd have battle on our hands.

I rubbed my brow, pain suddenly searing across my scalp.

Ewan cleared his throat, but I ignored him. How could I actually form words with my mouth to articulate the king's bidding?

James was a fool.

Behind the Plaid

But not just any fool. *Blood of my blood.* James was my brother. My *younger* brother. Aye. 'Tis *I* who should be king.

I am the twin brother of King James V of Scotland. When the long-dead queen—my true mother—birthed twins, the oldest was thought to have been stillborn and whisked away from the royal house before anyone would know of it. The truth was, I was much alive, although not as hearty as the second born child—James. Those in service made the decision alone, although they later told the king—my true father—the reality of our birth night and where the babe had been sent. On his death bed, when my brother and I were still babes at the breast, the old king begged his advisor to keep the secret, however, the advisor did confess to the new young king, my brother, who then sought the truth—finding out I was much alive.

King James visited Gealach on the eve of my foster father's death. Never knowing that my parents were not my own, the news struck deep, stilled caused discord within me. My foster mother's heart actually stopped upon seeing the king grace her threshold. I remember the way her face had turned ashen, her eyes rolling in the back of her head. I'd rushed forward, my arms outstretched to catch her, but she fell to the stone floor in a limp heap. Dead.

From that moment, I loved my brother for who he was, but hated him at the same time for causing the loss of my mother. My identity. I was not who I thought I was. My entire world collapsed into a great black stinking hole. James demanded my allegiance or death. I wanted to live. I wanted to get to know the man who was my brother. To get to know those who were my true blood.

Blood of my blood.

But it came with a price. My rightful claim.

James bade me guard a chest, his treasure. He did not tell me the contents—and made me swear to never open it, unless he was killed. My brother had stared up at the tapestry my mother commissioned of my foster father and my true father. "Fitting," he'd muttered. I'd not realized until that moment that the man and woman I'd thought were my parents actually knew all along who I was. And not once had they said anything. Unless my mother thought to ease her conscience by showing that the king had given them a great gift. Indeed his heir.

I'd knelt before the newly crowned King—my king, my brother, the usurper. I knelt and offered him *my* fealty. And he threatened me. If I did not agree to the alliance or strayed in any way, I'd be condemned to death on the spot, no trial, and the people of my clan would all be executed—women and children included.

I could have run him through. Could have ended it there—but I would have also been ending my own life and everyone else's that I knew. I made a choice. A conscious decision. I was given a different path. Raised to be a guardian, not a king. As a gift, I let my brother keep his life. And in turn, he let me keep mine, for I was fully aware that he, too, could have pulled his sword from his pretty gilded scabbard and run it through my heart. He said as much, followed by a brief explanation. *Because we are brothers*, James wished me to remain alive and well. And a promise—if I ever became a threat, the axe would fall heavily and bluntly upon my neck.

Having only one choice, I forged an alliance with the king. An alliance that I swore to take with me to the grave. I've been loyal to my brother. Steadfast. And in return he has given me gifts and the power to protect his crown. I protect our secret, the treasure buried in the bowels of Gealach, and Scotland, with every ounce of power I possesses.

We are constantly under attack, for there are many who know I was given a treasure to guard, but none who have the knowledge of what that treasure is. Because of this, I am always on edge. Consumed with the need for control which wars with my longing for harmony—a longing I do not ever see an end to... Except when I'm with Emma.

A shadow passed under the library door. No doubt we'd seen many as we holed up with the door barred. Prowlers, all intent on hearing a whispered word. We are safe when they know nothing. Threats are only ever dangerous when presented as indisputable knowledge. I'd never give them the chance.

I nodded to Ewan who turned to the specially made door with his sword in hand. He slipped the pointed edge into a death slit. Before he could open the small eyehole to peer through, I called, "Wait." For a moment, my heart stopped as I imagined Emma on the other side.

Ewan stilled his sword.

No one passed by this door save spies. But hadn't Emma lurked outside my door the other night? I pushed from my chair so forcefully it tumbled backward, and in two large steps I was at Ewan's side.

"Emma," I whispered.

Ewan raised a questioning brow and I chose to ignore him. I flipped off the bar and yanked open the door. It wasn't Emma, but another faceless spy who scurried down the corridor and out of sight.

Ewan took off after the figure who'd already melted into the shadows. My guard was silent, he would find them and he would finish the job I'd stopped him from completing when thoughts of Emma broke into my conscience.

With a growl I slammed the door shut, stalked to my desk and ripped the parchment from its surface. I skimmed the note until finding the place where I'd left off before.

If you are loyal to me, which I know you are, you will use discretion with Laird MacDonald and heed my directive. He must return to his castle in the north. There is much we need to discuss, which I would not dare to write within this letter no matter how trustworthy the messenger is.

I will call on Gealach soon. Be ready.

Your Sovereign,

James, by the grace of God, of England, Scotland, France and Ireland, King, Defender of the Faith

Sovereign. As if I needed the reminder. Every waking moment of my life was a reminder. The anger in me only rose. James was keeping things from me. How the hell was I supposed to protect him and Scotland when I knew naught? When our enemy was allowed to go free?

This was one of the times I wanted to tilt my head back and roar the indignities of life that had been heaped upon me. A moment when I wanted to gather an army and storm all of my enemies' castles and annihilate them. When the briefest thought of taking what was rightfully mine flitted through my mind. Moments of insanity. For they could not be lucid thoughts. No sane man in my position would ever dream of destroying the lives of hundreds, thousands of people.

And that was when I remembered my duty. Honor. I had more than any man I knew. Even James. I would not bow to my enemies. I would not let my own weaknesses take all I knew, plunge me into the dark. I had a duty. A duty to my country. A duty to my king. A duty to my dead parents. A duty to my blood.

That was why I must remain strong. An indomitable force.

I lifted the missive to the candle and watched the orange flame lick at the corner, catching hold and lapping up the page until it turned black and disintegrated into ash.

Well, if my enemy was to be put back on his ship and sent to his abominable isles where he'd likely fill his ship with more warriors and return to me, then so be it. The last corner of the page disintegrated with a burning sting between my thumb and forefinger. Evidence gone. I clenched the flame in my fist, snuffing the candle out.

The dungeon guards nodded, opening the barred door without question. The stairs to the dungeon were well-lit.

Behind the Plaid

Precaution after MacDonald murdered my man—a fact the king didna know when he wrote his reply. A fact I was going to use to my advantage.

I pulled my *sgian dubh* from my boot and approached MacDonald's cell. I used the blade to pick at my nails, and leaned nonchalantly against the wall. I waited, refusing to be the first one to speak. Out of the corner of my eye I watched the man shift uncomfortably, stubborn jackass didna want to speak either. I'd wait all night. Hell, the longer I waited, the longer he remained behind bars and the threat of death by rat bite grew.

"What do ye want, Grant?" he growled.

I chuckled, though my laugh had no humor in it. I slid my eyes up lazily and focused on the man I wished to beat into a bloody, unrecognizable pulp. I didna stop fiddling with my blade, crossed my ankles over each other. "Well, 'twould appear ye have friends in high places."

MacDonald's grin was menacing.

"And I dinna mean God, for he still thinks I should slay ye where ye stand."

"Ye converse with the Lord?" MacDonald sneered.

"Pity ye do not," I answered.

"Fool." MacDonald turned his back on me.

I'd think the move unwise in any other man, but in MacDonald I knew it was only a show of his disrespect.

"I'm sending ye home, MacDonald. Sweet dreams, Laird of the Isles. Ye'll travel back to your lands on the morrow at dawn—in the utmost comfort."

MacDonald gave a triumphant laugh. It took every ounce of willpower within me not to wrench open the cell and thrust my blade through his eye socket. His sinister laugh followed me all the way up the stairs, and I swore I could still hear him through the thick wooden doors.

But I was the only one laughing as his ship sailed toward the north with him tied, shackled with his own irons, to the mast.

CHAPTER TWENTY-THREE

Emma

Shouts startled me from sleep.

Great wailing, angry cries. My eyes flew open and I stared up at the unfamiliar ceiling, shivers racing along my spine. I was frozen for a moment in time, unable to move, breathe.

Those cries... And then silence.

I was alone. A cursory glance told me I was still in Logan's room. But that did nothing to calm me because the visions of our lovemaking came tumbling back. If I weren't already lying down, I'd have to. Again I shivered, but this time not from cold. In fact, I was warm, hot.

And anxious.

Anxious to tell him my feelings. Yet determined not to reveal my innermost private emotions. Love was no sentiment to be easily bestowed, and here I was, a miracle of time travel, fucking some hot warrior's brains out and falling in love. I shook my head, part in denial, partly because I'd been an idiot to let myself fall.

I climbed from the bed and pulled the silky chemise that lay neatly over a wooden chair over my head. Not the chemise I'd worn when Logan brought me to his room the day before. It appeared I'd slept through the night and someone had left it, along with a gorgeous green satin gown, Logan's plaid colors embroidered at the hem, wrists and collar. Light colored pearls edged the bodice. A gown meant for a queen.

Not me.

This gown was in pieces, a skirt, sleeves and a bodice. Lovely silken stockings embroidered with thistles. Thick petticoats that would make the gown puff, and surely make me swelter once the sun had risen. I wouldn't be able to dress myself. I'd have to find Agatha first. This gown looked like those worn by ladies at a Tudor court. But this was no Tudor court. This was Scotland. The Highlands. And I refused to wear such garb.

The screams came again. Yells now, really. Angry bellows, returned shouts. I swallowed hard, fearing the castle had been invaded. Where was Logan? Had he left me here to go and fight? But in the back of my mind, I knew he left shortly after we'd both exhausted our bodies. I'd pretended to be asleep while he slipped away, unable to confront him having just realized what my own feelings were. I sensed he, too, needed to escape from the heady and heavy cloud that enveloped us.

A tiny slit of light seeped through the shutters, in stark contrast to the demon roaring. Instead of the devil coming with the dark, he came with the dawn. I snuck to the window, and eased open the shutters, trying my damndest not to make a noise. But the hinges didn't agree and creaked so loud I was sure Logan's door would be banged open any minute.

Behind the Plaid

I stiffened, unmoving, hands holding the shutters open, mouth agape, eyes wide, at the most beautiful sunrise I'd ever seen before. Pink and orange dashed across a purple backdrop meeting the crest of mountains. A few clouds hung as if waiting for direction to fall and create a mystic haze. The loch lapped lazily, the ships rocked. One ship's sails were unfurled and waving with the slight breeze that was always present. What was it about this place that made me want to lie on the ground all day and enjoy the splendor of its creation?

But there again, the shouts disrupted that moment of beauty, and no one came barreling through Logan's door to slam the shutters closed. A steady stream of warriors followed behind Logan, across the grassy overlook. Between them, a man was being dragged. A shackled man.

I gasped, disbelieving what I saw. So medieval. So unreal. A caravan of brutality. One of the men who walked behind the prisoner hit him and he bellowed, his cries echoing in the morning air.

Somehow I knew immediately that this man was the murderer. The way they all despised him, the way Logan had taken his dignity. While I knew Logan to be a brutal man if needed, he also seemed like one who would show mercy if necessary. One who, if you gave him what he wanted, would not simply slit your throat for giving answers. But I also knew with a fierce clarity, that he would not abide traitors. Traitors stood between him and his secrets. His treasure.

Watching them march the prisoner along the cliff's edge toward the dock stairs to the water below reminded me of how real this era was. The harshness of it. A stark reminder that I'd not dropped into fancyland. This was actually happening. There was no government like I was used to. There was no police, no one I could call to come and take me away or to protect me from anyone, including myself.

The man below, the laird of Gealach, with broad shoulders, glittering in his weapons, was the one I loved. Madly. Deeply. He'd somehow stormed inside my mind and possessed my very soul. And lucky for me, because he was the one marching a prisoner to God knows where across the dewy grass, tramping beautiful flowers, instead of the prisoner.

Two quick raps hit the door and then it was opened. I turned to see Agatha standing in the doorway, her hands folded over her middle. "My lady, his lairdship wished me to help ye dress, so ye might break your fast."

My stomach growled, a reminder of how little I'd eaten the day before. Logan and I had skipped dinner in favor of feasting on each other. I'd skip every meal for the rest of my life if he so much as grinned at me. Damn... I unclenched my hands, not realizing I'd been digging my nails into my palms. My body was already in agreement with my mind. Agatha would surely notice my hardened nipples. I'd keep my thighs tightly clenched, praying my tender, tingling, swollen lips would stop throbbing, else I wouldn't be able to stay still.

"I don't want to wear this dress, Agatha. I liked the other more simple gowns. I don't want you to have to dress me." I wanted to add that I was no one special, that I'd been dressing myself for twenty some years, no need for a regression. But Agatha stood stonily within the room, giving me a look that broached no argument. The longer I argued, the longer it would be until breakfast and my stomach was starting to churn.

With an exaggerated sigh, I threw my hands into the air. "Fine. Let's get it over with."

Agatha nodded once and walked to the chair which my new attire had been tossed over. I supposed I'd feel quite like a royal today. Most young girls dream of being royal and even some women.

"Arms out now, lass." Agatha worked around me, pulling on my stockings, and tying them with satiny ribbons above my

Behind the Plaid

knee. I had to admit they were the nicest stockings I'd ever worn.

"No underwear?" I asked as she moved to put on the thick underskirts, tying them at the back. They poofed out and I had the overwhelming urge to swing around and see them make a wide bell around my legs.

"Underwear?" she asked.

"Never mind." I'd not worn any up until now, but I thought it simply because of the simple gowns. With a fancier gown, I had hoped to get a fancy set of drawers too. I remembered something about easy access and when I used to think of it in terms of using the bathroom, I realized how much easier it would be for Logan to touch me without the drawers. God, I wanted him to touch me. I shifted on my feet.

"Stay still," Agatha said, several pins between her lips.

I did her bidding and watched with fascination as she pinned pieces of fabric into place. The green satin skirt rustled and crinkled as she pinned it, and then came the bodice, lined with something hard, almost like a corset as she tied it behind me, tugging and tugging until I could barely breathe.

"Ye've a tiny waist, hardly needed any tugging at all."

I grunted. Agatha didn't know what she was talking about, and if she did, then my sympathies went out to those with a fuller figure as it probably felt even worse. My breasts were crushed and spilling from the top—fleshy mounds. And quite honestly, I was impressed. The bodice had managed to give me cleavage and it was damned nice. I couldn't wait to see the look on Logan's face when he saw me. Wanted to see the hunger sparking in his eyes.

Next came the sleeves, two sets. First red, then green. Even these were pinned into place. If I moved in the wrong way, I was going to get stabbed. No wonder women had such a regal way of walking in royal courts—they didn't want to bleed all over their gowns. I was about to ask Agatha if she could take off one set of sleeves, it was summer after all, when she pulled the red satin through the green making poofy red and green stripes at my shoulders.

"Pretty," I murmured. Then promptly wondered how many other women had worn this gown.

"Aye, 'tis. Used to be the laird's mother's gown. He saved it all these years."

I didn't want to read into her words and what the interpretation would be of anyone else dwelling at the castle. I was wearing Laird Grant's family gown. Probably saved for his wife. I did, however, have a question that needed to be asked, and I didn't want to ask Logan. If Agatha had somehow chosen for me to wear this... I wouldn't be able to face him.

"Whose choice was it for me to wear this gown?"

"His Lairdship's."

Relief filled me at the same time as dread. Logan had no qualms in giving me his previous lover's gowns, but to give me his mother's? I didn't know much about his mother. Should I be flattered or not? Should I feel that his gift was one with great meaning, or was this yet again a case of not wasting fabric?

Too many times in my life I'd not been true to myself and for the last eight years, I'd lost sight of who I was and what I wanted. Before that, I'd caved to peer pressure. Perhaps when I was a young child I might have chosen my own path, but even then I was guided by others. But here, standing in the center of this room, I wanted to plot my own course. I wanted to be the one who had a choice in the matter. As much as I was kept here within the walls, as much as I was beholden to Logan for his safety, I was also free. Free to choose who I was going to be. Free to express myself and my desires. I knew that. Felt it.

So, standing here in this gown that meant either utterly nothing or made a whole world of difference, I decided I had to speak with Logan about us. Yes, I'd agreed to be his lover. Yes, I'd agreed to stay. Yes, I'd accepted his protection. But I'd also fallen in love, and I had to protect myself, too. If he was only using me and this gown was another way to not waste fabric, then I had to end this before I fell harder. Before I was utterly crushed, my heart forever damaged. Because I'd started to heal with Logan, could feel it in my soul. He completed me.

Agatha and I didn't say any more. She gave me a half-lemon and after slipping a pair of matching satiny shoes onto my feet, she beckoned me to follow her. The corridors were dark as usual, the stairwell lit by arrow slits every few feet, shafts of light stabbing into the dark like radiant swords. There was no one in the great hall, which I assumed was because they were all following Logan on his course with the murderer.

"My lady, should ye like to sit here?" Although Agnes asked the question, it was more of a direction. A place had been set—no, two places had been set at the table, one at the head and one to the left.

Just two settings. If Agnes was having me sit at the place set to the left, the other spot could only be left to Logan. Yet again, a big deal. I shook my head. I wasn't going to sit down. Not until we'd talked.

"When does his lairdship expect to return?" I asked. Judging from what I saw out the window, he could be gone all day.

"He'll be returning soon. He bade ye take your place here."

I frowned. "No. I'll wait." I turned from Agatha and walked to the hearth, empty of a fire, but logs already set in place should one be lit. The maid give a disgruntled mumble, but I ignored her. I'd let her dress me, but I wasn't going to sit at a table by myself waiting for Logan. I needed to pace. Needed to stand.

And there was that little issue with possibly stabbing myself with the pins of my gown.

I didn't wait long. Maybe twenty minutes of pacing and staring at the various tapestries, counting the candles in the grand candelabra hanging mightily from the rafters—one-hundred forty the first time, one-hundred thirty-six the second time.

He came into the great hall alone, surprisingly not covered in blood as I'd imagined. His eyes were automatically riveted to my cleavage, his appreciative gaze making me flush and tingle.

"Ye look beautiful," he murmured. He came toward me, confidence and power in each step. My thighs quivered, breath quickened. God, he was magnificent, oozed sexuality.

"Thank you." Heat suffused my cheeks, and between my thighs. I had to change the subject or else I'd lift my skirts before I had a chance to ask about them. "Where is…the prisoner?"

"Gone."

I nodded, not knowing what he meant, but assuming it had been clean. I glanced back toward the hearth, trying to form words for what needed to be said.

"He yet lives."

That caught my attention. "Why?"

"Should I have killed him?" Logan's expression was contemplative.

I shrugged. "I don't think that's really my decision."

"'Twas not my decision either."

"But you are in charge here."

He nodded. "But I still answer to my king."

"Oh." I'd somehow forgotten about that. Had to get used to there being a king, when I'd grown up without one.

"Are ye hungry?" he asked.

"Starved," I replied, but my appetite was for something entirely different.

"As am I." Judging from the way his lids turned heavy as his gaze fell once more to my breasts, Logan was not referring to food either.

Easy access. We both had it. A flip of his kilt and a flip of my many skirts and we could come together in the heated,

Behind the Plaid

frenzied passion I'd been craving since waking up. But before that... I had to know my place.

"Logan, I..." My voice trailed off as the words refused to leave my throat. "I need to know—" Dammit, this was harder than I thought.

"Know what?" Logan came forward, only a foot away. He smelled like the outside, and his dark hair was windblown, making him look roguish.

I took a deep breath. I just had to spit it out. "I need to know what is going on between us. Where I stand."

Logan swallowed, enough of a visible movement to show he dreaded my question. He pressed his lips together, and the desire filled his eyes evaporated. I glanced away, pain seeping from my chest up to my throat. I blinked, praying tears didn't fall even as they stung my eyes. Just as I'd suspected, I was nothing but a vessel with which to find pleasure. All of our encounters, the way he made me feel, the closeness and intensity that had developed—it was all in my head.

He stood silent, body tense.

Thunder rumbled overhead, then cracked, echoing ominously throughout the great hall. The morning had looked bright when I woke, and now the weather appeared to have soured with my mood. A storm.

My heart was broken. Any dreams I'd had of staying in this world diminished.

A storm.

The gate.

I ran. Lifted my skirts and took off toward the doors. Ignoring Logan's calls. Ignoring the sound of his pounding feet behind me. I ran. Out into the courtyard where rain fell in pelting droves. Sprinted until my lungs hurt and the gate was within my reach. Thunder rolled, lightning split the sky.

I reached for the postern, my hands brushing the wet stones as another shaft of lightning collided with the gate.

CHAPTER TWENTY-FOUR

Logan

"Emma, nay!" I shouted, watching her run through the courtyard, a blur of beauty in green and red satin. Lightning sliced through the air, threatening to hit either one of us again and again. Gealach was a beacon for lightning, struck every storm. And still she ran toward the gate, reaching her arms for something.

As if in slow motion, a bright golden light carved the once bright morning sky, aimed for the gate, and Emma. Terror filled me and though I ran at full speed, my legs moved at a sluggish pace.

"Halt!" I bellowed. But she ignored me, and anger mixed with my fear. I wanted to pluck her from the ground, punish her for disobeying me. Punish her for leaving me. Punish her for putting fear in my heart.

Behind the Plaid

Everything happened at once. The control I needed so desperately in order to breathe was wrenched from me by the hands of God himself.

Lightning struck the gate as Emma touched it. Sparks flew from the stones and she was tossed backward, crumbling to the ground in a heap of flesh and bone. I reached her, diving through the muddy ground and catching her head before it hit.

Her eyes were closed, dark lashes fanning over her cheeks. She looked peaceful, calm in her sleep and I was suddenly terrified that she was no longer among the living. So incredibly pale and still she was.

"Emma," I whispered, cradling her head in my arms, and then pulling the rest of her into my embrace. I pressed my ear to her chest, hearing the steady beat of her heart above the din of pounding thunder and rain. Acute relief filled me, abating my anger somewhat. She yet lived! Until that moment, I'd not realized exactly how much I would grieve for her should she leave me. Didna realize how deeply she seeped into my soul.

Lightning no longer struck, as if it had surrendered the moment it hit the gate.

Without effort, I stood, covered in mud and soaked through from the pounding rain. Water dropped from my hair, the tip of my nose, my chin. Emma's skin glistened from rain or tears I couldn't tell, a smear of mud was across her cheek. My boots squished through the mire. I looked up to the sky, letting the rain wash some of the mud from our faces. I wanted to bellow up to the heavens. My chest was tight. Stomach churning. Never had I felt this way before.

A glance out to sea saw the distant spec of MacDonald's ship and I prayed the lightning struck him too, sent him to the bowels of Hell.

Emma moaned against my chest. Her running was my fault. I'd forced her out with my silence. With my pride and my fear at answering her. This was not what I wanted but how could I open up, tell her she meant more to me than just a lover as we'd originally agreed upon? Wasna giving her my mother's dress, setting a place for her at my left, wasna all of that sign enough that I held a deep respect for her?

But I had an idea—nay I knew—Emma did not just respect me. And I did not only respect her. She'd burrowed into a place I'd kept locked up in chains since the day my brother came to tell me the truth of my heritage. My heart, my soul.

I am a brutal warrior. The guardian of Scotland. I am the king's brother. I am the rightful king. And yet, I am a coward. Too weak to admit to a woman that I have powerful feelings for her.

And here she lay in my arms, soaked to the bone.

The door to the castle was opened already by worried servants. Ewan stood in the vestibule, concern etched over his face. I shook my head, not willing to explain what had happened. I needed Emma upstairs. Safe within our walls. Warm and dry. The lightning had struck the stones, but she'd been touching the stones and sparks had flown. There was no telling what damage had been done. I had to make sure she was all right.

A slew of servants followed me into Emma's chamber, clucking, lighting the hearth, pulling out linens. I laid her on the bed, hovered over her and would let no one touch her. Her eyes had not yet opened, and she murmured, clutching her gown.

"My laird, let them undress her. She's soaked through," Ewan murmured. The voice of reason when my mind was a torrent of thought. "The healer is here."

I backed away and Emma was swarmed by maids and the healer. Ewan turned his back dutifully to give her privacy and I was glad for not having to order him to leave. Or challenge him to a duel for gazing at her luscious form.

"She wanted to escape," Ewan said, more of a statement then a question. He crossed his arms over his chest.

Behind the Plaid

I took a similar stance, but I faced Emma. "Aye. But 'twas my doing. I forced her to run."

Ewan shook his head. "I dinna believe it."

"I am weak."

Ewan chuckled quietly. "Nay, ye are the strongest man I know."

I gave a disgusted grunt. "When it comes to Emma..." I shook my head. Before Emma, I was fully aware of my weaknesses—need for control, inability to trust, being denied my past, fear of losing Gealach to my enemies. Never had I thought a woman would sweep the world from beneath my feet. Not a manly quality to discover. And one of a warrior's greatest values was his masculinity.

"Tell her," Ewan said.

"Tell her what?" I frowned.

"Tell her what she needs to hear. Make it right."

I grunted. What did Ewan know? Nothing. He was my second, not the reader of my soul, nor Emma's.

"She doesna appear to be hurt from lightning, my laird," the healer said. "'Haps a little shocked 'tis all. Nothing a bit of tisane or whisky canna help."

I nodded.

When the room was empty and Emma opened her eyes, I sat beside her and gripped her hand hard in mine. They dressed her in a chemise with ivory ribbons. A plaid blanket covered just up to her hips. Her skin was pale, and I wanted to kiss the life back into her, make her pink with passion. Instead, I held a hot tisane to her lips, the herbal scent calming. Emma sipped daintily.

"Are ye hurt anywhere?" I asked.

"Just stunned."

Our eyes locked in a heated stare. I could see pain in her eyes, pain that mirrored within me.

"Dinna leave me, Emma."

Her lips parted and she searched my eyes. "Why? Why should I stay?"

"Because I need ye." It was the most of a confession she was going to get from me. More than I'd ever told another person. I, Logan Grant, Laird of Gealach, Guardian of Scotland, didna need people. They needed me.

Emma nodded. "I need you, too," she murmured, a tear slipping from the corner of her eye.

Silent emotion passed between us. More than I was willing to voice, simply because I'd never uttered them before. In truth, I was still a coward. Fearful of her rejection. She didna know who I truly was. Even my own father, upon being told of my birth, rejected me. How could I be sure this woman who affected me so deeply, wouldna also reject me?

One look though…and I knew. Emma would only leave again if she was forced to. And I'd be damned sure that I wasna the one who pushed her away. No way in hell I'd let anyone else hurt her, either. The pain that seared my chest when she left was too much.

Scotland was in a world of unrest. Threats around every crag and bramble. Secrets and treasures buried within the walls of Gealach and hundreds of thousands of lives hanging in the balance. And in all of that, I'd found peace, my safe haven, within Emma's arms. Having her near made this world bearable. Reinforced my belief that though I'd been robbed of my birthright, there was a reason behind it.

I could never let her go.

Emma

"You're making me wet," I said. A sense of boldness filled me more so than all the others. Lying upon my bed—and yes, it was *mine*—I felt safe and like I'd truly arrived home.

Logan's eyes widened, his jaw muscles clenched.

"You're soaking wet, my laird." I flashed a teasing smile, knowing what Logan had thought I meant.

His silence in the great hall had hurt me. Pushed me away, made me run to the gate, but even though lightning struck, I was still here. Not only was that a sign, but Logan's confession, his need for me, filled me with warmth. I couldn't push him away. I wanted to pull him in closer. I yearned for him. The thought of leaving him made my heart hurt. I had to stay. And apparently Fate agreed with me. At least for now. Yes, the world was different from my own—in fact, worlds apart. Yes, I was technically married to an asshole in the twenty-first century. But this was the sixteenth century, and sitting beside me was a real man. Steven was nothing compared to Logan and I would gladly give up five hundred years of technology to spend as long as I could with him.

Goodbye, Mrs. Gordon. I was never going to be her again.

Logan stood, and for a moment, I swore he was going to strip out of his wet clothes, and my mouth watered at the prospect. But he didn't. Instead, he walked over toward the wood-paneled wall, and twisted one of the many decorative etchings. The wall slid open. Yet another secret panel. This castle was full of them. I leaned up on my elbows and stared through.

Logan's room. The identical bed to mine, directly across. All this time, we'd slept facing each other—a secret panel our only barrier.

He slipped through the door, keeping his back to me. Stopping, he pulled off his shirt, the muscles surrounding his spine rippling in sensual currents. Shoulders bunching, biceps curling. Hot damn, what a man he was. He unhooked his belt and unfurled his kilt. Oh my God...his ass was molded perfectly. I wanted to scramble from the bed, just so I could stroke it. A man's behind had never held me so captivated. I blew out a breath, surprised by how fevered the vision of him stripping naked made me.

And then he walked away.

No. No, I couldn't let him just walk away. Not when my sex was already slick and clenching. Not when my nipples ached to feel his touch. Not without touching that ass. I was a new woman. Emma of Gealach.

I whipped back the covers and ripped off my chemise. I made quick work of grabbing the sheer black gown and slipping it over my head. The fabric was luscious against my skin, and with primal need I stalked toward the panel.

I paused at the outside, feeling almost like if I walked through this door, there would be no going back. This was the path I'd be choosing, and I could sense that power in the air. The same one that radiated from Gealach when I was in the cab. It was an inescapable draw. I caught my breath.

Shoulders squared, chin lifted, I stepped through the door.

"I wondered how long it would—" But Logan's words stopped when he saw what I was wearing. He visibly swallowed. Leaning against the wall, arms crossed over his chest, cock hard and lifted toward me, he was the epitome of raw, male sexuality.

My response froze in my throat. Logan might be raking his scorching gaze over my body, making me shiver, but I was doing the same. I dropped to my knees, in front of him, his huge cock at eye level and without asking, I flicked my tongue over the tip.

Logan grabbed a fistful of my hair and groaned when I sucked him in deep.

"Emma..." he moaned.

I gripped his cock, using the slickness of my saliva to stroke up and down in rhythm with my mouth. The muscles of his thighs and abs flexed. I gripped his hard ass with my free hand, massaging the tautness of it, feeling him flex with each suck. With a loud groan, Logan yanked away, his hand still curled in my hair.

I gazed at him, my lips tingling.

He pulled me up by the hair, crushed his mouth to mine, gripping my buttocks firmly and pulling me tight against him. His hard shaft pressed between my thighs, sending delicious shudders all over me. Logan's tongue swept possessively into my mouth, tasting of mint and spice. I held nothing back. Wrapped my arms around his neck, and lifted a leg to curve around Logan's hip.

"Oh, aye, lass. I want ye so bad."

"Please," I murmured against his mouth, nibbling at his lower lip.

Logan gripped my buttocks with both hands and lifted me up. He pressed me up against the wood-paneled wall, the sudden chill of the wall a shock and I shrieked. Logan chuckled, slipped a hand down my thigh to the hem of the sheer gown.

"Ye look like a seductive nymph in this gown." Logan's Scottish burr and the sexy things he said sent frissons of delicious pleasure through me. He tugged at my ear lobe, and I gripped his shoulders, nails digging into his brawny flesh.

"What does that make you?" I asked wickedly, scraping my teeth against his neck.

"The man who's going to fuck a nymph."

My clit throbbed in answer, and I ground my hips against his, hooked my feet behind him. Logan managed to scrunch my gown up around my waist and a hand slipped between my thighs. I moaned, thighs quivering as his fingers glided between the slippery folds of my sex, and then plunged deep. Back arched, I cried out, ground against his fingers.

"That's right, nymph, ride my hand." His lips captured mine again in a searing kiss. One that made me shudder and sigh and murmur his name.

When once I'd thought this a dream, a moment of fantasy, now I knew how real it was. Somehow the fates aligned and brought me here, away from the nightmare that had become my life so I might carve out a bit of peace and pleasure and love in this world filled with turmoil. Logan had begun to heal my heart, and in the same respect, I was healing him.

Logan fingered the ribbons at the dip in my throat. I'd not bothered to tie them as I hurried to toss it on. He slid his fingers inside to my bare shoulder and tugged. The gown fell off my shoulder, my small breasts spilling out to his waiting hand and mouth. He flicked his tongue wildly over one nipple and then the other, all the while thrusting his fingers deep inside me, swirling his thumb over my clit. My head fell back against the wood, moans ripping from my throat with primitive need.

"Aye, lass, cry out for me."

"Logan, please. Please..."

"Please, what?" he teased, drawing my nipple between his teeth.

"Please take me."

"Och, aye." His fingers slipped out, and were replaced by the head of his hard shaft. "Is this what ye want?" He stroked his cock over my clit, between my folds, the head pushing just an inch inside me.

I rocked my hips against his, desperate for more. "Yes!"

Logan thrust forward, all the way to the hilt, his balls bouncing against my buttocks. Both of us cried out in unison, and I writhed, flush against him. My clit rubbed against his pelvis, fiery sensation rocketing through me. The passion that ignited between us was even greater than the sparks from the lightning. It was miraculous splendor. Pure ecstasy. Raw, powerful, animalistic.

He thrust deep, pulled out slow. Teasing me, tormenting me with his heated body and expert touch. He completely dominated me in every respect and I wanted nothing more than to submit to each demand. That was where the real power was—Logan gave it all to me—he never asked of me anything I didn't want to do. He dominated my mind, but I possessed his soul—entwined with my own.

His pace increased, and delirium took over. I held on tight, writhing against him. Pleasure consumed me and I cried out, my body tightening as it exploded.

"Oh, Logan," I moaned.

"I love ye," he said, shuddering inside me. His face fell against my shoulder, lips pressed to the crook of my neck.

My heart constricted. I threaded my fingers through his hair and tugged until Logan pulled back enough to look me in the eyes. "I love you, too."

Neither one of us could hide behind the plaid any more.

While this may be *The End* for now—'tis not truly over…
Look for the next installments of Logan and Emma's story:
Bared to the Highlander (8/15/13) and **The Dark Side of the Laird** (12/15/13)

If you enjoyed **BEHIND THE PLAID**, *please spread the word by leaving a review on the site where you purchased your copy, or a reader site such as Goodreads or Shelfari! I love to hear from readers too, so drop me a line at* authorelizaknight@gmail.com *OR visit me on Facebook:* https://www.facebook.com/elizaknightauthor. *I'm also on Twitter: @ElizaKnight Many thanks!*

Eliza Knight

Book Two: *Bared to the Highlander*

Secret obsession makes for the sweetest of sins.

Overwhelmed by her new life in another era with the Laird of Gealach, and the feelings that threaten to consume her, Emma determines she must return to her own time and a semblance of sanity. Having heard of a magical circle of stones atop the ridge overlooking Loch Ness, she manages to escape from the castle and the desire and intensity of Logan that's held her captive.

When Logan realizes Emma is missing, he is enraged and terrified. He seeks to find her and when he does, he will punish her exquisitely for leaving him, and for inexplicably exposing his scorching fascination and adoration.

Together again, their passions are reignited and a new stunning level of sensuality and self-discovery invoked. But underneath it all, both still wrestle with their inner demons and the impending danger of angered clans and traitors among them. Revealing how they feel about each other could bring about cataclysmic crash within their hearts and the realm. The blade is sharp on both edges, but they know not which side to choose, for one promises sweet, decadent surrender and the other, irrevocable damage—and they aren't certain which is which. Will baring her soul to the Highlander forever change the course of history?

Book Three: *Dark Side of the Laird*

Bound by passion. Freed by love.

When the damaged and tormented Emma first meets the equally broken Logan, they embark on a torrid, emotionally provocative affair that irrevocably changed their lives. Emma has sacrificed her entire being and just when she thinks Logan is willing to do the same, he holds back. Reluctant for their love to be a thing of shadows, Emma issues an ultimatum: commit or say goodbye. Fearful of losing her, Logan agrees.

In order to keep her, he must gain permission to marry from the one man he's sought to avoid: his brother, the King. His appeal is denied and instead, Logan is seized and sent to the dungeon with no hope for escape. While in Hell, Logan's dark past haunts him, threatening to consume him. He must fight to remain the man he's become with Emma by his side and relinquish the control he's held onto for a lifetime.

Fearing her lover is dead, Emma decides once and for all she must leave history where it belongs and return to the present. But when she tries once again to break the bonds of time, she is struck down. Emma must choose her destiny. Must answer the cries her body makes in the dark for her laird. They've always been strongest when together, but now Emma must find the courage on her own to see her fate fulfilled—and Logan returned to her.

ABOUT THE AUTHOR

Eliza Knight is the multi-published, award-winning, Amazon best-selling author of sizzling historical romance and erotic romance. While not reading, writing or researching for her latest book, she chases after her three children. In her spare time (if there is such a thing…) she likes daydreaming, wine-tasting, traveling, hiking, staring at the stars, watching movies, shopping and visiting with family and friends. She lives atop a small mountain, and enjoys cold winter nights when she can curl up in front of a roaring fire with her own knight in shining armor. Visit Eliza at www.elizaknight.com or her historical blog History Undressed: www.historyundressed.com

Printed in Great Britain
by Amazon.co.uk, Ltd.,
Marston Gate.